# DRAGONS DON'T EAT MEAT

## BOOK I OF THE VALKYRIE BESTIARY SERIES

KIM MCDOUGALL

Dragons Don't Eat Meat


Published by Wrongtree Press, www.WrongTreePress.com.
Cover and book design by Castelane, www.Castelane.com.
Cover art by Pamela Francescut.



Paperback ISBN: 978-1-9994107-8-0
Hardcover ISBN: 978-1-7772144-9-4
eBook ISBN: 978-1-9994107-9-7

Version 1

FICTION / Fantasy / Urban
FICTION / Fantasy / Paranormal

## Books by Kim McDougall

**The Hidden Coven Series:**
Inborn Magic
Soothed by Magic
Trigger Magic
Bellwether Magic
Gone Magic

**Valkyrie Bestiary Series:**
Three Half Goats Gruff (Novelette)
Dragons Don't Eat Meat
Dervishes Don't Dance
Hell Hounds Don't Heel

**Writing as Eliza Crowe**
**The Shifted Dreams Series:**
Pick Your Monster
Lost Rogues

*For Larry, who taught me the secrets of Abbott's Agora.*

# CHAPTER 1

After a long day chasing pookas, moon-frogs and one particularly stealthy gremlin, all I wanted was a cup of tea and a hot bath. Not necessarily in that order. I sniffed myself. The bath would definitely come first. The gremlin had rolled in garbage to mask his scent. But he was Hub's problem now. That was the best part about taking commissions from the city. I was only responsible for trapping the nuisance critters, not re-homing them.

I pulled up to a storefront that had once been a mechanic's shop. A hand-painted sign over the office door proclaimed "Valkyrie Pest Control." The space was all mine and I was duly proud of it. I'd worked hard, building the business up from a part-time job I'd done mostly as favors to friends. I'd always had an affinity for animals. Bugs didn't faze me and when the fae came to town, it turned out they didn't daunt me either.

Too tired to unpack, I left my gear in the truck. A quick peek at the moon-frog caught on my last job showed the critter happily chewing the bars of his cage. About the size of a cantaloupe, he had bumpy, blue-green skin, big eyes and a wide mouth. Moon-frogs are voracious eaters with mildly acidic saliva. They can cause damage similar to termites, if termites were the size of rabbits. During most of the month, they're sluggish and easily caught. But when the full moon hits, the critter puffs up like a balloon covered in needle-sharp thorns that release a powerful hallucinogen. Nasty and dangerous but good for a quick high, they were hunted to near-extinction in the sixties. I hoped the cage would contain him for the night.

Thankfully, my apartment took up the back half of my office. I wouldn't have to haul my aching bones far before I could peel off my jeans and drop into a hot bath.

The sun had long since set. The fickle street lamp on the corner of my parking lot flickered, throwing more shadows than light. I grabbed the moon-frog's cage and lugged it toward the office. A movement at the upstairs window told me that Mr. Murray was at his usual lookout.

"Hello, Mr. Nosy-pants." I waved to him and the curtain fell back into place.

Ryleah's car was parked beside the door. As the latest in a long string of assistants, I didn't have high hopes for Ryleah making it to the one-month mark. I wasn't a demanding boss, but the job could get a little hairy. And slimy. And bloody. My last assistant, Tiffany, fainted the first time I brought back a vampire slug. Who knew those things could move so fast?

After I bandaged her, Tiffany quit. Before her, John could not deal with cleaning devil-rat blood off my tools. Before him…Well, there'd been other messes and other assistants who couldn't handle them. That Ryleah was still here, after eight o'clock on a Friday night, showed some gumption.

Inside, the office was dimly lit and silent. Two desks and a small sitting area filled the main room. Case files for past jobs were piled high on my desk. Cages, aquariums and terrariums lined two walls. Dozens of eyes peered from the gloom. My rescues were unusually subdued tonight. Even Clarence, my hyperactive basilisk, simply watched with wide eyes from his pen.

"Ryleah?" I dumped the moon-frog cage on my desk.

"Kyra! Shh! Over here." Ryleah peered from under her desk. "They're watching me!" Makeup was smeared under her eyes and a gob of green goo puckered her cheek. Gleeful chittering erupted from the shadows and two plump fur balls zoomed by, heading for the old garage-turned-gymnasium.

Ryleah squeaked, then choked back a sob.

I sighed.

"Alvin and Theo! I'm going to sell you as bait if you don't stop it right now!"

More chittering and a hunk of green cud landed on the floor by my feet. The madras knew I was bluffing. The mischievous rodents resembled guinea pigs and liked to chew hay into cud to throw at unsuspecting passersby. They had good aim too. I'd lost more than one assistant to their antics. And clearly, the new lock I'd spent a small fortune on did nothing to keep them in their cage. Little Houdinis.

"Come on." I helped Ryleah stand. "I'll catch them later. Any messages for me?"

She straightened her skirt and smoothed down her hair. I didn't mention the cud on her face.

"You've got no appointments this weekend, but Monday's turning out to be busy." She hiccuped as she flipped screens on a tablet. Her hands shook. "Three jobs in the morning, and…"

The bars of the moon-frog's cage gave way, and the fat critter plopped onto the desk. It jumped, landed on Ryleah's chest with a slimy splat, stared straight into her startled face and shrieked like its ass was on fire.

Ryleah shrieked right back.

I grabbed the frog before it could puff up and eject spiny thorns full of hallucinogenic venom right into her heart and dumped it into the wastepaper basket. Ryleah fell back, knocking over a chair while she clawed at the slime oozing into her cleavage.

"I'm…I'm…d-d-done." Her eyes blazed fiercely, but her chest heaved with the beginnings of hyperventilation. "N-n-no more." She grabbed her purse and ran out. I heard her car door slam and the engine flare to life. Tires skidded as she tore out of the parking lot.

"You can pick up your last check next week," I called weakly, knowing there was no way she'd ever be back. I'd transfer the money.

I righted the chair and sat. Exhaustion deflated me. I would need to hire another assistant. Where would I find time for interviews? But if I didn't make time, I'd be in a worse way. I couldn't manage the day-to-day office affairs and trap critters too. Business was booming. I should have been happy.

I gazed at the creatures in cages that lined my office. Fae beasts, otherworld rodents, lizards taken straight from mythology, birds, bugs, and some I had yet to classify. Each critter in my care was orphaned or injured and could no longer survive alone. We had a symbiotic relationship. I cared for them and they filled my need for family.

The madras returned to twine around my ankles.

"This is all your fault." I picked up Alvin. His round butt settled in the palm of my hand. I stroked his silky brindled fur and he leaned into my touch. His face was rounded like a guinea pig's, but his lip split to show two prominent front teeth. Intelligent eyes watched me with affection. I had no idea what world he came from, but if the ley-net caught on, madras would be the next go-to pets.

"You scared poor Ryleah. I'll be lucky if I don't get sued for mental trauma again."

Alvin head-butted my chin. He knew I couldn't stay mad. I put him down and carefully transferred the moon-frog to another cage. No way I could wait until tomorrow to release him. I'd have to go tonight. I turned to unlock the door leading from the office to my apartment.

"Gita! I've got to go out again," I called into the dark apartment. Muffled sobbing answered from the coat closet. I knocked on the door. "Gita, did you hear me?"

The door opened and the scent of ocean brine hit me. A gray face with red-rimmed eyes peered out. Green-brown hair hung like swamp moss to her waist. Though technically another rescue, Gita was the closest thing I had to a live-in nanny and housekeeper. Banshees didn't make the best roommates, but I needed help with my charges, and I'd grown used to her crying.

"You should change yer shirt." She sniffled and tucked a lock of gray hair behind a gray ear. "You smell like shite."

"Thanks. Can you feed the horde?"

Gita nodded, wiped her nose on a soggy handkerchief and slammed the closet door. The wailing escalated until Mr. Murray banged on his floor with a broom.

"Sorry, Mr. Murray," I said. "We'll try to keep it down." Gita must have heard him too, because her cries quieted to hiccupy sobs.

I grabbed a glass from the cupboard in the kitchen, found Hunter, my pygmy kraken nestled inside it and dumped him back in the aquarium, then rinsed the glass and gulped down as much water as I could hold. That would have to fill my stomach until I got home.

In the bedroom, I pulled off my shirt and picked another from the questionable pile of clothes on a chair. On a whim, I pulled out the braids that kept my hair out of the way while I worked and yanked a brush through my hair. Then I dabbed on lipstick.

I was no good at fooling myself, and I didn't even try to pretend the lipstick was for the moon-frog.

I was headed to Dorion Park. My trek would take me right by the home of Henry Mason, alchemist, Guardian and gargoyle. I'd last seen Mason over a year ago. We spent some quality time bleeding on each other after fighting a rock troll and shared one toe-curling, night-sweat-inducing kiss.

In the months since, he hadn't called. Typical. He'd left me hanging. Now, if I saw him—even if I found him in battle with a hell spawn—I wouldn't deign to throw a dagger his way.

But a little lipstick never hurt.

*Valkyriebestiary.com/gargoyle*

## Gargoyles Among Us

(*June 24, 2079*)

I want to thank everyone for their well-wishes. Yes, I am recovering nicely from my first encounter with a rock troll. If you missed that post, you can read all about it in the ***Archives.*** Many of you asked for more information about the mysterious "Guardian" who faced the troll with me earlier this month. I did some digging and he is a gargoyle. For privacy reasons, I'll leave out his name, but here's what I've been able to dig up on this elusive race.

Gargoyles are neither fae nor traditional shape-shifters, though they have characteristics of both races. Alchemists created the first gargoyles in the 15th century. They were stone statues carved by master sculptors and animated through alchemy. Some research indicates that the myth of the philosopher's stone originates with the gargoyles and the drive to bring them to life.

Traditionally, gargoyles take the shape of grotesques, fertility gods or green men. They can also resemble humans and animals (usually apex predators).

They are imbued with a sentient spirit to animate them, perhaps even the spirit of the alchemist or sculptor? This is just a working theory. The art of the gargoyle was lost long before the Flood Wars decimated the great alchemical library in Paris. The few remaining texts are decidedly cryptic, alluding only to the "spirit in the stone." Certainly, the gargoyle differs greatly from a simple golem (see ***Archives*** for more on golems).

Montreal has long been home to gargoyles, but they keep their activities private. Census records show that they vote for the Alchemist Party, which aligns with my observations that they seem to live mostly on the west end of the island, in the alchemist domain. They prefer the term "Guardian" to "gargoyle" but this might be a local affectation.

It is true that gargoyles come alive only at night and rest in a kind of stasis during the day. No other information about their abilities (magical or otherwise) could be found in the Montreal archives. So I'm opening up the topic to you, my readers and fellow cryptozoologists. Anyone else encounter a gargoyle? Leave your findings in the comments below and I will add the data to this entry.

## Comments (5)

I love your blog! Thanks for posting and glad to know you're on the mend.
*Karen_Tyrone (June 24, 2079)*

I encountered a gargoyle once—saved me from a mugging. So maybe the "Guardian" thing isn't just local?
*Kang_Master (June 24, 2079)*

Gargoyles are an abomination under heaven. Fae lovers like you make me sick.
*CreamPuff1489 (July 1, 2079)*

Have you actually seen a real gargoyle? The whole half-man, half-stone thing sounds so romantic!
*DaddysGirl (March 23, 2080)*

> I'm not sure about the romance, but they make good watch dogs. We are lucky to have them in our ward.
> *Valkyrie367 (April 25, 2080)*

# CHAPTER 2

The street lamp flickered out, leaving me in darkness as I dumped the new cage into the truck bed. I'd left the truck unlocked. No one would bother stealing it. That was the advantage of driving a pile of junk. But when I eased behind the wheel, I found a dervish perched on the passenger seat.

"Jacoby, what do you want?" I turned the key and the truck coughed to life.

At nearly two feet tall, Jacoby was large for a fire dervish. His thin face drew attention to his drooping ears and bulbous eyes that glared through a fringe of gray fur. He walked upright on two legs, but more gray fur covered his agile body and long limbs, like an elf crossed with a poodle.

"Wants to come with you, Kyra-lady." Determination clenched his jaw. Jacoby had been following me like a bad penny for days. Fire dervishes were tough and normally solitary creatures, but something had spooked him.

"I told you that you can't live with me. I have too many rescues already."

Jacoby was perfectly capable of surviving in the city. I only took in animals that couldn't care for themselves in our world, and preferably those that wouldn't set my building ablaze if they got too excited.

He gripped the seat belt with both hands as if I might try to dislodge him. I was too tired to argue, so I ignored him for the moment and navigated the maze of potholes in my parking lot. He clung to his seat as I sped through the dark streets. I swerved to make the exit for Gallop Bridge and then slowed to a stop in the line of cars waiting to leave the ward. I turned my attention back to my stowaway.

"Leave it alone." I slapped his gnarled fingers away from my radio as he scanned through dozens of static channels with one hand and cranked the volume with the other. The little dervish actually pouted. He fidgeted with the belt buckle. Something was up.

"Tell me why you're here or I'll drop you off in the middle of the bridge." I wouldn't really. Jacoby could teleport short distances. If I tried to kick him out of the truck, he'd just pop back inside.

Fuzzy eyebrows lowered over big eyes.

"I feels bad."

"You're sick?"

"No! I feels bad coming. Like a storm."

The sky was clear enough to show a brilliant range of stars, so Jacoby's storm had to be metaphorical or existential. I didn't discredit his feelings out of hand. Dervishes are nosy creatures that roost in chimneys, often spying on their unsuspecting hosts. That makes them a great source of information.

Maybe I could billet Jacoby with my equally nosy upper neighbor.

"Fine. You can stay with me for now, but I'm going outside the ward, into the Inbetween."

Jacoby sucked his long fingers and didn't say a word. We drove the rest of the way in uneasy silence.

Dorion Park lies outside the ward proper, but only a few kilometers into the Inbetween, the lawless terrain that fills the gaps between the few city-states left after the Flood Wars. I wasn't too worried though. The alchemists used the park as a testing ground for their mage-tech. They patrolled it and kept away the bandits and other large predators. Hub, Montreal's centralized governing body, had authorized me to use the park as re-homing grounds for any class three fae creature that I deemed dangerous to the general population.

Public access closed at dusk, but the utility roads were always open. I drove through a tunnel of immense trees, seeing only as far as the few feet of road my headlights illuminated. It wasn't a real park, but twelve hundred acres of dense forest, gurgling creeks and abundant wildlife.

I skirted around the east end and crossed a wooden bridge. To the right, trees blocked the light of the rising moon. On the left, a Gothic house reared up behind an overgrown garden.

I slowed the truck to a crawl to get a good look. Built of dark slate,

Guardian Manor was more castle than house. Small windows topped a large balcony hanging over front doors that opened onto a circular drive. And it had turrets—honest-to-gods turrets—strangled by creeping vines. The house was once an inn on one of the few roads leading into Montreal Ward. Now it was owned by Henry Mason, captain of the city's gargoyle vigilantes known as the Guardians.

I could have stopped near the park entrance, but I always took this longer route, telling myself that it was safer to dump the critters deeper in the woods. My traitorous heart hoped to glimpse Mason or one of his gargoyles. At this time of night, there was a good chance I might see one flying over the trees or perched on his rooftop.

I wasn't sure Mason could actually fly like the other gargoyles. I'd only met him once. Though he turned to stone with the sun like other gargoyles—I'd witnessed this freaky trait myself—he didn't have wings like the others. Nor did he have the traditional grotesque face. Just one more of his many mysteries—mysteries that had kept me thinking about him for nearly a year.

Who was I kidding? It had been three-hundred and twenty-one days since we fought the troll together. A girl didn't forget a man like Mason or the kiss he planted on me before the sun rose and turned him to stone.

It had been one hell of a night.

We'd fought a troll and tricked a gang of satyrs into burying it. When that didn't work, we fought the troll again. I was hurt. Badly. I spent four days in the hospital, the next three weeks wondering if I should call him and the following months trying to forget him. I'd mostly succeeded.

Driving by his house wasn't a desperate attempt to connect with a man who was obviously less impressed by my kiss than I was with his. It was a surrender to memory—a memory I could take out and polish off once in a while, then stow away for safe-keeping.

"There are some nice chimneys for you, Jacoby." I slowed to a stop and pointed at the roof of Guardian Manor.

Jacoby peered through the windshield. His long fingers pressed against the glass.

"Oooh. I likes towers."

"It's owned by a gargoyle." I thought he'd enjoy living with another nonhuman.

Jacoby whipped around as if I'd stung him.

"Gargoyles are mean! I can't lives with gargoyles!" He hunched back in the seat.

No quick-fix for my dervish problem then. I pulled away from the manor and headed deeper into the woods while Jacoby pouted.

The moon was only a sliver, its light barely penetrating the dense canopy of trees. I drove as fast as my old truck would let me and skidded around the corner, throwing up gravel as I turned into a clearing at the side of the track. Killing the engine, I found the flashlight that had fallen between the seats.

Jacoby followed me, bouncing from foot to foot as I unloaded the moon-frog.

"Where Kyra-lady goes?"

"In there." I nodded with my chin in the general direction of the trees and slung my sword harness across my back. No way would I go into the forest at night unarmed. My Aunt Dana, who had trained me in the fine art of killing, would say that even with a sword, I was as good as unarmed. And then she'd prove it by beating me bloody and taking my weapon. Dana was a giver like that.

Even though I might not be lethal by Valkyrie standards, my sword and I could probably fend off any nasties we might encounter in the woods. Probably.

"No, no, no!" Jacoby tugged at my sleeve. "Nice Kyra-lady should not goes in there." He pressed against my leg like a shy toddler, and I resisted the urge to shake him off.

"I won't be long," I said. "You can wait in the truck."

Jacoby stuck one multi-jointed finger in his ear and scratched. He looked at the truck, he looked at the dark forest, and must have decided his odds were better with company. He followed me as I hauled the cage up the path that led into darkness.

A ley-line river of pure magic ran under Dorion, and the park exuded a sense of unease that went beyond shadows cast by old trees. Every footstep felt hushed, as if the musky undergrowth swallowed my passing.

I was used to dealing with the darker fae and I had an affinity for forests, but I wanted to rush through these woods, looking over my shoulder for the Bad Wolf, Big Foot and Jack the Ripper. Even a mundane, someone whose magic was dim enough to be called intuition, would feel jumpy under this canopy. And I knew what else ran in the shadows along with chipmunks and opossums. After all, I'd released many of those darker creatures into this forest.

The moon-frog chose that moment to express displeasure at his captivity. Moon-frogs don't have a cute *ribbit* or even an impressive *galumph* like a bullfrog. No, they screech and honk like a rooster on crack. Every creature in the forest heard us coming. As the screeching faded to a low whine, three bony fingers slid into my hand, and I suppressed a grin. Right about now, Jacoby was wishing he'd stayed in the truck.

We girded a hill. The path turned left and emerged into a clearing at the bank of a large pond.

I have an extraordinary perception of magic. My mother called it the keening. It means I can sense even the smallest life-magics, down to a burrowing beetle. This sensitivity came in handy when I was looking for infestations of termites, but it could be overwhelming if I didn't keep filters around my psyche. Right now, my keening hummed along nicely, reacting to the lush foliage and wildlife in and around the pond. It was the perfect spot for a moon-frog.

I put down the cage and unlatched the door, which was mostly eaten away. The frog plopped onto the ground. It honked once, leaped into the pond, and was immediately lost under the tangle of vegetation.

Glad that was done, I turned toward the truck and saw a turret rising through the trees to the east. We were practically in Mason's backyard.

"There's the manor house we passed, Jacoby. Look at all the chimneys for you to roost in."

Jacoby glared at me and I smiled innocently.

"You're not afraid of a few gargoyles, are you?"

"I not fears nothing!"

A screeching roar tore the fabric of the night. Jacoby yelped and teleported away.

# CHAPTER 3

The roar was inhuman and not from any animal I knew. It was a scream of pain, a blast of red-hot fury laced with spicy magic I didn't recognize.

I left the empty cage and retraced my steps—eyes darting left and right, heart jumping at every shadow. Jacoby was gone.

As my path broke from the trees, the night fell silent. I don't mean the wind died. I mean crickets hushed, rodents quit rustling the underbrush and earthworms stopped tunneling through the dirt underfoot. The night had become utterly still.

The first rule for critter wranglers: when forest creatures stop moving, something bad is near.

Ahead of me, the trees thinned and large bodies moved in the light between branches. I ran toward the clearing and nearly tripped over a low stone wall. I crouched, rubbing my banged knee. On the other side, several odd shapes loomed out of the darkness. Headstones. The wall marked the boundary of an old cemetery.

My heart echoed in my ears. One beat…two beats…three…

A crimson beast stepped into the clearing, lifted its snout to taste the night air and spread leathery wings.

A dragon.

Not a bad thing then, but awesome in the old sense of the word, as in inspiring awe and a little fear. I'd never seen a dragon except in blurred photos, but they fascinated me. I collected every ley-net article of possible sightings. Rumors suggested that, like many other mystical creatures, dragons returned to our world when magic did, during the Flood Wars. Where had they been during the long magic drought? No one knew.

But there was one right in front of me now.

I was fumbling for my widget to record the beast when a second dragon emerged from the shadows, this one darker, blue or green, it was hard to tell in the dim light. A third one followed, a youth by its size. More dragons broke from the shadows. I counted thirteen in all. A thunder of dragons.

And they lived up to that name as they crashed around the cemetery. They seemed drunk as they stumbled over gravestones. Wings snagged on shrubs and tails lashed like whips. They grunted and snarled, snapping sharp teeth when one bumped into another.

All in all, I had imagined dragons would be more...graceful. And bigger. The biggest one—the queen, I guessed—was no larger than an elephant. And the smallest would have a hard time holding its own with a golden retriever.

But still, dragons. Wow.

Crouching outside the fieldstone wall, I watched the beautiful creatures mill around a few dozen graves. Most of the limestone markers were crooked or fallen over. Dragons snuffled around them, not grazing, but rooting like pigs after truffles.

Watching with a critical eye, I noticed the differences that marked males and females. The females had smaller, arrow-shaped heads and longer tails. The males were stouter with broad foreheads. They ranged in colors from the red of the queen to blues, greens and browns. Moonlight highlighted the tips of their scales, so they seemed to glitter.

And each dragon wore a collar of dull silver metal. Were they pets? They didn't seem tame. But someone had put on those collars.

A small brown dragon dug beside a headstone right in front of me. Her paws were clawed and strong as shovels. Dirt flew up from the busy work and her head soon disappeared into the deep hole. The others sniffed around, making more holes beside headstones.

These old graves were close to the surface. I heard brittle wood splintering as dragons broke through caskets.

*Oh, no.*

Were they necrovores? I sifted through my mental bestiary. I couldn't recall any myths about dragons eating dead flesh. Even if they did, it made little sense. There were no fresh corpses in this cemetery. The names engraved on the stones were worn away by wind and rain. There would be little flesh left to feed a necrovore.

Still, the dragons tore up graves and feasted on whatever they found—mostly jewelry and trinkets, treasure buried with the dead to make their passing easier. Grave adornments were often imbued with strong sympathetic magic, sometimes on purpose, sometimes unconsciously through the potent prayers of loved ones. And for centuries, these items had been buried in ground soaked in magic by the ley-line that ran under the park.

As the dragons crashed through coffins and crunched on relics, magic billowed around the yard like storm clouds. It assailed my every sense, tasting like burnt sugar, humming like a thousand bees and smelling like rot and fruit zest all in one.

My stomach roiled.

The dragons weren't necrovores. They tracked and ate magic. And someone had brought them here to dig up the magic of the old cemetery.

My keening went into overload as the dragons unearthed massive amounts of magic. Nausea swept through me, and I doubled over, clutching my gut.

Usually I kept the keening locked down tight. Most days, I needed only minimal wards to block out the constant barrage of tiny magics all around me. I hadn't been prepared for this onslaught, and it nearly knocked me out.

I closed my eyes, took several deep breaths and began the painstaking process of erecting the psychic barrier that would keep my mind from imploding. After a few moments of deep breathing, I brought myself under control and turned back to the amazing sight of dragons feasting on magic.

They used wedge-shaped bones at the tips of their tails to bash brittle coffins, then tore through rotten shrouds and pulled out anything buried with the ancient bodies, leaving the bones mostly unscathed.

The low rumble of a vehicle made me freeze. At the far end of the yard, the red lights of a transport truck flashed as it backed through the cemetery gates. The engine stilled and two figures jumped from the cab.

I ducked into the shadows, then crept along the wall, moving back into the trees when I needed cover. At the edge of the yard, I peered over the wall again, close enough now to make out faces.

Two young men stood beside the back end of the transport, one tall and muscular with white-blond hair tied back in a warrior's queue, the other shorter and darker with whip-like scars across his face. They wore leather jerkins over black pants, and held long iron rods, like cattle prods. The truck was parked in front of a sleeping dragon and the men seemed to be arguing about it.

"Why can't you ever do as you're told," the blond man said.

"Joran, man, I'm sorry, okay? I thought it was going to kill me." Scarface jabbed the dragon. His prod made a zapping sound and the body jerked, then lay still.

Not sleeping. The dragon was dead.

"Let's just gut it here and take the gold. Then we can leave the carcass," he said.

"Don't be a fool," said the one named Joran. "We can't leave any evidence behind."

Scarface laughed. "They're going to know that someone was here. Look at the mess the damned beasts made!"

Joran shook his head. "Just help me get the others loaded and we'll figure out what to do with this one afterwards."

Scarface held up a device like a remote control. Magic popped and I felt more than saw the containment field around the truck dissolve. The poacher hit a switch at the back of the vehicle and a heavy door zipped upward, locking open. Fancy stuff. These guys were backed by some serious money to have that kind of mage-tech.

Joran began rounding up the other dragons. Some were sated with magic and lumbered drunkenly around the yard. Others were still in the frenzy of the feast. He prodded them toward the transport. The queen hissed and snapped her jaws. Her collar flared red at the same time as Joran prodded her, and the tip of his rod sizzled with energy. She yelped and jerked away.

The bastards were controlling the dragons. But why? The littlest dragon, a blue beauty, stumbled by, trying to keep up with the others. He stopped to cough up a piece of gold filigree. Joran grabbed the gold and prodded the dragon onward.

Were they poachers? Dragons would bring a fortune on the black market, dead or alive. But they seemed more interested in the magic relics, and the only way to retrieve those would be to slaughter the beasts. What in the hells could be so profitable in an old cemetery that they would sacrifice an entire thunder of dragons?

And something else nagged at me. Why didn't the dragons just fly away?

None of it made sense. All I knew was that I wouldn't let them kill another dragon. I watched, assessing my enemies, looking for a weakness to strike at. I scanned the perimeter of the yard for guards, but the two poachers seemed to be working alone.

I couldn't overpower both of them. My best chance would be to wait until they had the dragons loaded, then disable the transport. With the men inside the truck's cab, they'd be at a disadvantage. And if I could take out one before they realized what was happening, it would be a fairer fight.

The transport posed another problem. It wasn't a truck exactly, just a long metal box with a cab in the front. No wheels. It was one of those hovercrafts that were popping up on the streets of Montreal lately, a new design from the alchemists. I wasn't sure how I could disable it.

The men were impatient. Dragons grunted and snarled at the glowing prods. Scarface waited at the truck, ushering the slow dragons through the opening in the containment field. Joran dragged the recalcitrant queen by her collar and several of the other dragons followed.

The queen balked at the rough handling. She snarled and her tail lashed out, catching Scarface with a glancing blow on his head. He retaliated by jabbing her hard in the soft spot under her wing. She screamed.

I'd had just about enough of this.

I leaped over the stone wall, headed right for Scarface and knocked him into the open gate at the back of the truck. Then I hit the switch. The door shut with a bang. Magic exploded in a brilliance of color and a rending scream as the containment field kicked on automatically. The screaming was cut off as the cargo door slammed shut.

Scarface was trapped inside, but his severed leg fell to the ground with a thud.

# CHAPTER 4

Six dragons remained in the yard. The other poacher came at me, fury blazing in his eyes.

"What did you do?"

Joran's accent was faintly European. He tossed the prod to his left hand and pulled a wicked-looking knife from his belt. His gaze found the leg on the ground, and a strangled growl escaped his throat.

Then he lunged.

I parried his first strike. My sword clanged on his metal prod. Dragons snarled and shuffled away.

He slashed again and I jumped back. The ground was full of holes, dug up by the dragons. I leaped over a torn open grave but the poacher was right behind me. I felt the passing wind of his prod as he swung for my head.

I turned to him, putting a headstone between us. My sword hummed with glee, happy just to be swinging free.

"I don't want to fight you. Just leave the dragons and go."

Joran grinned. He had big, rough-cut features. In a few years his face would be craggy, but now it bore the solid arrogance of youth.

"Perhaps I want to fight you." He leaped over the headstone to press his point. The small blue dragon squealed as I flinched backward and trampled his foot.

*Oh, why can't you just fly away already?*

The poacher took advantage of my unbalanced stance to drive the point of his prod at my ribs. I knocked it down with my blade. My hands shook. I hadn't been in a real fight since Aunt Dana beat me unconscious in the Valkyrie training ring. That was twelve years ago. But my muscles remembered even if my mind had tried to forget. The poacher jabbed and I parried. My sword arm came up on autopilot. He circled left, hopping nimbly over a fallen headstone. I followed, my eyes never leaving his face.

He broke our standoff with a hard overhand strike of the prod, then swung around fast and came up under my guard with the knife. I blocked each move, though the effort cost me. I needed to go on the offensive, but couldn't bring myself to do it.

Twelve years ago, I vowed never to take another life with my sword. I wouldn't let this scumbag make me break that vow.

I kicked out, catching him on the wrist, and his knife spun away. One weapon down. One to go.

He grinned and twirled the prod like a cheerleader with a baton.

His arm swept back but he checked the swing and jabbed upward instead, aiming for my stomach. I recoiled and blocked a second strike at waist level, but I fell and barely scrambled away before the prod struck the ground where my head had been. I surged to my feet in time to bring up my sword and block him again. The clash of prod against blade reverberated through my arm. He shoved with brute force. I held my ground and pushed back.

"Where are you taking the dragons?" Even in my rage, I wouldn't injure this man with my Valkyrie sword. I had to disarm him.

Joran grinned, the way a gorilla bares its teeth. He pushed me backward and leveled his prod at my chest. The tip flared with red-hot magic, but the broken ground of a grave separated us. He couldn't get in a killing blow from that distance.

But I could.

I slammed my blade down on the shaft of his prod. At the same moment, I called the magic pooling in the earth at our feet and sent a burst through the blade. My sword sliced through the metal like tin foil. It was a trick I'd been practicing for months.

The poacher gaped at his stubby six-inches of broken handle.

"How…?"

I leaped forward and kicked out his knee. He fell, screaming. They never expect girls to play dirty. I kicked him again in the kidney. That would hurt.

He wasn't finished though. His reach was long, and the broken prod came up fast, even through his pain. Its magic was disabled, but the jagged tip could still do some damage. I barely deflected it. With shear effort, he forced me away and stood. Back on two feet, though clearly favoring his left leg, he held his stumpy blade like a street fighter.

The small blue dragon stumbled into him. Joran cried out as his injured knee caved and he dropped his broken weapon. The dragon yelped and took off in a zig-zag run. But the damage was done. The beast had knocked the poacher into me. My sword impaled his right arm.

"By the One-eyed Father!" I swore and pushed the man away. His knee could no longer support him and he crumpled to the ground. Blood stained his sleeve. It was a minor wound, but the poacher was as good as dead. I leveled my sword at his throat. He clutched his injured arm and stared at me in defiance.

"Where are you taking the dragons?" I asked again. "Who sent you here?" He gritted his teeth. "Tell me!" I yelled, but the man squeezed his eyes shut, waiting for death.

I reversed my blade and clubbed him over the skull. He slumped into unconsciousness, and the world was better off.

He looked smaller laid out on the ground than he had looming over me. Blood soaked his shirt and vest. Magic leaked from the wound too.

Blood is the medium for a man's life-force, his strongest magic. That's why so many of the dark rituals call for it. One might even call it a soul.

And this guy was leaking his all over the dirt.

My muscles jittered with over-exertion, and I felt battered from the excess magic in the air. My sword hummed too, yearning to finish the poacher. Valkyrie blades didn't do things halfway.

*Damn him for blooding the blade!*

My hands shook even as I pointed the sword at the unconscious man's chest. A wound by a Valkyrie sword was always fatal to a mortal. The poacher might live for days or weeks yet, but he was a dead man walking.

A Valkyrie isn't just a warrior. She is judge, jury and executioner. We were the clean-up crew on Viking battlefields of old. Our blades are deadly, but after death, a second strike—if the Valkyrie is feeling generous—releases the soul from the body and sends the warrior to Valhalla, paradise, heaven,

Arcadia or whatever his pleasure. A Valkyrie's blessing is akin to last rites. Without it, souls must find their way alone. Sometimes, they wander for ages, haunting this plane.

I didn't want this godly power. I was no judge to decide if a man should be granted eternal life in paradise. When I'd spouted this altruism in the training yard, Aunt Dana, the Freya of Asgard, had beaten me within an inch of my life and left me as a warning to the other novices.

A Valkyrie who wouldn't blood her blade was dead to her.

But I didn't die. I healed, at least in body. But more tragedy awaited me and I left Asgard soon after. I left my family, my sick mother and the only home I had. I left when the Aesir were on the verge of war with the Titans, and in my rage, I burned Bifrost, the rainbow bridge, on my way out. The only road from this world to Asgard was now permanently closed, thanks to my temper tantrum.

It hadn't been my finest hour.

And this poacher dragged all those turbid memories to the surface because he wanted to sell magic trinkets on the black market. I kicked his unconscious body.

*Asshole.*

I kicked him again, rolling him onto his face. Let him eat dirt.

My sword throbbed now. Its desire to finish the kill was palpable and infected me too. I wanted to jam the blade through his ribs and twist until his heart burst like a bag of pudding.

I shook with restraint. I wasn't a killer. I didn't even kill rats if I could help it. I was a humane pest controller, not a Valkyrie executioner.

But I couldn't let him live either. His wound would only fester. No medication, magic or otherwise would heal it. His body would rot from the inside out. No one, not even this scumbag deserved to die like that.

I raised my sword for the killing blow.

And the clumsy little blue dragon bumped into me again.

"Quit it!" I said, turning my attention away from the unconscious man.

The dragon sat back on his haunches and watched me curiously. His stubby wings flared open and closed like bellows breathing air into his lungs. He stood no taller than my hip, with dark blue scales on his limbs, grading to lighter blue on his pear-shaped belly. He had the big, copper eyes of an anime character and a blunt snout, speckled with silver freckles. A soft fluff of blue feathers crested his head.

He was ridiculously cute.

"This is your fault." I pointed my sword at the unconscious poacher. "You made me cut him." The little dragon puffed his wings.

By now, the other dragons had settled after the commotion. They watched me warily but didn't try to leave.

The queen had a burn mark where the poacher's prod had stung her. I made a move to inspect it, but she hissed and backed up, eyeing my sword like it might spring to life and bite her.

"Hey!" I dropped the weapon and held up my empty hands to soothe her. "Look. I won't hurt you."

I had no idea how sentient these creatures were. Some stories pegged them as intelligent beings with spell-craft and even mind-speak in their arsenal of talents. Others claimed they were just beasts, stronger than most and fire-breathing, but not capable of communication.

Tone of voice mattered more than words with most creatures, so I kept mine even and reasonable.

"You're free now. You can go. These men won't hurt you anymore. I promise." The red dragon cocked her head, as if trying to see me better. I stepped toward her. The other dragons ruffled their wings or moved away, but the red stayed her ground.

"You're a pretty one, aren't you? Red scales like fire. I would name you Ruby." The dragon—Ruby—followed my every word with slightly hooded eyes. I kept up the flow of mindless chatter. It was my best weapon.

"There you go. Such a pretty beast. I bet that wing is sore. Can I look at it?"

Ruby's head dipped low. It was a sign. Animals have tension release indicators. Horses whuffle. Cats blink slowly. Basilisks fan their combs. I bet that head dip was a release of tension and stepped forward again, this time stretching a hand to touch her.

"Such a magnificent queen." I took another step. "You're very strong. And I know you want to protect the others. Why don't you all just fly away?" I placed my hand on her shoulder and she moved back, not alarmed, but not tolerating the touch either.

"Does your wing hurt? I can help you." I didn't make another move to touch her, but I didn't back away either. We stood eye to eye, at an impasse. The little dragon wasn't as cautious as the queen. He ducked under my hand and let me scratch his feathery crest. I rubbed his ears and his neck, coming up against the hard collar.

The collar.

I crouched beside the little dragon to examine it. The dull metal felt oily to the touch, though no residue came off on my fingers. Something about it set my teeth on edge. My mental wards were still buttoned up tight, and I let them go just enough to sense the collar's magic. But there was nothing to sense. It was a total absence of magic, like a void in the vast web of life all around me.

The collar was a magic nullifier. This is what kept them from flight and from using any other magic they might have.

I groped around the collar but could find no clasp. It was one solid ring. Leaning back, my hand found the grip of my sword.

"This won't hurt. I promise. But you have to stand still. Understand?" The dragon licked the end of my nose. That was good enough for me. I held the tip of the blade against the metal. It burned with black, noxious smoke, and the collar fell away. The dragon bounced up and down, clearly happy with his new freedom.

I turned to Ruby, still holding my smoking blade.

She stared at me fiercely, then lowered her head. As soon as her collar fell away, she lunged past me, spitting fire on the spot where Joran had fallen.

But he was gone. Sometime, while my back was turned, he'd recovered consciousness and slunk away.

*Gods dammit!* Now I'd have to hunt him down and finish the job.

But first I had a thunder to free. Ruby stood watch while I cut off the other collars. Then I headed for the truck.

Magic came off it in waves. The containment field was a powerful ward, but nothing my sword couldn't cut through. I glanced around the yard first, making sure that Joran had truly disappeared. I'm not shy about my magic, but it wasn't a good idea to let anyone know that I had a weapon capable of cutting holes in wards. Not when the triumvirate that ruled Montreal Ward thought their protection of the island was unbreachable. Best to let those in charge believe in their supremacy.

I nudged the severed limb out of the way and dosed my blade with a bit of magic as I pressed it into the crack around the hatch. The sword wasn't happy at this continued pedestrian use. It wanted blood. But metal melted and when the hinges broke, the hatch fell away.

A green dragon tumbled out. The others eyed me sleepily from the back of the transport. The queen chirped and they lumbered forward, trampling Scarface's body. I didn't need to check him for a pulse. His sightless eyes told me all I needed to know.

I freed the rest of the dragons from their collars. The queen flexed her wings and launched into the sky. It wasn't a graceful flight. Her wings beat clumsily as if she hadn't used them in years. The others followed in her wake. One let out a howl of triumph and pent up rage, and they disappeared over the treetops.

All but one fat, little blue dragon. He jumped, stretched his wings, floated a few seconds and thumped to the ground. He ran for the stone wall, climbed on top of it and tried again, but his stubby wings couldn't hold his weight. My heart broke as he whined and watched the rest of his pack fly away.

"Nice job." The deep voice startled me and I whirled, ready to take on another fight. My blade stopped an inch from his neck. It wasn't another poacher.

It was Henry Mason.

# CHAPTER 5

His heart beat like the tolling of a church bell. I would recognize his magic signature anywhere. Mason, the man I'd dreamed about, cursed, and tried to forget for nearly a year was standing at the tip of my sword.

"What are you doing here?" My arm shook. The blade wavered at his throat. I'd been blasted by magic, beaten, held at knifepoint and generally abused today. I was holding on with the last of my strength.

"Stand down, Kyra."

I could look only at the tip of metal, where it gently nudged his flesh.

"Kyra!"

The voice drew my eyes to his face. His mouth was set in a grim line and his nose was painfully aquiline. But gods, those eyes! They were silver-gray, dark souls fringed with lashes longer than any man had a right to. I wanted to climb inside that gaze and curl up with hot cocoa and a good book.

Slowly, like stretching into the maw of a big cat, he reached for my sword and pushed it sideways.

"What happened here?"

"I don't know. Poachers. There were more dragons. A whole herd of them."

Magic had been spilled—from the dead man, the dug up graves and the broken containment field. It still slithered around the cemetery in a furious hush. I shook my head, trying to clear the unpleasant sensation.

"Thunder," Mason said. He watched me closely, as if I were a fugitive who might run.

"What?"

"A herd of dragons is called a thunder."

*Thank you, Mr. Know-it-all.*

"I've never seen dragons in the park." A breeze tossed his black hair over his forehead as he looked at the night sky. My fingers itched to brush it aside.

"That's because there aren't any, normally. These were Maltese dragons, I think. They're a long way from home. The poachers brought them here." I was babbling again. It didn't have the same effect on Mason as it had on the dragon queen. For another moment, he watched me with his infuriatingly bland expression, then turned to survey the yard—dug up graves, bones and rotting clothes, upended headstones, and a fat blue dragon who seemed to have forgotten that his posse abandoned him and was happily chewing through an unearthed trinket box.

"They brought them here on purpose," Mason said.

"Yes." I sheathed my sword and crossed my arms. It seemed a better defense against the lure of the man standing before me. And I didn't want him to see my hands shake.

"How many?" he asked.

"Two. One got caught in the tailgate when I disabled it." I motioned toward the truck. "I knocked out another one, but he ran away while I was dealing with the dragons."

"I'll have the Guardians track him," Mason said. I followed his gaze to the far gate where two figures stepped into the yard, one small and broad, the other tall and stooped.

"Berto, one got away. Can you and the boys track him?" The taller Guardian nodded. He had the typical gargoyle face, an elaborate grotesque with thick lips and a bulbous nose. He turned away without speaking and left the yard.

The second Guardian huffed up to us. He was short and squat with skin like bark and brambles for beard and hair. Stocky wings jutted from his back. They looked like tattered leather stretched over bent branches.

"There be beauty in the eyes of the gods tonight, milady." He horked a wad of phlegm onto the grass, hiked up his pants and scratched his ass.

"Uh, yeah," I said. His magic felt off, like an animated character whose sound was slightly out of phase with his image.

"Kyra Greene, meet Angus," Mason said.

I nodded and Angus winked. He was an authentic green man, an ancient spirit of fertility and prosperity, probably sculpted in the sixteenth century and brought to life during the Renaissance by an alchemist.

In the last year, I'd done my research on gargoyles.

I glanced back at Mason. Broad shoulders with no wings, classic good looks, unruly black curls. He was a different sort of gargoyle, one I hadn't quite figured out.

Angus bent and picked through the debris left at a grave. He held up one of the broken dragon collars.

"Damnation and roses," he swore. "Something tore this place up an' good!" When he spoke, his lips spread like a knot in a tree. It was difficult not to stare.

"The dragons," I said. "I think the poachers brought them here on purpose to find artifacts."

"They eat magic," Mason said. It wasn't a question; it was a revelation. His eyes darkened and narrowed onto the far end of the yard where the little blue dragon was chowing down on some dug-up treasure. His nose unearthed a metal box. It must have been warded because when he bit into it, magic exploded.

The dragon barely noticed, but I was at the limit of my strength. Too much magic spent. Too much sensory overload. While the dragon munched on his newfound treasure, I threw up every mental defense I could muster. It wasn't enough.

A tsunami of magic hit me.

My breath stopped. I gagged, fought for air and doubled over to retch in the grass.

"Kyra?" Mason's voice came from far away, through a haze. I fought to bring my keening under control and hung limply on a headstone, retching onto the grass.

Mason crouched beside me and gently rubbed my back.

"Are you all right?"

I nodded, not trusting my voice. He pulled a handkerchief from his jacket pocket and wiped my chin. Excellent. I snatched the cloth from him and turned away.

*I am a sexy, intelligent, strong woman.* I stared at the hankie in my shaking hand. His initials were monogrammed on it in cursive needlepoint. I closed my eyes and almost puked again. *I am beautiful and honest. Bodily functions are a part of my beauty.*

"You've got a sensitivity to magic," Mason said.

"No shit."

I could still feel the magic pulsing through the yard, but I managed to reconstruct my psychic wards. They were flimsy, but stable.

Angus offered me a sip from the flask hanging on his belt.

"A little fire in the belly might help," he said, but I just shook my head. Alcohol was the last thing I needed.

I swayed and Mason put a hand on my shoulder.

"I'm fine." I shrugged him off. The last time he'd touched me, I'd been bloody and wounded from our battle with a rock troll, barely hanging onto consciousness while we waited for the paramedics to arrive. And then a year of silence. It seemed I needed to spill some bodily fluids to get the man's attention.

He eyed me again, as if he didn't believe I wasn't about to crumple into a pile of sobbing goo. Then he crouched by the grave that the blue dragon had dug up.

The dragon was done with all the excitement. He curled into a ball, tucked his nose under a wing and fell asleep. Mason ignored him. He let dirt filter through his hands and ran a finger over the worn writing on the headstone.

"Did you know the person buried here?" I asked, thinking the dragon had disturbed a loved-one. Mason was old. This could be the grave of his child, parent or wife. Immortals could rack up a significant number of wives and children.

"No. I took over this land after the war. It was abandoned." Mason's tone was somber, but not sad. I couldn't get a read on this guy. "It's not about who was buried here." He touched a bit of rotted cloth, probably a shroud that poked through the dirt. "But what."

"Hey, Bossman, isn't that the grave where we buried a wee magical stone a few months back?" Angus peered over his shoulder.

Mason nodded. "Fifty-four years ago."

"Hellfire's arse." Angus whistled. "It's been so long?"

I'd lived with immortals in Asgard. They had a warped sense of time. My cousin Aaric once told me that after a while, the days, weeks and months fused to a blur and only a good fight or a bad woman stood out in his mind. So it didn't surprise me that half a century could feel like months to Angus.

Mason picked through the broken coffin, pushing aside bones and brittle cloth.

"It's gone." He sat back on his ankles and frowned.

"What was it?" I asked.

"A bloodstone."

That told me nothing. But he didn't elaborate. I left him to search for his lost treasure and turned my attention to the dead. Let Mason waste time looking for some gemstone.

My grumpy sword hummed with anticipation of a kill. I could give it something to chew on.

Gently, I touched the dead dragon with the tip of the blade. Magic eased up it into my hand. Blood magic. Life. I pressed the sword into the yielding flesh to release the dragon's soul. This was just a formality. Strictly speaking, animals rarely needed the services of a Valkyrie. Their spirits were much less complicated than humans' and more accepting of death. The dragon would have found a way to move on. But I felt it needed some kind of tribute, and this was the only way I knew how to pay homage to its lost life. The unbound spirit swirled around my head like a thank-you kiss, then flew gracefully into the trees.

I did the same for Scarface. He didn't deserve it, but I wouldn't judge him. Some other godly power would have to do that.

"Feel better now?" asked Mason. I must have looked insane, poking corpses with my sword. I pulled myself up to my full five-foot-seven inches and smiled.

"Yes, thank you."

Mason shook his head. "You are an odd duck, aren't you?"

I shrugged. I'd been called worse.

"Did you find what you were looking for?" I asked.

"We think your little porker over there ate it." Angus jerked a thumb at the sleeping dragon. It was possible. If my keening wasn't so close to overload, I could have tried to sense it.

Instead I asked, "Is it dangerous?"

"Yes," Mason said, not exactly forthcoming with knowledge.

"Dangerous like a poison?" I looked at the dragon, worried he'd swallowed something that would make him sick.

"Dangerous like end-of-the-world dangerous." Angus scooped up the sleeping dragon. "But don't worry. We'll get it back."

"Where are you taking him?"

"It's not over until the dragon poops," he said.

"You can't be serious." I looked at Mason, who nodded.

"We need that stone."

"So what, you plan to keep the dragon as your prisoner until he produces the stone? Well, joke's on you. Dragons eat magic. It's probably dissolving in his stomach juices right now." I tensed, silently cursing my big mouth. I'd just given Mason every reason to slaughter the dragon.

I wouldn't let him do it. I was already tired and heart-sore, but I'd fight them both before letting anything happen to the last dragon.

"The stone is indestructible," Mason said. "Believe me, I've tried. Fire, acid, crushing. Nothing works. That's why I buried it. Now we have to get it back. Don't worry. We won't hurt him. He'll be my guest until the stone passes."

I narrowed my eyes, wishing my keening could decipher his inscrutable expression. Would he really keep the dragon alive until it produced his precious gem? Or would he take the easy way out like the poachers?

"You know nothing about caring for dragons."

"How hard can it be?" Angus said. "It's a baby. Feed it, burp it, let it sleep."

"He's not just a baby. He's malformed." I grabbed the sleeping dragon from Angus. He snorted, but didn't stir from his food coma. "Look at the shape of his legs. They're bowed. And his wings aren't nearly as strong as they should be. I think those collars stunted them all, but he's worse than the others."

"Well, we could stand here and talk until the cows turn blue," Angus said, "but that won't bring the stone back any sooner." He turned and lumbered out of the yard.

Mason and I stared at each other. There were three-hundred and twenty-one days of silence between us, silence that couldn't be broken by niceties.

"You're not getting the dragon," I said.

He rubbed the back of his neck and considered me. "You'll look out for the bloodstone?"

"As soon as I find it, you'll have it." I turned away, but Mason caught my arm.

"Kyra, be careful. Those poachers won't give up easily."

Our eyes met and his look reminded again of the last time we'd been thrown together.

As the sun had come up, Mason called for a medic. His expression told me my injuries were serious. He wanted to stay, but the sunrise was his bitch, and he'd gone to stone, leaving me broken and alone next to the remains of the rock troll.

He wore the same expression now, like he wanted to save me from something horrible but was powerless to do so.

I nodded and held the dragon closer to me as I headed back through the trees, thinking, j*ust what in the hells is a bloodstone?*

*Valkyriebestiary.com/banshee*

## Wailing Banshees

*(June 12th, 2076)*

*Banshee: from the Celtic root Bean and Sídhe, meaning Woman of the Faeries.*

Like the family gods of ancient Rome, banshees act as conduits between the living and the dead. They are generally retained by the well-to do family of Celtic or Gaelic descent.

The Banshee's cry—a horrible mix of piercing wail and a wolfish moan—has been known to sour the milk in a woman's breast and call up storms from the deep. However, "screaming banshee" is a pejorative misnomer as the banshee screams only to herald the death of a family member who is far from home. Her screams are more of a community service than a haunting. The banshee's everyday communications consist mostly of muted sobs and blubbering.

More active in the winter months, banshee sightings are still rare. She has appeared at the bedside of those in the throes of the plague, though her knowledge of medicine has long been suspect. Mostly, she can be found on the moors, wailing and dancing a sad dirge. Her gray complexion easily blends into fog-shrouded hillsides. Her foot leaves no prints, but her breath can wilt spring blooms. Discoveries of banshee nests have diminished in the last hundred years, an indicator of their declining numbers. The nest is often a small cave or hollowed-out hillside that may be a doorway to the underworld. In urban settings, banshees prefer dark, confining abodes.

A banshee male has never been found. Perhaps his absence is the root of the banshee's distress.

On a personal note, I found a banshee wandering the shores of the St. Lawrence. She was clearly out of sorts and lost. She's settled in nicely with my other rescues. I'm almost used to the constant crying :) And she brews a mean cup of coffee.

## COMMENTS (8)

Banshee tears are great for infusions. I have a recipe for a good-fortune elixir. PM me for details.

*cchedgewitch (June 29, 2076)*

> Thanks!
>
> *Valkyrie367 (June 29, 2076)*

Is it true that a banshee can break glass with their scream?

*Newfienews (July 5, 2076)*

> I haven't seen that yet. I'll let you know.
>
> *Valkyrie367 (July 5, 2076)*

Let her lose in the woods. Give her a good head strt and put 1 between her eyes. I'd love a banshee head on my wall with my other trofies.

*BigGameGuy (August 12, 2076)*

> Go on with you! You couldna catch any woman, let alone a banshee. But I'd like to see you try. Not too attached to those testies of yours, are you? They'd make a great soup.
>
> *CapeBretonBanshee (August 13, 2076)*

I'm praying for your soul. May God forgive you for harboring the wicked.

*Lighthouse45 (November 3, 2077)*

You always have the best information. I'm bookmarking this article.

*DaddysGirl (October 11, 2078)*

# CHAPTER 6

Habit normally woke me before dawn. Some critters were best routed in the pre-dawn hours, and I was usually on my first case before most people poured their coffee. But I'd dragged my tired body home just before sunup to catch a few hours of sleep before a strange rumbling noise woke me.

The dragon slept flat on his back at the end of my bed. I'd left him curled on the floor, but in the night he'd crawled onto my bed. Now he snorted and pedaled the air. Poor thing was still running from the bad guys even in his sleep. His legs churned, then he crashed and jolted awake.

"Hey buddy, have a bad dream?"

He whined.

"You don't look so good. Hungry?" His ears twitched. Did he understand my words or was he reacting to my tone?

"Come on. Let's see what we can find you to eat."

My apartment was small—one bedroom, a living area, tiny bathroom and a kitchen tucked into a corner by the front door which led directly into the offices of Valkyrie Pest Control. Every available space was cluttered with cages, aviaries and pens. An exterminator with the soft heart of a dryad was bound to collect a few critters, but my apartment had begun to look like a zoo. Shining eyes watched me from every corner. A clawed hand reached through the bars of a cage and snagged my pajamas. The dragon shied back.

"It's okay. That's Kur. He's an ice sprite. You'll like him. I'll let him out to play later." Willow, my gray cat, slept on top of Kur's cage and I scratched her head. She opened one eye in greeting, then tucked her nose under her tail and went back to the busy work of being a cat.

As I headed to the kitchen, I passed Hunter's aquarium. The pygmy kraken poked a tentacle from the water and I gave him a fist bump. Through the glass, he watched the newest arrival to the Kyra Greene wildlife refuge as the dragon tried to keep away from all the staring eyes and reaching claws. That wasn't easy to do. Every time he backed away from one cage, he bumped into another.

From the office I could hear Clarence, my basilisk, slithering nut-ball crazy around his pen yelling, "Gobble-gobble!" The madras were tormenting him again. That mess would wait until after coffee.

I herded the dragon into the kitchen.

"You were too late for decent folk, last night," Gita said with her Cape Breton burr as I stepped into the kitchen. Her eyes were red-rimmed, but she seemed alert.

"I had to drop a moon-frog in the park." I poured a cup of coffee. Gita made it strong enough to jolt, just the way I liked it. She frowned, suspecting I had more to tell, but I knew better than to worry Gita with details.

I sipped the scalding coffee.

"And you brought home some other mouth to feed, I see." She pointed a spatula at the dragon who had plunked down in the middle of the kitchen to chew his toenails.

"He's only visiting. He'll be gone soon."

Gita pursed her lips. "That's what you always say."

She was right. Most of my charges had been temporary guests that somehow ended up as permanent residents—Gita included.

"I suppose Ollivicenzanhe-axl is hungry too." She began pulling plates of food from the warm oven.

"Olli...what?"

"That'd be his name. Ollivicenzanhe-axl."

"Right." I didn't ask how she knew the dragon's name. She might have made it up, but Gita had an uncanny ability to communicate with just about any creature. She wasn't quite telepathic, at least not the way she described it. She just *knew* things.

"I see. That's a bit of a mouthful. How about if I just call him Ollie?"

Ollie flexed his wings in a gesture that I was coming to associate with pleasure, like a dog wagging its tail.

"I guess that'd be alright," Gita said. "Eggs?" She thrust a plate of eggs, toast and ham in front of me before I could answer. Ollie sat at my feet, watching with big, eager eyes, wings slowly billowing in and out.

I offered him a piece of ham. His hands were almost human like, with four nubby fingers and a thumb, all ending in sharp claws. He took the ham almost delicately, stuck it in his mouth, then made a face and spat it out.

"Don't like ham, huh?" I gave him a bit of toast. He chewed this for a few moments before spitting out a wad of wet dough on the floor.

"Not bread either? We'll have to find you something to eat. I don't have any bits of magic gold lying around for you."

After several tries, we found that he liked apples. He went through all the apples before belching once and curling up on the linoleum for another nap.

I would have to make a run to the market for more fruit. It probably wasn't a good idea to have a hungry dragon as a house guest.

After breakfast I made my rounds, checking each of the cages, aquariums and terrariums. I fed the rats. They were the only animal that Gita wouldn't touch if she didn't have to. And yes, I get the irony of an exterminator keeping rats. I let the madras out of their cage with an admonishment for them not to wake the sleeping dragon. Then I sorted my laundry, found Hunter at the bottom of the basket and dumped him back into his aquarium. Next, I slathered a stinking hunk of rotting beef with hairball remedy and threw it into Clarence's cage. He screamed, "Gobble-gobble!" and tore into the flesh with his wicked sharp beak.

"Cock-a-doodle-doo," I said. "You're a rooster"—well, half rooster, half snake, anyway—"not a turkey." The basilisk was a mimic, like a parrot. I'd been trying to get him to speak, but he refused. He tore up the meat, swallowing big chunks.

"He be out of sorts," Gita appeared at my side like a specter of death.

"It's just a basilisk stone," I said, glancing back at Clarence, whose muzzle was covered with gore. "The hairball remedy will help. Once he passes it, he'll settle down." Every few months, Clarence produced an opal-like stone in his feces. The stones were unique to basilisks, as far as I knew, and I wasn't sure if they were a gizzard stone ground to shining effect or if, like an oyster, the basilisk produced the stone to protect itself from a foreign body in its system. Whatever the case, they were quite pretty and I kept them in a jar on my desk.

Gita sniffed. "I smell sickness. Gita knows." She tapped her nose with a long, bent finger. "Before the week 'tis out, there be death in this house!" She wailed and ran to her closet. Clarence shrieked, "Gobble-Gobble!" Mr. Murray banged on his floor with a broom handle.

"We'll be quiet, Mr. Murray," I called. I knew he could hear me. Mr. Murray spent his days with his ear pressed to the air vent, listening to my business, then complained when we were too loud—which was often.

I didn't worry too much about Gita's prophetic words. She predicted death every day and twice on Tuesdays. But she believed each one, and I'd learned not to argue with her.

The rest of my chores went quickly. Kur, the ice sprite, panted, even though the apartment felt cool to me. I filled his bowl with ice cubes and he settled over them like a hen to roost.

I scooped up dirty bedding from cages, then headed to my office to tackle the mess on my desk.

A sleepy dragon waddled into the room. He saw me and chirped a greeting.

"Hey there, fella. You feel better?" I reached out to pet his fluffy crest and his eyes closed as I scratched behind his ear. He'd been sleeping for hours, but he still seemed listless. The entire thunder of dragons had been stunted and sickly, but this little guy was worse than the others. I suspected that, as the smallest of the herd, he didn't get to eat as often. And if those poachers were keeping them captive, they might have starved them as a means of control.

I coaxed Ollie to sit between my feet while I perched at the edge of my desk chair. Last night's events had blasted my usual psychic wards. The little sleep didn't help. I felt fragile, as if the barest breeze of magic could crack me down the middle. But I had to know if Ollie really had swallowed the bloodstone.

I let down my wards and laid my hands over his belly. As I leaned in, he licked my chin. His breath smelled of apples and burning coal. A shiver ran through him as my hands met his skin, but he didn't shy away. He gazed at me with trusting eyes.

"This won't hurt."

I searched, but found nothing.

Huh.

In the cemetery, Ollie had chewed through the warded box containing the bloodstone and the release of magic had nearly floored me. Now? Nothing. Maybe the dragon had some natural warding. That made sense. If the stories about fire-breathing were true, they had to keep that magic secret somehow or their prey would keen them coming.

I patted him on the head and his wings billowed.

"I guess, we'll just have to wait and see. You and Clarence are in the same boat." It would be a fun week, sorting through excrement, searching for stones. The joys of animal husbandry.

I fed Ollie the last of my fruit store then let Clarence out of his cage. After a bit of exaggerated bravado on Clarence's part, the two of them settled in for some play time. I threw a rubber ball. Clarence grabbed it in his beak, then taunted Ollie to chase him. Alvin and Theo joined in. Chase was Clarence's favorite game. He never gave up the ball, but at least with it in his mouth, he couldn't scream "Gobble! Gobble!" and wake up Mr. Murray again.

I listened from my office to the thumping and crashing sounds in my apartment. This was why I didn't have nice things. An angry hiss told me that Willow had made an appearance, and this game did not please her. But Willow could hold her own, so I let them be.

Tidying my cluttered desk took only five minutes while I listened to my messages. Most were from potential clients. I resolved to call them tomorrow. This no assistant thing was already a hassle. I fired up my ancient computer and placed an ad on the Montreal job boards.

*Needed: Office assistant. Those who are squeamish about blood, slime or bug guts need not apply. Bookkeeping background a plus.*

That would have applicants busting down the door.

I had plenty of work to do, but while I had the computer out, I couldn't resist a little worthwhile procrastination.

I touched the screen to activate the search and typed "llw.valkyriebestiary.com" into the browser. As the search engine twirled its rainbow cursor, I shot a bit of magic through my fingertips into the computer. The llw or Ley Line Web was the supernatural designation that brought up a whole different class of sites. This was the ley-net with magical teeth, a dark web that skirted the boundaries of Montreal Ward to reach out into the big world beyond. On the llw, I could find fae and other-worlder information that wasn't available to the general public. I could talk to people in other wards, even those that Hub deemed hostile, and I could purchase just about anything on the black market, for the right price.

I had many questions about last night, but before searching for information about dragons, I added a quick post to my blog about the moon-frog.

After a few months of saving mystical creatures, I'd realized that there was very little information available about the care and feeding of them. Most people only wanted to know how to hunt them or harvest their organs for exotic dishes and fabled medicines. My knowledge about caring for critters came from trial and error. Many errors. Clarence had spat out every mouthful of food before I learned that he preferred raw, rotten meat. And chocolate, but a basilisk on a sugar rush was not a good thing.

But these creatures were here to stay and someone needed to care for them. I kept a blog of my experiences. It was mostly for my reference, so I could go back and remember what worked and what didn't, but soon I'd gathered a small following online—others like me from all over the globe who were scrambling to care for these unusual creatures.

I hit "Post" on my moon-frog article and scanned the comments on my other pages. I hadn't been keeping up with the blog in over a month. The comments were the usual mix of encouraging support and racist hate. I answered the deserving ones and ignored the others. Someone with the tag *Daddysgirl* recently posted a comment on my gargoyle article, even though it was almost a year old.

*Have you actually seen a real gargoyle? The whole half-man, half-stone thing sounds so romantic!*

Mason and his posse were about as romantic as cholera. But it was nice to get comments on the blog and Daddysgirl was a regular poster, someone who admired the diversity of Terra's creatures as much as I did, so I tapped out a quick response.

Next, I drafted a second article about my encounter with the dragons, but I hesitated before posting it. Those poachers would look for the dragons that got away. My little blog was only a blip in the virtual atmosphere, but I didn't want to take chances with Ollie's safety.

I saved the post in my drafts and searched for "bloodstone" but only came up with hits on jewelry and charms. Nothing that screamed "end of the world."

The magic box of binary code would not give me any more help on the subject. Before putting it aside, I checked my ad. Already, three people had posted their resumes, and I set up interviews for the following days.

My mind circled around Mason, dragons, bloodstones and back to Mason again. Now that I was away from his velvety eyes, that guy irked me. He was too used to bossing around his Guardians and expected everyone to do his bidding. And I had no illusions about his ruthlessness. If I hadn't forced the issue with the dragon, Ollie would be hanging from a meat hook back at Guardian manor right now.

Again, I felt the burning need to understand the bloodstone's importance.

I glanced at the bright day outside my window. The gargoyles would be stone for several hours more. Just enough time for me to get a jump on them. If Mason didn't want to tell me about his mysterious bloodstone, he'd soon learn I had other resources. I could track it down without his help.

But first, I had to take care of business. I had clients to call and jobs to postpone so I could hunt down dragons and one dead poacher walking.

# CHAPTER 7

Willow lounged in her bed on my desk. The bed was just a cardboard box with a folded blanket inside, but it was her castle and no other housemate would violate its sanctity. For the last hour, Ollie had been trying to get her to play with him by running around the desk then nudging her box with his nose. Willow watched him with her tail thumping slowly on the desk.

"There's nothing left in the fruit drawer for you." I scratched Ollie's ears and he leaned against my leg. "I'll make a run for the market."

That perked him up. He zipped around the desk twice with wings pumping and landed at my feet.

"You have to stay here. Sorry fella. The bad men might be looking for you." He tugged on my pant leg with his claws. I still wasn't sure how much English he actually understood. "You stay here with Willow. Keep her company." The cat opened one eye at the sound of her name, but was otherwise unmoved.

I left Ollie pestering Gita in the kitchen while she prepared the evening feedings. I felt reasonably sure that it was safe to leave him.

Reasonably.

The market was only a few blocks away, but I was going to haul a lot of produce back home, so I took the truck. I unplugged it from the ley-line charger and turned to find Jacoby sitting in my passenger seat. Again.

"I should really start locking that door."

"You stinks like dragon," he said as I started the engine.

"And you stink like rotting garbage, so we're even."

He nodded like that was fair.

"Vinny threws out a whole pizza." He rubbed his fuzzy stomach. He'd been dumpster diving behind Vincent's Pizzeria on Main Street.

"If you were hungry, you could have come to me," I said.

Jacoby peered at me, the gray fuzz that framed his eyes sticking straight out.

"You lets me stay at your house?"

"No. We've been over that. You can't stay. But you'd be welcome for dinner anytime."

He pouted. "But dragon stays."

"The dragon is a temporary guest. Just until I find his thunder."

Maybe if I said that enough times it would actually be true. I really didn't want to take in a stray dragon.

At the market, I headed straight for the fruit and vegetable vendors. The pickings were slim this early in the year, but there were plenty of hothouse melons and some squashes that didn't look too pathetic. I placed a large order for those and had them stowed in my truck.

To the south of Montreal Ward, the orchards and farms are all protected by the city's militia. We have acres of greenhouses too. Other wards are not so lucky, and we produce enough to trade. Fresh produce isn't cheap though, and my bill was an excellent incentive to find Ollie's pack mates soon.

Next stop was Abbott's Agora, a section of the regular market reserved for purveyors of all things arcane. Unlike the rest of the market, there are no brightly colored awnings in the Agora. Instead, clusters of hovel-like stalls sit against the backdrop of twentieth-century buildings that were once a college and now house offices for the alchemists.

An antique asphalt road winds through the Agora like a lost river. Every turn brings fresh scents of burning herbs, dark potions and cured animal hides as well as the sweaty, spicy smells of the vendors and customers. Vendor wares hang from wooden trellises or lie across tables. Some stalls sell delicate or dangerous goods, and these have doors covered in rawhides or hand woven curtains. I've roamed the Agora for hours and never seen the same scene twice. It is impossibly large for the small space it inhabits. I have no idea whose magic started it, but over the years the market has taken on a sentience of its own and doesn't need anyone's magical intervention now.

I wandered, touching an interesting texture of weave here or sniffing a smudge stick there. You can't let the Agora know you have a particular destination in mind, or you'll find yourself lost for hours as the road contorts like a Mobius strip. So I let Jacoby browse the odd wares. Like a toddler, he had to touch everything and more than one vendor glared at me before I snatched some precious artifact from his fingers. I wasn't fast enough when he found the bags of wind. He plucked one from a bin and opened it before I could react. A hot gust blew him off his feet and he tumbled, cackling and hooting into the merchant's tent, knocking over a display of animal-tail key chains.

"So sorry!" I transferred ten bucks for the bag of wind. The vendor, a fossil of an old woman, glared and I gave her another ten. "We'll take a second one." Jacoby grabbed for the bag.

"Not here." I held it just out of his reach. "Promise me you won't open it until you're outside the city ward."

Jacoby jumped for the toy.

"Promise!"

"I promises." He grumbled, snatched the bag and tied it to his belt.

Next, we stopped in front of Nesi's, my go-to guy for outrageous critters. If I had a double-horned cerastes, Nesi would re-home it. A venom spitting sloth-spider? No problem. Nesi could find me a collector. The first few times I sold him creatures, I'd done my due diligence and checked out the buyers. I wouldn't let my captures go to slaughterhouses. I didn't care how much mucus a sebaceous salamander could cough up. It was still a living creature and deserved to finish its existence in peace. But Nesi was on the up and up. He sold only to those who truly admired critters in all their living, fire-breathing, bile-vomiting, venom-spitting glory. Mostly they went to private zoos, but as long as they were cared for, I didn't make a fuss. I had only so many options for re-homing creatures. They couldn't all go back to the Inbetween where they might harass the farmers tending the ward's only food source.

Nesi's store was little more than a leaning shed with a tattered afghan hanging in the doorway. The table out front held cheap clay idols of ancient gods, rabbit's feet, catnip balls and dream-catchers. The serious stuff was inside. His little shack hid enough magic to purchase the crown jewels of a small empire.

I left Jacoby outside with the less breakable items and found Nesi hunched over a gemstone with a jeweler's loupe pressed against one eye. Magic oozed off the pinkish stone in his hand. Cages of every size were piled against the walls of his shop. A baby jaculus slithered in one, wings still too fragile to lift its serpentine body into the air. A large aquarium burbled quietly in one corner. Dark shapes slunk in the water, but I wasn't foolish enough to poke my nose in for a look. Rare birds in wrought-iron cages hung from the ceiling. They were quiet now, but I suspected Nesi didn't get to sleep past dawn. Inside another glass terrarium, dozens of leontos clung to pieces of egg carton. The small cricket-like insects were known as lion-killers, but since there were few lions in Montreal Ward, Nesi sold them as bait. My eel and bearded monitors loved them too.

"Hey, Princess." He didn't look up from his examination of the stone. Nesi believed I was a princess from a water planet in the Pleiades star cluster. Most days it was just a fond nickname and I went with it, but Nesi's mood could instantly shift to rambling incoherence or worse. He was prone to fits of ranting paranoia, and I'd learned to leave him alone when he was in one of those moods.

I slipped a hunk of egg carton and a few dozen leontos into a plastic bag while he finished with his pink rock. After a few moments, when the only sounds in the shack were the shifting of wings and scaled feet, Nesi popped the rock into a bag and turned his attention to me.

"Got any tasty critters for me today?"

He seemed lucid enough.

"Caught a moon-frog yesterday," I said, "but I let it go."

"Too bad. I could use a good high." He flicked up the loupe so it rested on his forehead like a third eye. Gray hair exploded from his head and fell past a long beard that he kept in two tight braids. His cheek bones were a shade past gaunt. One blue eye pierced me with a canny gaze. The other was milky white. He liked to spin tales about it. The blindness was the result of a spell gone awry. He claimed it was messed up from a lucky shot by a spitting glow-gecko, or a parasitic viral infection. But the truth was less glamorous, if no less tragic. Nesi had fought in the Flood Wars. He didn't talk about it.

"So no critters. Just came for those?" He took the bag of leontos from me and tied it shut, leaving a bubble of air for the bugs to breathe.

"Not exactly." I fidgeted with some rings displayed on a small table. I wanted to tell Nesi about the murdered dragon and the bloodstone, but wasn't sure how to do that without mentioning Mason, and his secrets weren't mine to give. I started with something less ambivalent.

"I found a dead dragon yesterday."

"Dragon and a moon-frog. Busy day." He had no idea. "Did you bring me anything? Scales? Horns? Wings? I can get a good price for dragon leather."

"No. I didn't bring you dragon booty. There was a whole thunder. Someone killed one and the others got away." I wouldn't tell him about Ollie yet.

"Poachers then. Shit." Nesi made the word two syllables. Shee-it. "Sons of bitches, all of them. But I didn't hear about any dragon parts on the market." His magic, which was usually a quiet hum, rang out angrily for a moment, before settling back to a simmer. I didn't know where Nesi came from or what kind of power he had. It isn't polite—and it's sometimes even a little dangerous—to ask a supernatural about his heritage. But he was old. The Flood Wars ended over fifty years ago.

"They weren't poachers exactly," I said. "I think they were using the dragons to find treasure. Did you know that dragons eat magic relics?"

"'Course." Nesi snorted. "Where do you think all the stories of hoarded dragon treasure come from? You think the beasts really like to lounge around on a pile of gold. Damned uncomfortable, if you ask me. No. They eat it."

"Seems like a lot of bother to transport an entire thunder of dragons just to find some magic relics," I said.

"Most people can't pick out magic the way you can, Princess."

"I know that, but they were going to kill the dragons and gut them for the relics. And they'd stunted them somehow."

Nesi squinted at me. "What do you mean?"

"The dragons all wore null collars to keep them from flying. And they'd been wearing them for a while. Their wings were atrophied."

"Like I said: SOB's."

"Well, I rescued one of them." Nesi perked up at this news. "No, he's not for sale. I'm looking for his thunder so I can return him to the wild."

"Ambitious."

"Necessary. He's just a baby. Have you heard of any dragon sightings in the area?" Nesi had a vast network of trackers, hunters and coyotes both inside the ward and throughout the Inbetween.

"Not yet. But if the rest of them got away, I'm sure I'll hear something. Want me to put out a call?"

I thought about that for a moment. I needed intel, but I didn't want to shine a beacon on Ollie's whereabouts either.

"Okay," I said, "But be discreet. I can trust you not to mention that I have the dragon, right?"

Nesi's withered hand covered mine. "Princess, you can trust me with your life, your heart and your lunch."

I pulled out of the awkward hand-holding. Nesi watched me pick through his collection of gemstones in silence. He was patient. I wasn't sure how much I should tell him.

"One of the dragons dug up a gemstone," I said finally. "I didn't get a good look, but it was potent. Nearly knocked me on my ass." Nesi was one of the few people who knew just how sensitive I was to magic. We'd worked together for too long, with too many bizarre magics for him to be unaware of it. But just because he knew my secrets didn't mean I could trust him with Mason's. I had to be careful here.

"I was told it was a bloodstone. Have you ever seen one?"

His one good eye stared at me for a moment, but he didn't ask who told me. Instead, he unfolded his thin legs from the stool and reached above him to a shelf lost in the shadows of the dim shop. Nesi's library was impressive, if discreet. He had many books I wished I could get my hands on, but he was miserly with the information they contained. He dropped a huge tome on the table and opened its cracked spine. Ancientness wafted up from the pages. Even through my wards, the hum of magic rising from the book made my teeth ache.

"You really should scan those and put them on the ley-net." I thought of the paltry information available online. "It would be so much easier to access."

"Easy isn't always better." The pages creaked like the door to a haunted house when he turned them. "Besides, I've tried to scan them. Doesn't work."

"What do you mean?"

"I mean, I put them on the scanner, the scanner runs across the page and then, nothing. I was able to scan some lesser volumes. I blogged about it." He pointed to the stack of cards on the counter with llw.NesiWares.com printed over a glowing geode. "But it seems the stronger the magic, the more resistant it is to tech."

"Maybe the alchemists could help you with that," I said, but Nesi's milky-eyed glare told me he would never trust the alchemists with his precious library.

"Here. Maffeo Polo talks about bloodstones." He stopped at a page illuminated with two paintings in opposite corners. One was a pile of colored stones that looked like a clutch of dragon eggs. The other was the scaled face of a dragon with a red jewel on its forehead, right between its golden eyes.

"Maffeo Polo?" I asked.

"Marco Polo's lesser known uncle. He was an accomplished explorer too, and a prolific writer. Marco learned that skill from him."

"Why do we never hear about him then?" I couldn't keep my fingers off the page. I traced the scroll work frame around the dragon's face. The text was gibberish to me.

"Why do you think? They banned him. In his time, it was one thing to write about giraffes, hippos and other exotic creatures, but don't go spouting off about things like ogres and demons. They'd shut you down right quick. Believe me. I know."

His bushy brows lowered over his eyes. Nesi was always ranting about the collective "they" as if some shadowy evil organization was out to get him. "They" were watching him. "They" would bring down the economy. "They" opposed space exploration because "They" knew what was truly out there. I didn't want to know who "They" were. Nesi had secrets. Dark ones. I believed that all knowledge was good. But when I looked into his eyes, one damaged and milky, the other haunted, I wasn't sure I wanted Nesi's knowledge.

"Does it say anything about the bloodstone being a weapon?" I asked.

He ran his fingers along the glossy black text. The words shivered at his touch, their magic quiet and authoritative.

"Not a weapon. A…dish. No, that's wrong. A vessel."

"Like a cup?"

"Yes. Or a container. Just something that holds something else. Huh. Says here they're a special kind of scale, taken from the forehead of a dragon. No, that's wrong too." He took down another book and flipped through what looked like a dictionary of sorts.

"Not taken from a dragon. Forged in the head of a dragon. That sounds messy. But technically they are magically inert. Nothing more than a box."

"That can't be right. I felt its magic like a punch in the gut. And the dragons went after it too."

"Well, a box is just a box. What's important is what you put inside it."

"So the dragon wasn't drawn to the bloodstone, but the magic inside it?"

"Seems so." He shut the book. "Now tell me what kind of trouble you've gotten yourself into."

I wasn't sure if it was the blue eye or the white eye that saw right through me, but when Nesi turned them on me I felt like a little girl caught in an act of naughtiness.

Jacoby's shrieking got me out of answering. We ran outside to find the dervish gleefully spinning along with a toy top he'd found among the junk for sale. His arms whirled as he spun faster, his shrieks edging toward maniacal. Dust and bits of leaves coalesced around his feet, the onset of a full-on dust funnel.

*Oh, no…No, no, no.*

I handed Nesi my bag of bugs and dove for Jacoby, locking his arms to his side to abort his burgeoning maelstrom.

"Stop!"

Jacoby stared at me with huge, unfocused eyes. His thin chest heaved as he panted. His feet still tried to turn him despite my firm grip.

"Jacoby, you need to stop!" I yelled again, more because of my frazzled nerves than to reach him. He was in the throes of a whirlwind and wouldn't hear me.

"Is that a fire dervish?" Nesi asked.

"Yes." I was losing my grip.

"How marvelous."

"Find me something to bind him with before he goes nova!"

Nesi disappeared inside his hut. I spoke in soothing baby-talk tones, hoping to calm Jacoby. Other than being able to teleport short distances, dervishes had one other remarkable talent. They could spin themselves into a fiery tornado frenzy. If unchecked, Jacoby's whirlwind would grow to encompass half the market. He could take out an entire city block.

Nesi returned with a syringe.

"Hey!" I protested as he plunged it into Jacoby's arm. The dervish's eyes rolled back and he went limp.

"I said to bind him, not drug him."

"Come now, Princess. I've been dealing with wild beasts since before you were born." That was possible but unlikely. I was older than I looked. "Better to sedate the little guy than risk hurting him."

He had a point. And Jacoby finally got his wish. He was coming home with me.

# CHAPTER 8

As soon as I unlocked my door, I knew something was wrong. Gleeful chitters followed the sound of breaking glass. Clarence paced in his pen, screaming, "Gobble! Gobble!" The madras cage was empty. Again. Crap. I put the unconscious Jacoby on Willow's bed and hurried through to my apartment.

The place was in shambles. My couch was tipped backwards, the cushions lying scattered across the floor. The mug I'd used that morning lay broken in a puddle of coffee. Magazines, clumps of dirty hay and clothes from my bedroom were scattered around. Willow perched atop the curtain rod over the patio door, watching the chaos unfold with wide eyes.

And the mayhem was ongoing. Ollie ran around the toppled couch and leaped over the wreckage. His wings fluttered and he hovered for a second before landing with a thump.

He was trying to fly.

Alvin and Theo egged him on by pelting him with gooey wads of chewed hay. From somewhere deep inside her closet, Gita wailed.

"Hello?" A voice came from the office. No time to sort out the disaster now. I closed the door on my apartment and faced a tidy young man.

Looking at my harried state, he said, "I'm here about the job?" He made it sound like a question, as if he couldn't believe this was the right place.

"Of course. You must be Frank Myers?" I indicated that he should take the chair beside my desk.

A crash from the other room told me that my floor lamp had just died.

I closed my eyes and prayed for patience. Frank glanced nervously at the closed door.

"Is this a bad time?" he asked. "Should I come back?"

I almost said yes, but the need to fill the assistant's position overruled.

"No, no. It's fine," I said. "So do you have any clerical experience?" I sat and tried to look professional by sorting through the folders lodged under the passed-out dervish. Finally, I found Frank's resume. Jacoby snorted and rolled in his sleep, tossing one long bony arm across the folder.

"Is that an elf?"

"A dervish. More in the brownie or bodach family." I was always amazed at how the mundanes could live in such a diverse ward and still know so little about other species.

"So, clerical experience?"

"Uh, yes. I worked for a small nonprofit, managing the office." Frank sat rigid in his chair.

Another crash from my apartment and an unholy shriek.

"Bookkeeping?"

Crash and the howl of a really angry cat.

"No bookkeeping." He was looking kind of pale. "Do you maybe want to check on that?"

Gita chose that moment to come out of her closet and yell at my misbehaving charges. Banshees can really rant. Mr. Murray thudded on his floor, demanding quiet. And Clarence screamed, "Gobble! Gobble," from about three feet away.

"Maybe I should come back another time." Frank's chair fell over as he ran out the door.

I put my head on my arms and just sat. There was nothing else to do. My life had dissolved into madness.

Eventually, flight practice ended and Gita's wailing faded to sobs.

I rose and went to see the damage.

"He'll be the death of us!" Gita pointed at the little blue dragon, who now nested on one of the fallen couch cushions. His co-conspirators were sound asleep beside him. Ollie chirped and put a protective wing over the madras.

"That creature is the devil himself!" Gita said, but her rant lacked luster.

"Come on. Let's make tea."

After getting Gita settled, I returned to find Ollie fast asleep. I scooped up Alvin and Theo. Their fat, furry rumps fit perfectly into the crooks of my elbows. Alvin stretched up and butted my chin.

"It's a good thing you're so cute." I tucked them back into their cage, though I don't know why I bothered. They could get out any time they wanted. I found a garbage bag and filled it with ripped magazines and broken crockery. The lamp could be fixed, I hoped.

I cleaned up as best I could and brought the wreckage of my apartment out to the dumpster. It was dark already, but the street lamp outside my warehouse hadn't come on. The electrical grid on my block was patchy at best. I'd complained to the town a dozen times, but no one bothered to answer.

I dumped the ruins of my apartment in the bin outside and turned back to the door, only to smack into a lurking figure.

"I've come for the dung," Mason said.

I paused only a second to let my heart stop hammering, then said, "Does that line work for you often?"

He grinned. "Only on the really dirty girls."

Mason pressed one hand against the wall beside my head, leaned into me and whispered, "And you are one dirty girl."

My heart squeezed. He was standing so close. And he smelled so good. He plucked a wad of madras cud from my hair and raised one eyebrow in a question. My self-esteem went from sexy tease to filth-encrusted waif in an instant.

"Thanks." I took the ball of chewed hay and ducked under his arm at a full retreat.

Luck was with us. Ollie had blessed us with a nice pile of steaming dung, right on my living room carpet. Gita stood over it, weeping. "I suppose you expect me to clean this up?"

"Don't touch it," Mason said urgently as she leaned down to scoop it up. Gita took exception to his tone and ran for her closet.

He watched her leave with a worried expression. "I didn't mean to offend."

I shrugged. "Taking offense is a national sport for banshees."

"I didn't realize that banshees had their own nation."

"Of course they do," I said. "It's Bansheeland."

Mason took a widget from his pocket, pressed a few buttons then said,

"No, Ireland is the closest thing they have to a homeland, but it seems they're spread across the globe now."

"Impressive. I didn't think an old guy like you would know how to use the ley-web."

"I haven't let all my tools atrophy," he said. This would have been a much flirtier conversation if we weren't both crouched over a pile of dung.

"I'll…uh…get you a shovel," I said, "but I can already tell that the bloodstone isn't there. That dung is magically inert."

Mason poked through it with the shovel anyway. It was full of bits of gold and silver trinkets. The dragon had digested the magic and expelled the metals. I scooped up the mess and put it in a muck bucket destined for the composter.

"So we keep looking?" I asked.

Mason nodded. "We keep looking."

"I'm going to find Ollie's thunder."

"Ollie?"

I pointed to the sleeping dragon. "That's his name."

"And you know where the other dragons are?"

"Not yet, but I'll find them. I've got someone asking around."

"You didn't tell this someone about the bloodstone, did you?"

"No." My face is a terrible liar. "Okay, I might have asked him what a bloodstone is, but I didn't tell him about you."

"*Sacrament.*" Mason swore in old French and rubbed the back of his neck. "Can't you just stay out of my business?"

I stood straighter to look him in the eye. "Not when your business is bound up with his business." I pointed at the dragon. "I won't let you or anyone else hurt him. I *will* find his family."

Mason glared at me, then came to some private decision. "Fine. I'm coming with you."

"I don't need your help."

"I wasn't asking. I'm not letting that dragon go until I get the bloodstone back. Besides, I have contacts at Hub. If there have been any dragon sightings in the area, they'll know about it."

I knew Mason was a high-ranking alchemist, so it only made sense that he'd want to bring Hub into this mess. I wasn't so keen on the idea.

"I'd rather leave the authorities out of it."

Mason narrowed his eyes. "Why?"

"Because I nicked one of the poachers with my sword." I crossed my arms over my chest, my best defense against answering his questions.

"And that's a problem?"

I turned away and started tidying the rest of the mess.

"What are you not telling me?" he demanded, spinning me around to face him.

"About as much as you're not telling me." We stood nose-to-nose, well nose-to-chin because he was a good six inches taller than me. I could feel the slow tolling of his magic. It was deep and constant, like waves rolling onto a beach.

"Since it looks like we're stuck working together, perhaps an exchange of information is in order," he said. He wasn't going to let this go. But I could use his curiosity to my advantage.

"Fine. An answer for an answer. But coffee first."

I set the coffeepot to brew and returned to find Mason examining my menagerie.

"How do you ever sleep past dawn with all these mouths to feed," he asked. "And what is that?" He poked a finger in Kur's cage.

"That's an ice-sprite. And no, I don't get much sleep."

Kur gripped Mason's finger in both his tiny hands and tried to eat it. Mason pulled his finger back and inspected the next cage, which held two troll bats hanging upside down from a branch. He shook his head and smiled. Turning, he spotted the aquarium on the shelf next to the ruined couch. A red gelatinous head with baseball eyes peered over the rim of the tank. One tiny tentacle followed to grip the glass.

"What the hell is that?"

"Pygmy kraken."

"You mean an octopus."

The tentacle jerked upright, then waved slowly side to side.

"What's it doing?"

"Flipping you off."

"Nice."

The couch was still a mess, so I ushered Mason to my kitchen and we settled down at my 1950's style kitchenette with mugs of hot coffee. He didn't even wince when he tasted my jet-fuel brew. Impressive.

"You go first," I said.

"What's so important about finding the poachers?" he asked.

I retrieved my sword from the umbrella stand, unsheathed it and laid it across the laminate table. The two-and-a-half-foot long blade could hardly be called a sword. It was a knife with ambitions of glory. Aunt Dana wouldn't let me have anything bigger, not until I'd proven myself. And after I spent forty years fighting in the arena on Asgard, I still hadn't proven my worth in her eyes.

But other than its size, the sword had all the properties of a Valkyrie weapon. The double-edged blade, suitable for hacking, ended in a short grip and round pommel. And it was alive.

"You probably can't feel it, but that's one anxious sword," I said. "Since you're so proficient on the search engines, you can look up 'Valkyrie,' but I'll fill in the pertinent details."

I touched the dull metal with a gentle caress. Its magic hummed through my fingers, full of excitement at its recent blooding.

"Valkyrie blades are soul-suckers. It tasted that poacher's blood and it won't rest easy until it finishes the kill."

"So, you'll hunt him down and what? Just kill him?" Mason asked. I couldn't tell if he approved of that quest or not.

"It would be a mercy killing," I said. "The man is dead already. He just doesn't know it. A wound from a Valkyrie blade is always fatal for a mortal. It will fester. No mundane or magic intervention will heal it. Eventually, the necrosis will spread and he'll start to rot before he's even dead. It's a horrible, painful way to go."

"Interesting." Mason ran one finger along the blade. "So if I were to cut myself now, my long years of life would finally come to an end?"

I closed my eyes and the despair that was always simmering beneath the surface of my everyday face threatened to overwhelm me. A sour image flashed through my mind—an image of my cousin holding my hand in his, my blade gripped inside both hands, plunging into his heart.

I swallowed hard and pushed the past away. I was getting good at that. Maybe in another hundred years I'd almost forget that I'd killed my first love and best friend.

Mason watched me with intense eyes. He saw more than I wanted to share.

*Please tell me you aren't another one of those melancholy immortals, looking for a quick exit off this plane of existence.*

Aloud, I said, "Maybe. Its magic is erratic with immortals. It might kill you, or just give you really bad heartburn."

Mason considered that and chose his words carefully.

"So you want to track this man down and kill him before his limbs turn black."

"Yes, and I'd appreciate it if Hub didn't know about it."

I was pretty sure mercy killing was still murder.

"Fine, I'll keep that part out of it, but I still think we can use their resources to find the dragons. Unless you have a better plan."

Not unless Nesi's network produced results. Reluctantly, I shook my head.

"My turn." I had so many questions, I didn't know where to begin. Best to get the most bang for my buck and ask the one that I wouldn't find the answer to anywhere else.

"Why are you so desperate to get that bloodstone back?"

Mason didn't answer right away. Was he debating the wisdom of telling me the truth? Or was he simply trying to pick through the truth, deciding which bits were suitable for me? Since I had just done the same to him, I couldn't fault him for it.

"I created the bloodstone. It's my responsibility to make sure it stays safe."

An answer and not an answer.

"And keeping it safe means keeping it hidden," he said. "I would destroy it if I could, but that isn't possible. At least I haven't found a way."

"And why do you need to hide it?"

Mason smiled and held up two fingers. "That's two questions. My turn first."

"What did the poacher look like? The one you cut."

"He was young and blond with a face like a block of wood. Why? You know him?"

Mason shook his head. "Just wondering if an old friend finally found me."

I thought about that for a minute. It would make sense. That cemetery was targeted. And the only one living nearby was Mason with his crew of Guardians.

"Your turn." He was letting me off easy. I couldn't repay the favor. I needed to know.

"I know what the bloodstone does. It holds magic, right?" He nodded, but I wasn't done. "So what hideous thing did you hide in it?"

"Not hide," he said. "Imprison."

We were going to need something stronger than coffee for this conversation. I leaned over and pulled a bottle of whiskey and two glasses from a cupboard. I poured two shots and shoved one at Mason. He sipped it and only made a slight face. He was probably used to a finer age, but my budget could only provide the cheap stuff.

Ollie came into the kitchen, sleepy-eyed and hungry. I tossed him an apple from the bowl of fruit in the middle of the table. He settled down to chew on it, his tail swishing across the linoleum.

"You don't have to tell me," I said.

"Yes, I do." He gulped the whiskey and nudged the glass toward me. I refilled it.

"I'm not a real gargoyle, in case you hadn't noticed."

"You mean you weren't born a gargoyle?"

He laughed. It was a harsh sound that hurt my heart.

"See any wings?" He dipped his broad shoulders to show me his back, as if I might have overlooked his lack of wings. "A witch cursed me to this half-life."

"You must have really pissed her off."

"That I did." His smile made me ache. I wanted to trace the fine line that quirked his lips upward. Ollie seemed to sense the mood and laid his head across Mason's knee. Mason scratched behind his ear.

"The witch is caught in the bloodstone. I couldn't defeat her, so I trapped her. That was three-hundred years ago. Besides the Guardians, the only person who knows about her is Pierre Garnier, her lover. I think he might have sent the poachers."

"But surely, he's dead by now."

Mason shrugged. "I'm not dead."

"So you think the guy I cut is this Pierre Garnier?"

"No, he doesn't fit Pierre's description. But maybe he's working for him. All I know is that Pierre has been hunting me and the bloodstone for centuries. Polina, the witch, was a major power back in her day. How much more damage could she do now, with the ley-lines overflowing?"

The world had taken a sharp turn about eighty years ago. Everyone thought that the worst effect of climate change would be the flooding when the icecaps melted. And that was devastating. Cities fell off the map, but then the fighting started. The real war to end all wars. And it would have. But no one expected the Earth to wake up. As ley-lines swelled, the land took on a sentience of its own.

Terra fought back. Magic surged through the planet like lifeblood and there was no going back.

Our world was a very different place than Renaissance France. Mason was right. A witch who was powerful back then, could be devastating today.

I glanced at Ollie, who was enjoying the attention as Mason rubbed the scales around his crest. Did that little dragon really have the spirit of a dead witch in his gut?

"I guess you should join me then, to find the dragons," I said. "Any idea where we should start?"

"The transport truck that the poachers used," Mason said. "I have a lead on it. I should have an answer by tomorrow. Be ready to leave at sundown."

He stood to leave.

I stopped him. "There's still something you're not telling me."

"Right back at you." He winked before heading out the door.

# CHAPTER 9

Jacoby was gone when I woke the next morning. He must have recovered from Nesi's tranquilizer and gone looking for food. It occurred to me I didn't even know what dervishes ate, other than dumpster pizza. I made a mental note to ask him next time he showed up.

The day was all about waiting. Waiting for Mason to get information from his contact at Hub. Waiting for Nesi to get back to me with news from his network. And sitting through several painful interviews for a new assistant.

These did not go well.

Of the three candidates, only one wasn't freaked out by my menagerie. Candace (who preferred to go by "Candy" because she was "just so sweet") thought Alvin and Theo were delightful and even cooed over my snake-rooster when he yelled "Gobble! Gobble!" at her. Unfortunately, sweet-cheeks Candy had no relevant job skills on her resume and I suspected she couldn't type over ten words per minute with those long nails.

So a pass for Candy.

The phone rang as I was tidying my office.

"Can you get to Annequin Lodge?" Nesi said, before I could even say "Hello."

"Is that in the east end?" I'd never heard of Annequin Lodge, but my neighborhood was about as far west as you could get without falling off the island.

"No. It's a hundred kilometers north of here."

"In the Inbetween? You can't be serious."

"Do you want to find the dragons or not? There have been sightings in the mountains above the lodge. There's a trapper who works the area around it. She'll be expecting you."

Was it possible the dragons had found a way out of the ward and flown a hundred kilometers into the wilds in just a couple of days? I knew too little about dragons to dispute that, so I took down the coordinates for the lodge. The trapper's name was Simone. I didn't look forward to working with someone who hunted animals for a living, but desperate times and all.

"Thanks, Nesi. I owe you one."

"Don't worry. I'm keeping a tally." He hung up.

While waiting for my final job applicant to arrive, I took Ollie out for a stroll around the parking lot, hoping he'd do his business there and not in my living room again. I brought Clarence with us. He made the neighbors nervous—it wasn't often that you saw a basilisk slithering through the neighborhood—but he was due to pass the gizzard stone and could use the exercise.

Neither one obliged me, so I left them to play chase while I opened the back hatch on my truck and went through my kit, deciding what I'd need to bring on the journey to Annequin Lodge.

The Inbetween is the lawless land between protected wards. Looking at my usual pest control kit, I realized I wasn't prepared for such a trip. I had first aid—both mundane and a very expensive med-mage kit—traps of various sizes, tranquilizers and the usual rope, duct tape and flares. None of that would protect me if I met with a wraith or an ogre. Not to mention the bandits that preyed on travelers and refugees. And oh, the spontaneous bursts of magic that could manifest anything from monsters to storms. Fun stuff.

I left Montreal Ward regularly, but I never went farther than Dorion Park, right in Mason's backyard, under the protection of the Guardians. To travel through the real Inbetween I'd need weapons. And backup.

A car pulled up, parked next to my truck and a stylish young man stepped out. Ollie and Clarence skidded around the bumper of his car and slammed into him. The man stumbled backward and nearly lost his man-bun. Ollie hissed out a plume of black smoke and Clarence yelled, "Gobble! Gobble!" The visitor jumped back into his car. Tires squealed as he left.

That was the last of my candidates for an assistant. Well, I couldn't worry about it now. The ad would be up on the job board for another few days.

Maybe when I returned from the lodge, I'd have another batch to interview.

Ollie, sensing that he'd misbehaved somehow, nudged me with his nose and looked up with big, sad eyes.

I scratched his head.

"Don't worry, buddy. If he couldn't handle a little dragon fire, then he's the wrong guy for the job anyway." Ollie chirped and ran off to chase Clarence again.

I turned back to organizing my kit. I needed to pack light and choose weapons accordingly. Guns were unpredictable in the Inbetween, where pockets of raw magic could cause them to misfire or even backfire. Swords were a solid choice, but good only at close range. Bandits wouldn't be so obliging. I packed a slingshot and at the last moment I added my crossbow. Was that overkill? Probably not enough kill.

Mason might have some other ideas for protection. Alchemists always had the best mage-tech. I didn't relish the thought of traveling with him for days (or nights) on end, but he wouldn't give up his chance to recover his precious bloodstone.

Glancing at the sun that just peeked over the tree line, I had about two hours to get ready. It was strange to think that Mason was, at that moment, inanimate stone. Was he aware of his surroundings during his gargoyle hours? Did he sleep or was he trapped inside his stone prison, just counting down the minutes until he was free? I shivered at the thought. We all had our curses to bear, but imagining Mason stuck in stone made me irrationally angry.

Maybe Ollie would pass the bloodstone today. Mason would take his treasure and be out of my life again. I'd take Ollie to find his thunder on my own. That would be for the best, but a small, selfish part of my heart hoped that Ollie was constipated for a few days longer.

Just as I was wrangling the dragon and the basilisk inside, another car pulled up, this one black and sleek. A tall man stepped out. His pearly gray suit matched his long hair. Even his complexion was gray as if he didn't see the sun too often.

"Miss Greene?"

I nodded.

"My name is Dutch. I work for Mr. Mason. I am his daytime eyes, you might say."

"I remember you."

After our fight with the rock troll, Mason had sent Dutch to check on me in the hospital. Dutch seemed like a nice man, but seeing him brought back all those feelings of fear and rejection—waking up alone and in pain in the hospital, wondering if Mason was still alive, then realizing he wouldn't be coming to see me.

Ollie slipped around my legs to sniff this new visitor. Dutch patted him on his head and Ollie decided he was good people.

"What can I help you with," I asked.

"Mr. Mason wanted me to let you know that his lead about the truck transport has hit a dead end. He will keep trying, but asked if you had other news."

"I do. Dragons have been sighted in the mountains north of Annequin Lodge in the Inbetween. I'm leaving tonight and I could use some company."

Dutch nodded in an odd way that almost seemed like a bow.

"Of course. Mr. Mason will meet you here just after sunset."

And just like that, our fates were sealed.

*Valkyriebestiary.com/moon-frog*

## The Problem with Moon-frogs

*(April 25, 2080)*

*Moon-frog: Class 3 Fae.*

Though moon-frogs are amphibian, they're not actually related to the frogs of Terra. Cryptozoologists speculate that they found a hole between worlds during the Flood Wars. Several mentions in texts to "puffer toads" or "peace toads" suggest that they may have arrived in our world as early as 1960.

While exhibiting no natural tendencies for magic, the moon-frog reacts to the full moon by swelling its body and producing venom-laced spikes on its back—possibly part of a mating ritual, though I have witnessed this behavior in response to stress.

A mature moon-frog weighs about 5 kilos. Fully expanded, its body is about 40 centimeters in diameter. Its skin is mottled blue, green and brown and looks glossy, as if it would be wet to the touch, though in my experience, they are usually dry and sort of velvety.

**Warning: Use extreme caution when handling moon-frogs. While their venom is more hallucinogenic than poisonous, an overdose can be fatal. Don't lick the frogs!

In my travels, I have trapped and re-homed a half dozen moon-frogs, but they have always been solitary creatures. Does anyone know how they reproduce? Are there moon-frog tadpoles? Leave your moon-frog experiences in the comments below.

## Comments (5)

I have never come across a moon-frog. But my sister-wife says that a brew from their venom is very good for fevers, especially those derived from a virus.

*cchedgewitch (April 27, 2080)*

> Good to know. Thanks!
>
> *Valkyrie367 (May 27, 2080)*

Gotta get me some frog love!

*PeachOut (April 29, 2080)*

You mean people get high from licking frogs? That's hilarious!

*DaddysGirl (April 30, 2080)*

What is wrong with people? Licking frogs?

*SiriusBlue14 (May 7, 2080)*

# CHAPTER 10

"We're not taking that." Mason pointed at my truck like its very existence offended him.

"Would you rather let a dragon tear up your sweet leather upholstery?" I asked. Mason drove a modern alchemical wonder—a sleek, black, magic-efficient model. No way he'd let the dragon spoil it.

He crossed his arms. "A car is just a car. If it gets me from point A to point B, I don't care what the upholstery looks like."

Well, that was a refreshingly unmacho point of view. The gargoyle had layers.

"So why can't we take my truck, then?"

"Because two miles into the Inbetween it will most likely break an axle. It looks like it's being held together by sheer willpower and dental floss."

"Duct tape," I muttered. "Not dental floss."

Mason was right, of course. And my truck guzzled magic. With no charging stations in the Inbetween, we'd need to haul a dozen batteries with us. Mason's car would be more efficient.

As I transferred my kit to his trunk, Ollie raced around the parking lot. He knew something was up. I let him burn off excess energy because it would be a long drive with a hyped-up dragon. Angus, the green-man gargoyle I'd met at the cemetery, encouraged the dragon to flap his wings and try to make lift off. He pumped his stubby wings and hovered a few inches off the ground to show Ollie his technique. Ollie tried to copy him until I was finally ready.

Angus shooed Ollie into the backseat. I hopped into the passenger seat and Mason drove. As we pulled out of the parking lot, I waved to the shadow in the upstairs window, and Mr. Murray jerked the curtain back into place. I sighed, hoping Gita could keep my charges under control until I returned.

We drove toward the North Gate in silence, each within a cocoon of our own thoughts.

The line of cars leaving the ward was much shorter than those waiting to come in. Crystal Bridge spans the gap between the island of Montreal and the mainland to the north. The bridge, made of glittery white stone, is one of only three gates through the ward that protects the city.

A few years after the Flood Wars, three friends—one fae, one human and one alchemist—came to Montreal and began the painful process of boosting the island's natural wards. Other city-states had carved out their piece of the post-war landscape, but none were powerful enough to overtake Montreal. And so the three founders had years to build up their ward, until it covered the entire island, creating a haven where different races could live together. I won't say in perfect harmony. That would be idealizing things. But we mostly got along.

The fae held Crystal bridge, and they were responsible for maintaining its security.

Mason rolled down my window as we approached the checkpoint. The guard bent to peer inside. He was tall and elfin in appearance, with smooth golden skin, white blond hair braided in an elaborate knot and brilliant green eyes. But that could have been a glamor. For all I knew, he was short, fat and covered in warts. The class one fae were masters of glamor and could take on any appearance they wanted.

"Hey, Holistayr. What's with the crowd tonight?" Mason asked.

"Nothing to worry about," the guard said. "Just rumors of vamp activity to the west. Some homesteaders decided it would be a good time to visit the big city."

Homesteaders were a paranoid lot. They gave up the safety of a ward to live free in the wilds of the Inbetween. If they were heading for the city, the vampire attacks had to be more than rumor. I wanted to ask the guard more, but he waved us on, impatient to keep the line moving.

As we drove over the river, I felt like we were driving off the edge of the world. To the west lay the Floods, a vast plain of swampy land now hidden by the long line of refugees coming into the ward. A few cars lit the night with their headlights, but most travelers were on foot or riding in horse-drawn carts—a long stream of ragged humans and fae, seeking the protection of the ward. To the north and east, the vast no-man's-land of the Inbetween stretched into the darkness.

Mason drove slowly as we approached the far end of the bridge and the ward gate. To a mundane, the ward would appear only as a slight shimmer in the air. But it set my skin prickling. As the arch of the gate loomed overhead, my heart beat erratically and I fought for breath. Just as the screech of magic coming off the ward was almost too much to bear, we were through, and onto the busy thoroughfare that ran into Barrows, the rag-tag town that had grown up outside the north gate.

The streets were busier than usual. Groups of families squatted on any available patch of land. Other more disreputable sorts—fae and human—lingered in tavern doorways, their eyes watching all the activity.

Mason slowed the car to a crawl as we wove through the crowds. We parked in the alley behind Pack Station, an old inn on the farthest edge of town. It was the first place to greet incoming refugees and the last stop for outgoing travelers to stock up.

Ollie was sound asleep in the backseat.

"Keep the dragon out of sight," Mason said to Angus.

"No worries. I'll watch him with a fine-toothed comb." The green man propped his feet on the front seat and settled in beside Ollie. I was grateful for his vigilance. Slave traders and other black-marketers hunted in Barrows. A dragon would fetch a good price.

"We need extra batteries for the car," I said as we headed inside.

"Marcella should have some," Mason said.

"Marcella?"

"She owns this station."

I tried to imagine a reason for an alchemist to come through the fae-run Barrows often enough to be on a first-name basis with the innkeeper. I came up empty.

Inside, the common room was full, but not boisterous. Subdued travelers sat nursing mugs of ale around trestle tables. A young man played guitar in one corner, but no one seemed to pay him any attention.

Mason led us to the bar where a striking dark-haired woman was drying glasses with a rag. When she saw us she stood a little straighter, which thrust out her ample bosom, and she smiled.

"Henry!" she dropped the rag, circled the bar and kissed him solidly on both cheeks. "Ça va tu bien? You stayed away far too long!"

"I've been busy." Mason smiled.

"You always say that and I never believe you."

Mason shrugged as if it didn't matter to him what she believed, but Marcella didn't let go of his arm. She gazed up at him as if he were the light of the sun. Irrationally, I wanted to pluck her fingers from his sleeve and shove her aside a few paces.

"We're heading out and need some charging cubes," Mason said.

"Charging cubes are expensive, cherie. Where are you headed?" She spoke in that French accent that could make "Where is the toilet?" sound sexy.

Ooh, la-la.

"Annequin Hunt Lodge," I said.

Marcella finally noticed me. Her smile only faltered a bit before her innate innkeeper hospitality kicked in. Then she grabbed my hands in hers, and clutched me like I was the dearest of old friends.

"You must refresh before you go. Supper? Hot cider?" I shook my head, but she tugged me toward the bar. "Come. Sit and we will discuss."

Although Mason and I declined drinks, Marcella served up two glasses of hot cider. The smell rising on the steam was rich and earthy. I gave in and took a sip.

"Even if I had enough charging cubes to get you to the lodge—which I don't—the road past the north farms gets rough," Marcella said, "too rough for anything with wheels."

"Horses, then?" Mason said.

"Normally, yes." Marcella eyed the customers left and right as if someone might overhear. "I might have some mounts, but horses are scarce. You won't find any in town. The damned refugees have taken everything. To eat, you see. They are locusts. Last night I cracked open my last barrel of wine. What kind of inn runs out of wine? Locusts!"

"Where are they all coming from?" I asked.

"West. The opji are on the move. Many villages have been overrun already."

The opji were a race that once opposed the settlement in Montreal. The original triumvirate fought many bloody skirmishes with them before the opji retreated to Vioska, their home-base some two-hundred kilometers west of Montreal. Mostly they stayed there. But the opji were vampires. Or at least as much like the old vampire myths as to make no difference. They hunted humans traveling through the area for food. But I'd been back in Montreal for over a decade, and in that time, opji attacks close to home were rare.

"The guard at the gate mentioned the vamps," Mason said. "But they've always hunted between Montreal and Ottawa."

"Not like this." Marcella shook her head. "Something is different. Something is very wrong. They take stragglers, maybe attack a small caravan here or there. Now they take entire villages. People are scared." Her big brown eyes turned watery and her lower lip quivered. She seemed vulnerable and somehow even more attractive in her state. So attractive that even I wanted to hold her and give comfort. I flicked a glance at Mason. He seemed unmoved.

"Maybe there's been a sickness in the krowa," he said.

The opji ward, Vioska, was a bunker in the Ottawa valley. Like Montreal, they kept well-defended farms outside their ward. But their farms were nothing more than cattle pens. And the cattle—or krowa—were humans bred as food.

Marcella bit her bottom lip. "Sickness in their humans would account for the recent attacks."

"Or they're breeding extra *wojaks*," Mason said grimly. Wojaks were opji soldiers—humans bred just to be killed and turned into undead killing machines. More soldiers meant they were building an army.

"If they're decimating entire villages, something is up," I said.

Marcella laid a hand on Mason's arm. "You should not go out there. The Inbetween is not safe." Clearly, she didn't mind if I went.

"It never is." Mason downed the last of his cider and stood. "But we have to go anyway. Now you mentioned some horses?"

Marcella smiled. "I said, mounts, cherie. Not horses."

# CHAPTER 11

The barn behind Pack Station was empty except for the last three stalls, which housed a giant goat, donkey and…

"Is that an elk?" I asked.

"Reindeer." Marcella reached up—way up—to pat its nose. The beast was easily as big as a draft horse. The reindeer I'd seen at the petting zoo were half that size.

"They are Herne's beasts," she cooed, "creatures of the Wild Hunt. You go to Annequin Lodge? They will get you there safely. Like homing pigeons. Even if you died on their backs, they would still make sure your corpses arrived at the lodge. Very sturdy. Very reliable. And you pay only for the feed since I need to return them to Herne anyway."

"You can quit the sales pitch," Mason said. "You sold us."

Marcella pouted but accepted the two gold coins he dropped in her hand. Electronic money didn't work in Barrows. "That's for the feed and to rent garage space for my car while we're gone. And we'll need provisions." He dropped another coin in her hand.

"I told you food is dear these days," Marcella said.

Mason gave her another coin. "We'll take what we can get. And find someone to help us saddle these ridiculous beasts."

THE NIGHTS WERE long in April and we had several hours of riding before Mason and Angus would need to stop. I rode Lucille, a lop-eared, brindle goat with one blue eye and one brown eye. Her withers were as high as my shoulder. Angus rode an equally enormous donkey named Zsa Zsa with Ollie propped on the saddle behind him. Mason was graced with the reindeer, Norma Jean, a beautiful beast with a shaggy coat that ran from dark gray on her back to a frosty white on her nose. She'd recently dropped her antlers and her crown sported only two-inch buds.

I hadn't been on horseback in over ten years, and even with the modified saddle, Lucille wasn't built for comfort. After only an hour of riding, muscles I'd forgotten I had screamed for surrender.

We rode along an old highway, our mounts' feet echoing *clip-clop* with every step. The road was wide, three lanes coming and going. Grass and shrubs had grown up through the cracked pavement, forcing the mounts to pick a careful path. An old railroad track ran alongside, the train abandoned at the station and both wrapped in vines. In the distance, old buildings were barely visible against the night sky. Magic spurred the growth of flora that broke through masonry and pulled down ceilings, making these old structures unstable. Once, squatters had lived in these ruins and passing within their vicinity meant certain attack, but now even the most desperate bandits had moved on.

The Inbetween was a restless, quirky place. Winds whipped from different directions, sometimes cold and biting, other times bringing the scent of spring growth. I spotted several sets of predatory eyes gleaming from the shadows, and once, a Sasquatch-like creature stopped on the road ahead to assess our suitability as prey, then lumbered off.

And ghosts flitted along the road beside us. Hundreds of ghosts, invisible to the others. Lucille didn't even flinch as she clopped through an entire spectral family. I pretended not to see them. Ghosts were often drawn to my blade, as if sensing that their way off this plane of existence lay within its magic. But I could only help them if they were still tethered to their mortal bodies—if their mortal bodies hadn't yet rotted away to dust. Try explaining that concept to an angry ghost. So I ignored the sea of pale, beseeching faces and, as we left the remains of the suburbs, the ghosts trickled off.

A half moon lit our way and the night was warm for April, but a chill wind blew across the open highway. I pulled my scarf tight.

"Once there were enough cars to fill these roads, sometimes bumper to bumper for miles," Mason said.

"I remember. It seems like a lifetime ago." And it was.

Mason glanced at me, skepticism plain in his expression.

"You don't believe me?"

"You don't look old enough to remember traffic jams," he said.

"Neither do you."

"Point taken."

In fact, I was born near here, in a tiny town called St. Therese. Now it was underwater and part of the vast swamp simply known as the Floods. Later, my mother moved us to the big city, but we left that home for Asgard when I was barely eighteen, sixty years ago in Terra time, before magic blossomed from the ley-lines, and before the war that brought down governments.

I could only guess Mason's age from the research I'd done. He'd lived through the French Revolution, so he was at least three-hundred years old, maybe older. Possibly much older.

But I didn't ask and neither did he. We were still in polite mode, simply two strangers thrown together in an unlikely situation. We'd go our separate ways once Ollie reunited with his clan and Mason had his bloodstone back. Until then, we'd ride side-by-side and fight back-to-back if need be, but we wouldn't get personal.

I felt his presence beside me like the clouds of an impending storm. The slow beat of his magic coiled around him like a familiar weapon, one that he had faith in and could call upon at any given moment, but not one that he had to flaunt. His was old magic.

And I saw the little things: the way he held his reins with firm confidence. The straight cut of his dark pants that somehow looked as right in the saddle as they would in a boardroom. He never fussed with it, but the wind blew through his black hair, tossing it carelessly over his forehead.

*Get a grip. He's here for the bloodstone only.*

More importantly, I wasn't interested in another broody immortal. I'd fallen down that rabbit hole once already, and once was enough.

I turned my attention back to Lucille, who kept dipping her head to chew the weeds growing up through cracks in the pavement. I tugged on her reins and she grudgingly walked on.

Less than an hour into wilderness and, we no longer picked up the ley-net or any communications. Our widgets were little more than flashlights out here, and when their batteries died, they wouldn't even be that. I kept mine stowed in my pack in case the Annequin Lodge had communication lines. I hoped to contact Gita when we arrived.

Mason had also packed away his widget, but he held some other gadget in his hand. Marcella had given us a map with a few safe campgrounds highlighted. We needed to make good time to reach the first one by daylight. He checked the map, then his gadget, and altered our course, so we headed off the main road.

"Are you getting a signal out here?" I asked.

"Not in the usual way." Mason held up the gadget. It was a round brass contraption with a glass window, like an old-fashioned pocket watch. Behind the glass, a digital arrow rocked back and forth within a notched circle. The magic coming off it made me uncomfortable, like petting a cat's hair backwards. It was the same dissonance I sometimes felt from Angus's magic.

"A compass? But how?" Since the Flood Wars, Terra's magnetic field had flip-flopped so many times, conventional compasses were useless. And the few satellites still orbiting the planet had long since gone dark, so GPS systems didn't work either.

"It's geared to the Apex. As long as I can pinpoint that on a map, I can use it to gauge our position."

"You alchemy boys have all the best gadgets," I said. The Apex was a gemstone that capped the tower on Perrot Island just west of the ward. It harnessed the magic of the ley-lines to fuel Montreal's generators. I leaned over to get a better look at the compass. The battery was down to fifty percent already.

"Will it last long enough to get us to the lodge?" I asked.

Mason shook his head. "Just long enough to find one of Marcella's safe zones."

"Safe" was a relative term in the Inbetween. We wouldn't be truly safe until we were back inside Montreal Ward. Between us and the Annequin Lodge were hundreds of kilometers of wilderness that made Dorion Park seem like a child's playground.

As we rode along through that first night, my back itched as if it had a bright target painted on it. Lucille felt the tension in my muscles and shied away from shadows, which made me even jumpier.

Mason rode like he'd been born in the saddle. His straight back tapered to narrow hips and long thighs that hugged his mount without effort. Angus bounced along, barely hanging onto the saddle horn. Lucille turned out to be quite stubborn. She tried to pull me off the path to snag a few green shoots from a tree. I hauled on her reins and gave her a good kick.

"We're going to get left behind, you dumb beast." I kicked again but she only shook her ears as if batting at an annoying fly.

"You're not kicking hard enough," Mason said. He and Norma Jean stopped on the path ahead. "Don't be shy. You can't hurt her."

I kicked hard, shortening my reins and forcing the ornery goat to pull up her head and turn back to the path.

"I used to be good at this," I grumbled.

Mason smiled. "You'll find your seat. By tomorrow you'll be so saddle sore, you'll forget about anything else anyway."

"Terrific."

At first, Ollie had been excited about the trip, chirping and flapping his wings, but as the silence of the Inbetween settled around us like a wet blanket, the dragon became more subdued. He watched the passing shadows with round eyes.

A long howl broke the silence. It was a call of willful terror—a predator that knew its prey couldn't escape. I shivered and wished I was home in bed with a blanket pulled over my head.

The howl came again, undulating for nearly a minute before fading away. Ollie whimpered.

"Don't count your nightmares before they hatch," soothed Angus. "That beastie is far, far away." Ollie tucked his head under Angus's arm, his wings quivering.

We rode on. Twice I sensed creatures rustling in the underbrush and hoped they were more afraid of us than we were of them.

"Look at them fairies!" Angus said. Tiny lights flickered in the dense darkness between the trees.

"Those aren't fairies," I said. "They're pixies." The lights danced and zipped around the trees.

"What's the difference?" Angus said.

I could have given him the long explanation about the genomes of fairy versus pixies, two distinct designations that were often used interchangeably, but all I said was, "Fairies don't glow."

Pixies were common in Montreal Ward. The ward kept out only big magic, letting smaller otherworld creatures pass through, and pixies had just enough magic to make themselves glow. They could be a nuisance in a swarm, and I'd relocated more than one pixie nest from town.

The pixie song reached us as they came closer. It was a high pitched jingle like hundreds of tiny discordant sleigh bells. And then we were surrounded by the fluttering, flashing little beasts. They had vaguely humanoid bodies, but androgynous, with nearly featureless faces and long opalescent wings that glowed bright blue, green and yellow. They flitted over and around us, chittering out their odd bell-like song. One dove right at my face, but veered away at the last minute.

"Don't swat them," I said. "They won't hurt you." Angus ignored me and waved his hands wildly around his head. Ollie squealed with delight, jumping up and flexing his wings, trying to join the pixies in flight. He landed with a thud. The pixies tinkled loudly and swirled around his head before zooming off into the night.

Mason pulled his mount alongside mine.

"So you're the creature expert. What other kinds of nasties do you think we'll come across out here?"

I shrugged.

"I'm a wardie. I haven't been farther than Dorion Park in over a decade. There could be anything in these woods—brownies, ogres, trolls, not to the mention the human variety of monsters."

Mason mulled over this answer, then said, "And before that?"

"Before what?"

"You said you haven't left Montreal Ward in ten years. Where were you before that?"

*Home*, came my first thought. But Asgard wasn't home anymore and never would be again.

"I lived with my mother in Asgard."

Mason raised both eyebrows and it opened up his normally dour expression.

"Why so surprised," I said. "You know I'm Valkyrie."

"Yes, but I didn't realize you were a true-blood Aesir. I thought…"

"You thought 'Valkyrie' was an affectation like those idiots over in the Olympian ward pretending to be the descendants of Zeus and Hera."

"Something like that." His lips quirked up in a grin.

"Well, I'm only part Aesir. My mother's mother was human, a mortal that Baldyr fell in love with and kidnapped. And Mom had a passionate affair with a dryad."

That took him some time longer to process.

"So your grandfather is Baldyr? That Baldyr?"

I nodded, then realized he wouldn't see me in the dark. "Yes, the beloved son of Odin."

"And your father was a dryad."

"Yes." My family tree was ridiculously convoluted and this wasn't the time to go into it.

He grunted, giving away none of his thoughts, and we rode on through the darkness.

After another hour, as I struggled to rein in my mount once again, Mason said, "Let's take a break."

We hadn't yet found any water—no streams or ponds for the mounts—but Marcella had given us a collapsible bucket to water the hunt beasts from our supplies. They drank sparingly, too concerned with what was going on in the shadows to relax and refresh.

I took a sip from our rations and handed the water skin to Mason. He refused it.

"Drink more. You need it."

I took another small sip and pushed the skin to him.

"You're stubborn, aren't you?"

"We need to be careful. If we don't find a stream, those beasts could go through all our rations quickly. And I don't like the idea of finding our way through this forest on foot."

Mason pointed to his chest. "Alchemist, remember? If we need water, I'll find it."

"Good to know."

He handed the water skin back and I drank a big gulp before giving it to Angus who tried to squirt some into Ollie's mouth. The dragon thought it was a game and grabbed for the spout of water with his stubby fingers.

"Ollie, no!" I said. "You must drink it." I held his paws down while Angus gently squirted water into his mouth.

"He's a cute little fella," Angus said, "but not the brightest bulb in the drawer."

We traveled for another few hours. Mason navigated with his odd compass and Marcella's map. Sleep tugged at me, but every time Lucille felt my hands go lax on the reins, she headed off the path looking for last season's berries, so I fought with exhaustion to stay vigilant.

We came to a small lake that seemed frozen, despite the warmer weather. Around it, the forest grew thick and lush with only one visible path that led east, away from the lodge. I didn't relish the thought of cutting our way through that underbrush.

"Should we risk crossing over the ice?" I said.

"Maybe," Mason said. "If we can gauge its thickness."

At the edge of the lake, we peered through the ice. It was as black as the night sky. Then a body rolled by under the ice, and kept on rolling. One meter…two…three. By the time the beast's tail disappeared, I guessed it to be about ten meters.

"Let's walk around," Mason said.

"Agreed."

We took the eastern trail, hoping it would loop around again. After about half an hour, it finally swung west and the road widened.

"We're coming to a settlement of some kind," I said.

"How can you tell?" Mason asked.

"Ghosts." As we moved away from areas that had been densely populated before the war, the lingering spirits dwindled. I hadn't seen any in the last hour.

Now, a solitary man wearing an old-fashioned suit and tie ambled by, tipping his hat at us in greeting. I ignored him and willed my sword to be still. One or two eager ghosts I could handle, but the road ahead of us swarmed with them.

"You can see ghosts?"

I nodded. "Something bad happened here."

"It's the Inbetween," said Angus. "It was created by bad things happening."

"I mean something sudden. Something that wiped out a large population quickly. That's the only way to explain the number of ghosts." They were all around us now—old women, young women, men in suits, men in shorts and t-shirts, children. Many children. Our mounts flicked their ears as the specters brushed past them.

The road widened to become the main boulevard of a town that would have been quaint even in the twentieth century, and for the Inbetween, it was remarkably well-preserved. Most habitations we'd come across had succumbed to the forest. Magic favored fertility over desolation. The raging ley-lines fed the trees and shrubs, choking any ancient structure with vines and wildflowers.

But this town was untouched by magic. Little shops lined each side, their windows dirty, but unbroken. The pavement was uncracked and clear of debris. The sound of our mounts' hooves on the road seemed unnaturally loud as we walked the main street. Even the incessant wind died down.

"There's something at the end." Mason pointed.

Ahead, the street ended at a town square with a large monument at its center. The night was too dark to see it clearly, so we approached cautiously. Nothing moved. Lucille stopped in the road, and then tried to turn back the way we'd come. I yanked on her reins. By the time we caught up with the others, her eyes bulged and she tossed her head, trying to pull the reins from my grip.

Mason stopped at the street corner and dismounted. Lucille and I clopped up to him as he punched a button on the post of an old traffic light.

"What do you think this was for?" Mason asked.

"I think it was meant to make dummies stop and ask 'what's this for?'" I said.

He pushed the button twice more and grinned. "I just like to know how things work."

"You're an alchemist to the core."

Angus and Ollie waited ahead at the base of the monument, or what had once been a monument. A stone foundation was topped with a bronze statue of a man, maybe the town founder. Vines as thick as my wrist wrapped his body, and a giant seedpod obscured his head. On the ground below, the remnants of more seedpods lay split open and empty.

Angus whistled. "Looks like the shit hit the roof here."

Ollie whined and tried to crawl under Angus's arm.

It wasn't lost on me that the ghosts refused to enter this square. They watched us with mute curiosity, their translucent bodies making an eerie ring around the streets.

"I think we should leave," I said. Before I took another breath, a vine shot forward, wrapped around my chest and yanked me from Lucille's back.

# CHAPTER 12

The vine jerked me toward the monument. Its grip tightened and cut off my scream. The pavement scraped my knees, and I hit the stone base head first.

Everything went black.

I was out for only a moment but my vision came back hazy.

"Kyra!" Mason shouted behind me.

Hands grabbed my shoulders tugging me one way, while the vines pulled me the other.

"Don't!" I gasped.

"I can't cut them! They're too tough." Mason's face contorted in alarm.

"My...sword." The words came through the strangling vines. My sword could cut through anything.

Mason leaned over me and tried to pull the sword from the sheathe across my back.

"I can't..." His voice was strained. "The vine is too tight."

My head throbbed and my vision blackened around the edges again.

"Let go," I said. Mason's face appeared above me. His eyes filled with concern or maybe even fear.

"No!" He tried to gather me toward him.

*Yes!* He had to let go. Already, the vines were wrapping around his shoulders. Then I was wrenched upward and Mason disappeared. My feet dangled in midair and I came face to face with the seedpod.

Bigger than a bull's head, the pod dangled from one sturdy stalk. It glowed faintly in the moonlight and was ridged with deep purple veins. A slimy red nub hung from the bottom.

The whole thing vibrated as if ready to burst.

I thought of the hundreds of ghosts lining the square. What would come out of that pod?

*Run!* I wanted to yell it, to get Mason, Angus and Ollie as far away from this monstrosity as possible, but the vines covered my mouth. I gagged. My hand strained to reach my sword, even though I knew it was futile. Just one tiny cut would save me…

But I had other magic. Power I knew nothing about, given to me by my father, the dryad. Power over plants and trees.

Sometimes, when I walked through Dorion Park, I could feel the trees calling to a deep well of magic inside me. Now I drew from that well until my fingers tingled.

The vines reacted by easing their death grip, and I drew a full breath. Then I hummed the first bars of "All Through the Night," a folksong my mother used to sing to me when I couldn't sleep. I had no idea if this would work. I suffused the song with soothing magic. My head pounded and my throat ached, but I punched magic into my song and it rose, filling the night.

From below, Angus's deep voice rose to match mine. He sang the original Welsh version, and for once, the green man's magic seemed in harmony.

The seedpod was ready to burst. It swelled and throbbed, then shook as if in the throes of a seizure.

I poured more magic into my song.

The pod swayed, then drooped. The vines relaxed until I dropped to the cement, and they hung limply around the base of the monument. I kicked them off and Mason pulled me away.

"What did you do?" he asked.

"Subdued it for now. It's not dead. We need to leave."

Our mounts had scattered. Mason picked me up, throwing me over his shoulder and ran from the square, straight through a line of gaping ghosts. Angus followed with Ollie hopping behind him.

Outside the town, he let me down, and I soothed my bruised throat with small sips of water.

The mounts hadn't run far. We found them munching contently on a strange plant.

"Is that what I think it is?" Mason asked.

I crouched and examined the dark green vines. A few tiny pearl seedpods hung from them, miniatures of the giant in the square. I thought about taking a sample of the plant, but then remembered the ghosts. What would happen if such a plant grew to maturity inside Montreal ward?

"You think it'll kill the poor beasties?" Angus asked.

"I don't know," I said. "Goats will eat just about anything. We'll have to keep an eye on them." That sounded more positive than I felt. If the mounts got sick, I didn't think I could help them. And it was a long way to Annequin Lodge on foot.

We reached Marcella's campsite just before dawn, after walking through a tunnel cut into a dense hedge. We'd entered the tunnel under clear skies and came out to a snowstorm.

"The safe house should be just ahead," Mason yelled over the wailing wind. With the snow lashing us, I couldn't see more than a few feet ahead. We pushed through the storm until a large concrete bunker suddenly loomed out of the blinding whiteness.

The metal door opened with a screech. Inside, half the space was reserved for mounts with a water trough, bags of grain and straw piled against the wall. The other half had rough sleeping pallets and a wood stove with logs piled beside it. Someone kept this place stocked and in good repair.

As we untacked the mounts, Mason said, "I didn't have a chance to say it before, but you were amazing back there. With the singing. How did you know it would react like that?"

"I didn't, really. Dryads have always been able to talk to trees and flowers. I've never had a reason to do it, but it just felt right."

I brushed out Zsa Zsa's coat with a handful of straw and then turned to Lucille. Mason filled a feed bucket.

"We have to work fast," he said. "Dawn is coming."

"I can do this." I reached for the bucket. "Go have something to eat before you…" What was the term? Sleep? Petrify?

Mason's warm hand covered mine and he squeezed before releasing the bucket to me.

"You don't have to be shy about it. I'm a gargoyle. If we're going to travel together, you'll have to get used to it."

I nodded and turned away to take care of the beasts. When I finished, I found Ollie hopping and fluttering around Mason and Angus. Outside our concrete bunker, the sun had come up and they were stone.

The storm still raged by nightfall, and when the gargoyles woke, we argued about whether we should wait it out.

"The snow might only be falling around this camp," I said, exasperated. I wanted to push on. "We could walk a kilometer and find sunshine and roses. We have no idea what waits out there."

The Inbetween was fun like that.

"Exactly." Mason sipped his tea with no intention of moving. "We have no idea. So we'll wait."

I glared at him. I knew why he didn't want to leave. He thought I needed to rest after my ordeal with the killer monster lily. And it infuriated me. Any need to be coddled had been methodically beaten out of me by my Aunt Dana. I didn't want his mothering.

I grabbed a water skin and sipped. The cool water felt good on my bruised throat, but I wouldn't admit that to anyone.

"Fine. We'll stay," I said. "But only one day. We leave tomorrow as soon as the sun sets, whether the storm is done or not."

"Deal." Mason put another log in the stove and left the iron door open to give us more light. "At least the storm will keep the bandits away. We can all rest for a few hours."

Ollie came fluttering into the circle of light with Angus following.

"Anything?" I asked, hoping Ollie had finally passed the bloodstone.

"Nothing." Angus slumped on a stool by the fire. "That wee dragon is stopped up like a vintage bottle."

"Maybe he needs more fiber," Mason said.

"I dunno. He ate a whole pile of hay in the night. Enough fiber for a horse."

We all turned to watch Ollie, who seemed pleased with the attention and flapped his wings. Then he spotted Zsa Zsa's swishing tail and hopped away to chase it.

Angus reached into his saddlebag and produced a small bottle of whiskey. "Care for a wee dram?"

We passed around the bottle while Angus told stories about other journeys through the Inbetween. Ollie finally dozed off in the warm glow of the fire.

"But seriously, lass," Angus held the bottle up to me in a salute. "I never saw anything like that monster flower. It nearly ate you up."

The whiskey burning through my blood helped me forget the horror of that moment when I realized the seedpod was about to burst.

"I don't think it wanted to eat us. It was going to explode and release spoor. Of course, those could have eaten us." I shrugged and took the bottle from Angus. His brambly face—was brambly even a word? I hiccuped and giggled. His brambly face settled into a serious expression.

"Where did you learn that trick? The singing?" he asked. "That's dryad magic."

"My father was Timberfoot Greenleaf," I blurted.

Angus leaned back on his stool. "Is that right?"

Mason watched me, but his dark eyes were hidden in shadow and I couldn't fathom his expression. He'd drunk as much whiskey as Angus and me, but he seemed perfectly sober.

"So you know the dryad ways then." Angus rubbed his chin.

"A bit. I spent little time with the dryads. Just one summer. I wish I could use that magic more."

"I could teach you. The dryads and the green men, we're like kissing cousins." He puckered his lips and made kissy noises at me.

I laughed. "That's why your magic feels so familiar to me. Well, part of it anyway. The rest of your magic feels completely different. Like oil and water. You can shake them together, but they won't ever mesh. Not really."

I leaned in to stir the fire with a stick. In my drunken ignorance, I didn't realize that the room had fallen silent. Not until Mason swore and stomped away.

I looked up startled, then mortified. Had I just said that Angus's magic felt wrong?

"Angus, I'm so sorry!" I put down the whiskey bottle. Clearly I'd had enough."

"It's okay, lass." Angus's eyes were sad as he followed Mason to where he restlessly brushed the hunt beasts, who had already been thoroughly groomed.

Angus lowered his voice. "He's a bit tetchy about the subject. He's not mad at you, but at himself."

"Why?"

"You see, he made me. That is, he sculpted this body for me and then stole the spirit of a dryad to bring it to life."

My mouth formed a silent "oh."

Angus shrugged. "Twas the age of wonders. The Renaissance. Only men did'na wonder about whether they *should* do great works of magic and science, only if they *could*." His Gaelic accent had grown stronger, either from whiskey or emotion.

"Alchemists of that time were desperate to find the Philosopher's Stone. The ultimate mastery over life and death. That's what the first gargoyles were, attempts to create life from stone. And they worked. But the life was stolen, not created. And that is the conflict you sense in my magic. I have a little bit of Mason's soul—his blood and sweat that went into the carving—and the stolen soul of a dryad."

He leaned in closer. "In truth, it nearly drove me mad in those first years. And for that, Mason has never forgiven himself, though I forgave him centuries ago."

That was horrible. My hand covered my mouth, as if to keep that thought inside. I couldn't imagine a worse fate for a dryad—a being who thrived on freedom of the forest and breath of the trees—to be locked inside stone.

"They don't still do that, do they? Steal souls to make gargoyles, I mean."

Angus shook his head, but his bushy eyebrows lowered over his eyes. "Not so much, but you know those tech toys the alchemists like so much?"

I nodded, thinking of Mason's compass, with its oddly jarring magic.

"I think someone is using old Renaissance magic to fuel them."

"Does Mason know?"

"Not a bit, or he would'na use them."

"Will you tell him?"

"I need to prove it first."

"I can help."

Angus leaned back and considered me. "Maybe you can, when we get home to Montreal. And in return, I'll teach you a few dryad tricks."

We shook on it, then I stood up to follow Mason and found him mucking the animal stalls.

"I'm sorry," I said. "I didn't know. And what I said was rude."

"Might be rude, but it's the truth. I created an abomination. Just because Angus turned out all right doesn't excuse that." He looked back at the flickering fire and lowered his voice. "He won't admit it, but I know that his very existence pains him. Like a square peg living for all eternity wedged into a round hole. And I did that to him." He thumped his chest with a fist.

"He doesn't blame you."

"Doesn't matter."

It clearly didn't. Mason blamed himself enough for two.

"Goodnight." He stalked away, leaving me alone with my thoughts and an enormous goat that seemed oblivious to the tension in the air and only wanted to chew on my hair.

# CHAPTER 13

I slept for only a few hours and woke to to find Ollie eating hay. He methodically chewed the tough stalks while watching Angus. In stone form, the green man was paler, as if his bark-like skin had weathered in the rain. His usual flashing eyes were flat gray. Creepy. My gaze slid to Mason. His back was turned to me and I didn't want to see his face.

"Everything okay?" I asked. Ollie chirped but didn't take his eyes from Angus. "He'll wake up soon. Don't worry." I scratched him behind his bony brow ridge and he offered me a fistful of hay.

"Thanks, buddy, but I'll make my own supper."

Outside, the storm had stopped, but snow piled against the door. I struggled to open it wide enough to scoop a pot of snow.

I added wood to the stove, and melted the snow, going back for more until I had enough water to fill our canteens and make tea.

I ate a cold supper and drank my tea, then fed the mounts with Ollie zipping around my feet. He had the zoomies and I let him run it out. Better now than when we were in the saddle again.

I left out rations for Angus and Mason and waited, nervous about facing Mason again after my blundering insensitivity the night before.

The sun took its sweet time setting.

I felt Mason's presence before he moved. His magic resonated like an ocean current, strong and deep enough to change weather patterns. I turned to find him watching me.

"You're awake!" I said with forced cheeriness. "I made tea and left you some food, but the rest is packed and ready to go."

"Ah, I love having a woman take care of me." He grinned with forced humor. It seemed I had been forgiven.

"Don't get used to it."

He held his chest as if I'd shot him. "You wound me. Does that mean you won't bring me lemonade when we're doddering old ones, rocking our chairs on the porch at sunset?"

"You will never be old and doddering," I pointed out. "And I…" Well, I didn't know what the fates would decide for me. "And I don't like lemonade."

"When life gives you lemonade, make whiskey sours," Angus said. "Mmm, what I wouldn't do for a wee dram right now."

I groaned. I'd had my share of wee drams for a while.

Ollie stopped in mid-run and lunged at Angus, flexing his wings at the last moment so he didn't crash. Angus fluttered his own wings, rising an inch or two from the ground, and Ollie's tail whipped back and forth in his excitement.

"Yes, laddie, I promised to teach you some flying. But not here." Angus petted Ollie's head. "Night is falling like a lead hatchet and we should be on our way."

The mounts were eager to be moving again, and I had no trouble with Lucille for the first stretch, though I wasn't happy to be back in the saddle again.

Mason watched me fidget in my seat with a grin.

"I've got sores on top of my sores." I scowled.

"No worries. Those will callous over nicely."

"Terrific. I've always wanted a butt covered in callouses."

"I could rub oil on them." His grin made my girl parts go weak. "You don't have enough padding on your rump, that's the problem."

"Could we stop talking about my rump now?"

"As the lady wishes." He spurred Norma Jean with a kick and moved into the lead.

We left the snow behind like parting a curtain. One minute we tramped through billowing drifts; the next, we rode through a spring forest.

"Look at that tree!" I pointed to a massive oak, now mostly bare of its leaves, but covered in some kind of colorful moss or flowers. "I've never seen trees that flower like that."

"Not flowers," Mason said. "Look."

One of the brightly colored birds launched at us from the tree. Its wingspan had to reach eight feet. The rainbow-hued body ended in a scaled, whip-like tail. As it swooped over our heads, it let out a caw that chilled my blood. It seemed to check us out, then flew back to report. The others fluffed their wings and muttered when it returned, but didn't move to investigate us.

"Amazing," I said. "Do you think I could get a sample?"

"Oh, no," said Angus. "I wouldn't eat one of them with a ten-foot pole."

"Not a live sample. A feather would do. There must be some under that tree."

"I don't think it's a good idea to get too close," Mason said. "The beak on that thing is meant for tearing meat. And to them, we look pretty tender."

Mason was right. The only reason they left us alone was probably because they were too sleepy to hunt. Reluctantly, I turned away from the tree of rainbow birds and we pressed on.

The path was easy to follow, but dense trees pressed in on either side. The deeper we went into the wood, the more my nerves frayed. The trees were trying to tell me something. I didn't speak fluent dryad, but since meeting the deadly seedpod, I was more aware of this part of my magic, as if singing the killer plant to sleep had woken something in me.

Ollie hadn't worked out his excess energy and he bounced off Zsa Zsa's back, pumping his wings in an effort to fly.

"Keep that damn dragon under control," snapped Mason.

"Can't help it," grumbled Angus. "The little bugger is antsy. Can't say I blame him. These trees give me the jeepers creepers."

"We're nearing the edge of opji territory. We need to be vigilant," Mason said.

"Here, let me take him for a while." I reached for Ollie and tucked him into the seat in front of me. I scratched the softer scales behind his ears until he sighed and settled down.

"Do you think the opji will hunt this far from their ward?" I asked.

Vioska Ward was hundreds of kilometers west of us, but it wasn't unheard of for the opji to hunt as far east as the Quebec Plateau.

"Marcella said the opji are on the move," Mason said. "We have to assume they could be anywhere."

That ramped up my twitchiness. Now I could feel eyes watching from every shadow. Every rustling of leaves made me jump, and I was glad to leave the forest to emerge on a barren rocky plateau. At least here, I would see an attack coming.

Our path climbed steadily until we reached the head of an escarpment. With no discernible trail here, the night sky seemed like a wall of darkness ahead. Then fog rolled in, obscuring the path further. We trod slowly. The fog clung to my clothes and hair like damp cobwebs. My nose ran in the cold and I fumbled in my pocket for a handkerchief. Still distracted, I didn't notice when Mason stopped suddenly. Lucille bumped into Norma Jean and shied. Angus on his donkey rammed into us.

"Don't move," Mason hissed.

The wind picked up, and in that capricious way of the Inbetween, the fog dissipated.

We stood at the edge of a precipice.

Zsa Zsa's front hoof slid off the edge of the cliff before Angus yanked her backward. Rocks skittered down the cliff face, their echoes bouncing back for a long minute.

"Whoa," Angus hauled on his reins, trying to settle the donkey.

A faint eerie glow came from the valley below, reflecting off the cloud cover and tingeing everything green.

"What's down there?" Mason asked.

"Don't know," I said, but then sheet lighting raged across the sky and I saw a vast plain bordered on all sides by rock bluffs. Tall grass filled the valley. In the lightning's aftermath, the glow of the grass seemed even brighter, filling the night with an eerie green blush.

"That must be the Qualmish Plains," Mason said. "It's on Marcella's map. The Hunt Lodge is just past those mountains."

"Then we'd better get moving," Angus said.

The next flash of lightning revealed a path cutting through the grass, heading toward the mountains that were only a charcoal smudge on the horizon.

"A trail." I pointed. It was hard to tell if it was a caravan path or a simple deer trail from this height, but it was something.

Mason nodded. "We'll find a way down."

We dismounted and walked along the escarpment, peering into the darkness, looking for a safe passage down the shear cliff. Mason fished in his saddlebag and pulled out a gleam. He triggered it with a good shake and then tossed the orb in the air. It hung above our heads, casting a bright light.

"You alchemy boys always have the best toys," I said.

"Let's just hurry. That light will announce us to anybody in the area." He glanced into the wall of trees at our backs. The only people in the area would likely be opji.

After wasting precious minutes tacking back and forth across the ridge, frozen with the icy wind blowing off the plain, exhausted and jumping at every shadow, I finally spotted a dip in the rocks that hid a narrow trail down the escarpment.

"Here!" I yelled over thunder rumbling in the distance.

For once, I was glad Marcella had been out of horses. We let our sure-footed mounts take the lead, and they carelessly picked their way down. Angus hopped from rock to rock, buffeting each landing with outstretched wings and Ollie tried his best to follow.

"That's right," Angus said. "You might not be able to fly, but at least you can fall with style."

Mason and I were the slowest. He led, feeling each rock for solidity before setting his weight down.

"That one's loose," he said, but I had already stepped on it. The rock skidded under the scree, taking my foot with it. I slipped backward, then overcompensated and flung myself against his back. My hands clung to solid hips.

"I've been wanting those hands on me for a while, but please warn me before you grab my ass next time, so we don't fall to our deaths," Mason said. I could actually hear him grinning.

"Just keep that ass moving," I grumbled.

At the bottom, Ollie waited impatiently, bouncing up and trying to fly. Angus pulled on Zsa Zsa's lead but the donkey had parked herself by the luminous grass and seemed determined to ruminate on the entire plains.

"Blasted cur!" Angus yanked the reins.

Mason and I mounted, riding side by side into the grasslands. Zsa Zsa reluctantly followed. The trail kept to the eastern edge of the plains, moving north, close enough to the tree line that we could run into it for cover, but far enough away to see anything coming at us. The tips of grass swept my knees. Lightning flashed across the sky in great white sheets and the cold wind shifted continually as if stirring a great pot.

Inside the ward, we see vicious storms that wrack the landscape only from a distance—flashes of lightning or smudges of dark clouds on the horizon—because the ward keeps things temperate. Here, the weather was immediate, threatening and irrational. It followed no seasonal pattern. The wind could blow hot one moment, then turn around and slap you with an icy hand. So far, the storm seemed to be all talk and no action, but it felt menacing—as if it were stalking us.

"We're too exposed out here," Mason said.

I felt it too, that itch between my shoulder blades, as if someone had me in their sights.

The bilious green glow from the grasses made Mason look ghoulish, but he sat straight in the saddle, ready for any coming fight.

"Do you hear that?" he asked.

"Yes."

A sawing, crunching noise seemed to echo from all around. I turned in my saddle. Behind us, the grasses swayed erratically.

"Something's coming."

"Hold." Mason reached for his bow and readied an arrow. I pulled my sword. Out here in the Inbetween, it was easy to prime. The blade sucked in magic from the environment and hummed in my grip.

Ollie whined.

"Angus, keep him out of the way," I said, "and stay behind us."

"Aye." Angus pushed his mount between us and guarded our backs.

The sawing grew louder. I could make out three distinct trails through the grass now. Something was moving fast, trampling the tall stalks as it came. I saw a flash of black and white through a break in the grass.

"Orkins!" I said.

"You're not serious," Mason said. "I thought they were a myth."

"About as mythical as dragons."

The massive gastropods churned up the ground as they came. The peaks of their glistening black and white bodies just topped the grasses. Normally, they would chew through a field, digesting grass, weeds, insects and small rodents at a slow, steady pace, but something had spooked these.

"They're on the run." I lowered my blade, but didn't sheathe it. A flight of deer jumped from the trees, leaping through the field and disappearing in an instant. Mason jerked his bow in their direction but didn't shoot. Then a flock of white birds erupted from their night roost and filled the sky with caws before zipping away north.

The tentacles on the orkin's heads pointed forward. The massive slug bodies glided across the ground, flattening the grass as they zipped by. Ollie fluttered and chirped, excited by the spectacle. As the sawing of the orkins faded, he settled back on Angus's saddle.

The silence on the plains was absolute.

A wolf howled. We weren't done with the evening's entertainment yet.

Every hair on my body stood on end. We turned our mounts, forming a three-pronged vigil as we stared into the darkness and waited.

The first wolf broke through the grass and leapt at me, its mouth wide and eyes wild. My blade came up on instinct, but the beast shied right and disappeared into the night.

"Don't shoot!" I said. "They're not attacking!"

More wolves burst from the shadows. My clinical mind noted that some were big enough to be classified as dire wolves. Five, six, seven…an entire pack. Enough wolves to take down three riders and their mounts. But they weren't interested in us.

Angus swore in Welsh. My mount butted up against his as it shied from the beasts flying by on either side. Their howls agreed with my primitive need to flee. My knees tightened on Lucille's flanks. She stamped and snorted.

Rules for critter wranglers, number two: When scary things run away, something scarier is coming.

Then the vampires attacked.

# CHAPTER 14

They fell on us like shadows, propelled through the night sky with some uncanny magic. Mason took down two with arrows to the heart. I had only a second to admire his shooting before a bloodsucker was on me, fangs bared in a snarl.

He knocked me off my goat. I landed hard, with the vampire on top, his mouth snapping like a viper.

I hate vampires. By the One-eyed God, they are the worst vermin. Their magic feels…just wrong, like a bell with a sandpaper clacker. This one was a wojak, the mindless, undead drones that vampires use as soldiers and slaves. Wojaks have all the killing power of the opji elites with none of their finesse.

The tall grass stalks were as sharp as knives as we grappled over them. The wojak's bulging eyes locked onto the pulse at my throat. His gaunt face leered over me, pressing forward toward the vein that strained on my neck. Despite his skeletal appearance, I knew his jaws could crush the windpipe of a bear, and a wojak bite packs enough venom to render a victim unconscious, so they can feed in peace.

I couldn't let that happen. I knuckle-punched his windpipe and scrambled backward, tangling myself and my sword in the grass. He flipped me off-balance, then grabbed my hair, yanking me back under his control. Bared teeth came at me.

I blocked the bite with my arm and his fangs bit through jacket, skin and muscle. I screamed. Red eyes filled with lust and hate blazed down at me. Wojaks have little magic compared to their opji overlords. He wouldn't try to mesmerize me into letting him feed. He was simply going to kill me.

Behind me, I heard Ollie's high-pitched squeal.

I bit down on the pain surging through my arm and brought up my sword with the other. We were too close for a good thrust, but I nudged the tip of the blade between us.

He unlocked his bite, but held me fast in his grip. I grunted as he leaned on my windpipe. The gaunt face leered down at me, fangs red with my blood. Air was becoming a priority. The edges of my vision blurred. I pressed my blade. The angle was awkward, but all I needed was a little cut…

The blade jolted as it broke through skin. His magic signature changed from undead to fully alive.

The vampire's eyes widened and he jerked away. I gasped for sweet, sweet air and scrambled backward into the trampled grass.

He grabbed his leg and looked shocked when his hand came away wet with blood. A strangled word gurgled from his throat, but I didn't let him finish that thought. I hacked off his head with one magic-infused swipe of my sword. It fell with a wet thump and his body sagged. I stood over the corpse, my hands gripping the hilt of my sword so tightly they ached.

Was he dead? I was fairly certain that decapitation was fatal for vampires. Then his hand jerked. I jumped back, but it wasn't the corpse reanimating. Long blue tendrils curled from the ground and wound around his limbs. They made wet sucking noises as they encased the wojak's body in their web, pulling it into the earth. The head was getting the same treatment. I gagged and turned away.

The others were gone. I had to trust that they could take care of themselves. My bleeding arm throbbed. I took a moment to bind it with my scarf. How much venom had I taken in? My legs shook but that might have been from excess adrenaline.

A sound made me spin, sword clutched in shaking hands, but I checked my swing as Ollie jumped into the clearing. He mewled like a scared kitten and butted his head against my legs.

"It's okay, we're safe now," I said, though I still felt jumpy with raw fear. "Let's find Lucille and get out of here." I hoped for once that the goat's stubbornness would work in my favor. Maybe she was too thick-headed to be afraid of vampires, and I'd find her munching grass nearby.

Ollie squeaked as another vampire slipped from the shadows to block our path. He glanced at the headless body of his comrade—now half sunk in the ground—and grinned, displaying fangs as long as my little finger.

"Look, I've already killed one of you bloodsuckers tonight. Why don't you just fly on home now and give it a rest?" I was amazed at how calm I sounded when my guts were a pool of cold water in my shoes.

"That was a wojak. Just a bottom feeder. A cockroach." The vampire had a thick European accent. "I would not let you near me with that pig-sticker. You drop your weapon."

His eyes glowed, emitting magic that circled me like noxious vapors. This was an old vampire—an opji—the elite of the deadly Vioska ward. He was tall and handsome in a dark way, nothing like the half-breed wojak. His power was aged like a fine cheese and it stank just as much.

Against my will, my fingers relaxed and I almost let go of my sword, but its bond to me was greater than any vampire-trash magic. The blade refused to be dropped. My trembling fingers barely hung on to it.

The vampire smirked. "Your sword cannot hurt me. Keep it. But come to me now, so I can taste you."

My feet shuffled me forward, even though I sank all my will into standing still. Usually, the wards I built around my psyche blocked magic attacks, but my mind felt soft, like my thoughts flowed through pudding, and my feet kept moving. Ollie whined, confused by my complacency. I wanted to tell him to run, but my tongue stuck to the roof of my mouth and I could make no words come out.

The opji reached for my hand, his grip cold like granite. "You resist me." He grinned. "That is good. You'll make a fine slave. But first a taste, no?" His accent thickened as greed took over. My hair tie had broken when I fought the first vampire, and my hair hung around my face in a tangled mess. The opji brushed it aside, the touch oddly intimate. His magic spun a web around me, and suddenly I recognized why it was so odd. He had no heartbeat. Magic throbbed in his veins, but it was a poor substitute for true life. But I could give him mine. I *wanted* to give him mine—my life, my heartbeat, my blood…

He bit into me just above the collarbone. As my blood coursed into him, his venom hit me in a euphoric rush. Pure ecstasy swept me up and carried me on a wave of rapture. I let my head fall back, wanting to give him everything. From behind me, Ollie wailed in pure grief.

Then my sword pulsed in my hand, its magic like a bucket of cold water in my face.

My arm jerked up, catching the opji on the underside of his elbow. He jerked backward. The tip of my blade was black with his blood.

"What have you done?" He grabbed his arm, then his chest.

"You feel it don't you?" I rasped. My throat hurt. "I've stolen your immortality. You might as well be dead."

That wasn't entirely true. To a mortal, a wound by my blade was always fatal. With immortals it was unpredictable, but in the past it had broken whatever curse or spirit made them immortal. He wouldn't die by the wound, but the vampire would now grow old, just like any hapless human.

I rose and pointed my sword to where his hands clutched his chest.

"That's your heart beating like a human. Tickles doesn't it? Don't worry, I can fix that."

I swung back to lop off the bastard's head, but he jerked and fell forward, an arrow protruding from his back. Behind him, with blood smeared across his face and clothes torn, stood Mason. His bow was empty.

"I think that was the last of them," he said. "Are you okay?"

"I…" Along with the stimulant, vampire saliva has numbing and healing properties—easier to work a crowd and leave victims alive with no memory of being attacked. The wound on my neck was already healing, but the sense of loss at being torn away from the vampire's seductive magic remained. I ached to press my raw skin against his fangs again, to feel the rush of life flowing from me…

"I think so."

Mason strode forward to touch the punctures on my neck. I shivered and pulled away. He frowned, clearly wanting to say more, but I could only shake my head.

*Not now. Don't touch me now with the memory of that filthy creature still on me.*

Mason lowered his hand. "Angus has the mounts over there. We should go."

I nodded, suddenly very tired.

When I mounted, Mason propped Ollie in front of me.

"What are you doing?" My teeth chattered, and I gripped Ollie around the waist to keep my hands from shaking. I was going into shock.

"Kyra listen, ride as fast as you can to those mountains." Mason pointed north to the charcoal smudge on the horizon.

"But the dawn…the vampires will be gone."

"That's a myth. The opji don't like the sun, but they will bear it to hunt down someone that killed one of their own. Annequin Lodge is just on the other side of those mountains. You'll be safe there."

"What about you?"

"I'll go as far as I can before sunrise." He mounted the reindeer with one graceful leap. "But I'll break Norma Jean's back if I turn to stone riding her. I'll stop before then. You keep going."

"No! I won't."

"Kyra, please." He gripped my hand. "Take Ollie with you and go. Nothing can hurt me when I'm in stone form. Just run. Be safe and I'll catch up."

I knew that wasn't true. Gargoyles could die. Smash one into enough pieces and it wouldn't get up when the sun went down. But his eyes pleaded and I nodded. I gave Lucille a kick. For once she was glad to get moving, and we headed for the mountains.

Venom made my thoughts sluggish and I fought to stay in the saddle. Sometime after sunrise, I realized that Ollie and I were riding alone.

# CHAPTER 15

I gave Lucille free rein and had the presence of mind to tie Ollie to me before the hallucinations began. At least I thought they were hallucinations. In the Inbetween, one can never be sure. Were the hazy monsters walking beside us just my fevered imagination? Or were they something conjured by the unstable magic of the environment?

Worn out by the night's harrowing events, Ollie trembled in my arms. I tried to make soothing noises, but my mouth was dry, and they came out as clucks, which probably terrified him more. At least he didn't try to flee.

Sweat trickled down my back despite the cool mountain air. I clung to the saddle as waves of nausea washed over me.

Lucille followed a trail she must have taken many times, moving with purpose and sure-footed strength. As the sun rose, we crested the mountains at the lowest point and started down into a valley. The bright light speared my head. We rode on as the mountains broke into gentle hills. I squinted into the bright light, but saw no signs of the lodge in the picturesque valley.

I lost minutes to the fever, coming to with only a vague feeling of missing time. My stomach churned as I felt cold, then hot, then cold again. Still my mount plodded on. Then, scenting home, Lucille picked up her pace. Her faster gait rattled my teeth. I looked up, expecting to see the lodge but found only gentle green hills dotted with clumps of trees. Lucille trotted faster and I…was smacked in the face.

Ollie and I hit the ground as Lucille disappeared through an invisible barrier.

We had found the edge of the lodge's ward, but we weren't keyed to it. When Lucille returned with an empty saddle, would they send someone to look for us? I could only hope so.

Beside me, Ollie whined. I grabbed his paw and tucked it under my chin before passing out.

I WOKE IN a small room with a sloping ceiling. The one window let in sunlight, illuminating a tube protruding from my arm. My scratchy eyes followed the line up to a bottle on a metal pole.

"What the hell is that?" I rasped, trying to sit up and instantly regretting it.

A pretty young woman looked up from sewing some garment and tsk-tsked me.

"That is old school medicine. Before everything could be fixed with the wave of a med-mage, we used this. Don't worry, it's just fluids. A little concoction of my Gran's to get you on your feet."

She set aside her sewing and rose to lay a hand across my head.

"Fever's broke. You must be thirsty."

I nodded. My throat felt like sandpaper. She handed me a small horn cup.

"Drink it slowly. You've been out for two days."

Ollie jumped on the bed. His wings fluttered and he hovered for a moment before crashing to the mattress. He snorted out a thin stream of smoke in his excitement. I raised my free hand to pet him, and a wave of dizziness hit me.

"That's enough." The woman shooed Ollie off the bed. He sat on the floor and tucked his head under my free hand.

"Poor little thing. He's been worried about you." She had a bit of an Irish burr that made me homesick for Gita.

"Where am I?"

"You're safe. That's all you need to know for now. You've had some kind of drug overdose."

"Opji…" My voice trailed off as sleep took me again.

The next time I woke, another strange face was peering at me. This one was long and horsey, with bushy white eyebrows, mustache and grizzled gray hair. Nubby horns poked through the hair on his head.

"You're awake. Good." He sat back in a wooden chair that creaked under his weight. "I need to ask you some questions."

"Who…" My throat was too dry to speak. He handed me a cup and I drank slowly, giving myself time to examine my surroundings and remember what in the hells I was doing there.

The window was dark and a storm lamp glowed on a bedside table. The IV bottle was gone and so was Ollie.

"Ollie!" I sat bolt upright.

The man laid a big hand on my shoulder and pushed me back down.

"It's all right. The dragon is downstairs with that green man, drinking all my ale and telling vampire stories."

So Angus, at least, was safe.

"Where am I?"

"This is Annequin Lodge. I'm Herne and my daughter, Charlotte, has been tending to you. Seems you had a run-in with the opji."

"I was bitten." My hand went to my neck, but the wound had already healed.

Herne nodded. "Nasty creatures. You're lucky you got away with just a bite."

"My friend killed it." I wanted to know about Mason, but Herne had his own questions.

"How many of them attacked you?" His eyes bore into mine.

"I don't know. Six, maybe? The wojaks came first." Memories of the fight washed over me—the stench of wojak breath, the feel of my blade in his thigh, the strange tendrils wrapping him in their web. And the opji who was strong enough to break my magic wards and make me do his bidding. I shuddered and pulled the blankets around my neck.

"What does it matter?" I asked. My voice came out in a miserable croak.

Herne gripped my hand. "Tis very important. Vioska is two-hundred and fifty kilometers west of here. The opji rarely hunt far from their ward. I can only think of a few reasons they would come this far east, and none of them are good. So tell me everything you remember."

I nodded. He was right. The opji attack was ill news for everyone.

"There were at least six wojaks and one opji. We didn't see them coming. They flew in from the west. North-west. Mason killed two right away. I killed another. I didn't see what happened to the rest." I took a sip of water. "Then an opji found me."

"Just one?" Herne asked.

"That I saw. There might have been others. He wasn't just feeding. He said...I would be a good slave."

Herne stared at me in silence. Everyone knew the opji kept humans. The krowa were more than slaves. They were livestock. Certain krowa women were also chosen to breed with the opji to produce the disgusting wojak hybrids that were treated like grunts.

In the early years, after the Flood Wars, several altruistic wards, including Montreal, had tried to stop the opji and free their human captives. But the opji were too strong. Now the only thing we could do was try to keep people safe from their attacks. Refugees and travelers from other wards always moved in caravans with professional guards.

"When we left Montreal, the homesteaders were coming into the city," I said. "There were rumors of vampires in the area."

Herne grunted. "They're up to something and it can mean little good for the rest of us." He patted my hand and rose. "I think I'll go boost the wards around the inn."

"Wait." I clung to his hand. "You said Angus is downstairs. But we were with another friend. Henry Mason. Is he here too?"

Herne's eyebrows lowered. "Norma Jean came in early this morning. Alone. I'm sorry."

# CHAPTER 16

Charlotte wanted me to stay in bed one more day, but the sooner I was on my feet, the sooner I could go look for Mason. She protested but brought my freshly laundered clothes anyway.

"Be sure to eat before you go off fighting vampires again. There's a good venison stew in the pot tonight. Go down to the common room and Trixie will fix you up."

The common room was larger than my entire apartment and heated by a fire in a long hearth. Three long tables with benches and several smaller tables with chairs filled the space. Kerosene lamps hung from sconces around the room and I realized that I wouldn't be able to contact Gita to check in at home. Annequin Lodge was completely off the grid.

Herne fussed with a keg behind the oak-wood bar but gave me a quick wave. I scanned the room and found Ollie sleeping next to the hearth where a young boy stacked wood.

Trixie turned out to be a pretty server who laughed too loudly at Angus's jokes. He sat at a table in front of the fire. A couple of other patrons played cards nearby.

"Kyra!" Angus's voice boomed. "Aren't you just the cherry at the end of the tunnel!" His wings beat as he leaped the twenty feet separating us, then he hovered for a moment to give me a hug. Ollie woke and joined in. The other patrons couldn't help but smile at our odd little reunion.

Once I settled in front of the fire, Trixie set a plate of stew and a hunk of bread in front of me, along with a mug of some foul smelling brew.

"Charlotte's orders," she said. "Sorry 'bout that, but you're to drink it all."

I sipped it and was pleasantly surprised. Despite the aroma, it was spicy and sweet.

Angus related his adventures with the opji while I ate. The wojaks had left him alone. They hunted for human blood, and he had none.

"So they were easy pickings," he said. "I killed two while they attacked Mason and another two that had poor wee Ollie cornered."

"And the opji," I asked. "Did you see any of them?"

"Just the one that bit you. I reckon he's spindrill food now."

"Spindrill?"

"Did you not see them? Those fungus-like fingers that took the corpses. Charlotte called them spindrills."

"Right." I put that knowledge aside for a future blog entry. "And how did you get back here? After the sun rose, I lost you both."

Angus rubbed his leafy beard. "Well, I didn't want to hurt those hunt beasts, so I jumped off just before sunrise. Lucky for me, old Zsa Zsa thinks of nothing but food. I found her grazing nearby the next night. She brought me right here."

"And Mason?"

"Norma Jean didn't wait around. No worries. He'll make it on foot."

But I'd been unconscious for two days. Surely Mason would have made it back already, if he could.

I considered Mason's fate while I finished my food. I was letting Ollie lick the last yam off my fingers when a woman straddled the bench beside me.

"You the idiots who want to go hunting dragons?" she asked. "I'm Simone Bellantier. Nesi said to meet you here."

The nicest thing I could say about Simone was that she tried hard to look intimidating. She was too grim to be pretty and too small to be scary. Her clothes were a mishmash of brown and gray leathers that would blend into a forest background. Short black hair capped her head like a helmet and she fidgeted with a small knife, flipping it over her knuckles as if to impress her skill and dexterity upon us. The effect was diluted by the persistently twitching muscle under her right eye.

I pushed my plate away and folded my arms. "What makes you think we're idiots?"

"Heard that you already met with the vamps. Lost one of your crew. Now you want to hunt something ten times bigger that spits fire? Sounds idiotic to me."

We hadn't lost one of our crew. Mason was still out there. And the dragons I knew weren't that big. But I didn't contradict her. There was only one point I wanted to be clear on.

"We aren't hunting the dragons. I just want to find them and convince the queen to take on an orphan." We all looked at Ollie. He made a chirping noise.

Simone shrugged. "Like I said—idiotic. But if you must go, the dragons are two days north of here. My old ward is up there and I heard the beasts have been stealing cows from their grazing grounds."

"How do you know for sure they be dragons?" Angus asked.

"What else breathes fire and is big enough to carry off a cow? Look do you want my help or not? I came 'cuz Nesi asked me to, but I can find another job."

"We're waiting for a friend."

"Well, don't wait too long. I'm leaving tomorrow with or without you." Simone stood and walked away.

"I like a girl in leather," Angus said.

"Well, her sparkling personality won't win her any awards. Let's just hope she's a good tracker." Nesi wouldn't steer me wrong, but something more than her manner disturbed me.

"Dragons don't eat meat," I said.

"So you've said." Angus gulped down the last of his ale and waved at Trixie for more. "What of it?"

"Simone said that the dragons were stealing cows."

"Maybe they drink milk."

"Come on. I'm serious. Maybe this Simone is full of shit."

"Or maybe your little Ollie is an odd duck. In all the old tales, dragons eat whatever they want. People mostly."

I thought back to the stories I'd read about dragons. Yes, they did like to kill, but only those who went looking for them. Like we were about to do. Still, the stories were always about dragons sitting on mountains of gold and jewels, not bones.

I wasn't sure what to think, but Simone rubbed me the wrong way.

"Whether or not they're real dragons," I said, "I'm not leaving without Mason. I think we should go look for him."

"You're too wobbly on your pegs," Angus said. "Mason would want you to rest. Don't go throwing caution out with the bathwater. The captain will get here by hook or by ladder. I promise you."

As I tried to sort out this basketful of metaphors, my keening went into overload. Magic crashed against my personal wards like a mallet on a gong. I closed my eyes and built up my defenses, but I was exhausted and the effort nearly floored me.

Herne and Charlotte came rushing from the kitchen.

"What's all the bother?" Angus said.

"Someone's knocking at the gate," Herne said with a frown. "Bernard! Go let our guest in!" The boy who had been stacking wood jumped to attention and ran outside.

"Check for vampires before you open it, you lugger-head!" Herne bellowed, then turned to us with a smile. "It won't be vamps. I would know their magic anywhere. But the boy can be too impulsive."

Annequin Lodge had only one gate through the ward for safety reasons. Those who lived here were keyed to the magic barrier and could come and go as they pleased. All others had to use the gate, and heavy magic barred it at sundown.

I followed the serving boy. He was already down the path and opening the door in the stone wall that served as the inn's keep. This very real door also served as the gate to the ward.

After a few moments, Bernard returned with a dark figure limping after him.

Mason. His shirt was torn, hair messed, and he favored his left leg. Before I could question my motives, I ran down the path and threw my arms around his neck.

# CHAPTER 17

When Simone learned that we could only travel by night because of the gargoyles' unusual restrictions, she spewed out a string of curses that would have impressed my Viking cousins, then said, "We leave now, and my fee just doubled."

"That's insane," I said. Nesi had negotiated a fair deal for us, but I couldn't afford to double it.

"Do you know what hunts the Inbetween at night?" Simone crossed her arms. "No, you don't. I do. That's why you hired me. I will find your dragons, but night travel means hazard pay."

I was about to protest again when Mason said, "Fine. We leave in half an hour."

"Gold only. I expect half before we leave." Simone turned and left the common room.

"I can't afford to pay her double," I said as we sat at one of the long tables. Trixie put a plate of food in front of Mason and he ate like a starving man.

"And you don't need to be responsible for everything," he said.

"Ollie *IS* my responsibility."

"Only because you have a savior complex."

"I…what?"

"You think you need to take care of everyone. But those dragons were in my backyard for a reason. The bloodstone is my problem and I intend to fix it."

"That doesn't mean you need to pay to bring Ollie back to his thunder."

Mason put down his fork and pinned me with his glare.

"Just accept my help with a graceful 'thank you.'"

I really wanted to argue.

"Fine. Thank you." I went back to my room to pack my bag.

We left Annequin Lodge that night. Charlotte wanted Mason and I to rest, but Simone was adamant. Mason still limped, but he insisted that the sunrise would fix all his injuries.

I was in worse shape. The first part of the journey was an easy slope, but I grew fatigued quickly. And I couldn't get over the feeling that we were being watched. I sensed eyes peering from every shadow.

"Tell me again why we didn't bring the mounts," I said.

"Even the hunt beasts wouldn't make it through these mountains." Simone was impatient at the many breaks I called, but I couldn't seem to catch my breath. The vampire venom had taken a toll on my constitution.

"So how exactly are we supposed to cross something that even a goat can't cross?" I asked.

"Are we walking or talking?" Simone said. She was only a few paces ahead of us, but almost lost in the deep gloom of the forest.

"Can't we do both?" Mason asked, flashing her one of his best boyish grins.

Simone scowled. "No. You waste breath. We need to hurry."

Mason shrugged and we picked up the pace.

An hour later, we emerged from the forest to follow a gully that cut between two slopes. The ground was roughly pebbled like a dry stream bed. Hills on either side became steeper and more jagged as we moved on. Ahead was only blackness, but as we got closer, a sheer bluff rose out of the darkness, and it looked like the gully dead-ended right at its base.

"You don't mean for us to climb that, do you?" I asked breathlessly. We hadn't even brought climbing gear, and my legs were already shaking with fatigue. Simone shot me a sneering glance but said nothing.

"I'm going out on a limb to say she doesn't like you," Mason whispered. A hysterical giggle erupted from me and I had to sit down. I didn't care that we were in the middle of nowhere. I crumpled to the rocks. My limbs shook and my stomach was barely keeping down Herne's venison stew, but it was all so ridiculous. We were tracking through the Inbetween, looking for dragons, running from vampires with only an angry stranger as our guide. Another giggle escaped me.

Angus scratched his gnarled hair and said, "I think she's still coming down from the vampire high."

Ollie fluttered around my feet, and Mason pulled me up with both hands. "It's just a well-needed release of tension." He grinned.

"I'm fine." I stifled another laugh.

Simone watched my breakdown with arms crossed over her chest, that same muscle twitching under her eye. "We have no time for this."

"Why?" snapped Mason. "Do you have somewhere important to be? The dragons will keep."

"We have no time because you hold us back!" She pointed at Mason.

"Hey!" I said, all amusement gone. "I'm the one holding us back."

"Yes, but he's the reason we have to hurry. Dawn is only a couple of hours away. Already, we won't make it through the mountain by then, but if you don't stop this foolishness, we won't get to the camp in time. And it's not safe to camp in the open here."

"I apologize if my condition has set unreasonable constraints on you." Mason bowed formally. "We will endeavor to make up for the delay."

Simone squinted at him. Was he making fun of her? I didn't think so. Mason was born in another age, and his gentility came out when he was upset.

"I'm sorry too," I mumbled, but Simone was already walking away at a brisk pace.

The gully ended at the cliff face and we continued into the mountain, first creeping into a small opening, then moving more quickly as the cave opened up.

Simone took a torch that hung on the wall and lit it. We were going old-school. I almost suggested that Mason use his gleam, but Simone seemed to know what she was doing and I let it go.

The passage was well-used and warm air blew in from an underground vent. Within a few minutes, I shucked my jacket as sweat beaded in the small of my back. Simone didn't slow her pace.

I became disoriented as the path rose and fell, twisting at sharp angles. Several times, it opened into caverns, but Simone didn't stop. I was just about to swallow my pride and beg her for a rest when I heard the distinct echo of rushing water. We rounded another bend and came into an enormous cavern that sloped down to a river.

"We camp here," Simone said. "The water is fresh, but no fire. There are dangerous creatures in these caves. We don't want to attract them. The torch is enough."

The torch's light barely filled the cavern, and I didn't relish the all-encompassing darkness that would come when it burned out.

We filled our canteens from the river. The water was slow and black. I couldn't guess how deep, but at the end of the cavern, it disappeared into a hole with the sound of a waterfall.

Suddenly, I felt the weight of the mountain pressing down on me. I wanted to throw myself into the river and follow its path out of there. Fast.

"Breathe," Mason said. I shot him a quick smile. Was I that obvious?

"I'm okay. Just over-tired." He handed me a travel cake from his pack and I ate the dry bread mechanically.

After dinner, I started to pull out my bedroll but Simone stopped me.

"Don't sleep on the ground." She pointed to loops of old rope hanging from metal spikes driven into the rock walls. They turned out to be hammocks—two on either side of the cavern. One had rotted enough to be useless, and Simone cut it away with her hunting knife. Without another word, she swung into the remaining hammock on that side and turned her back on us.

The other two hammocks hung side-by-side about six feet off the ground. The only way to get into them was from a ledge along the wall that started near the cave's entry point.

"Let me get in first," Mason said, "so I'll be near the wall. I don't want to crush you." I nodded and he eased into the first hammock. It creaked under his weight and I hoped it would hold him after sunrise. I climbed over him. There was no way to do that gracefully or without rubbing my parts against his. My hammock had a longer reach to the metal studs, and it creaked and swung erratically.

By the time I settled in, Mason was grinning but at least he had the manners not to say anything. I shifted, trying to get comfortable while the hammocks bumped against each other.

*This should be interesting.*

"We'll perch here for the night," Angus said as he nudged Ollie onto the ledge. "Nothing will get past us."

Simone had left the torch burning, but it was nearly out.

"Do you still have that gleam?" I asked. Mason's hammock swayed. He pulled the orb from his backpack and shook it. The cave filled with light.

"Put that away!" Simone called from across the cave. "You'll call down every damned shusher in the place!"

I didn't know what a shusher was, but it didn't sound good.

Mason covered the gleam with his hands.

"Here." He passed it over to me, grabbing my hand to place it carefully. "It won't break if it falls on the rock, but tuck it under your jacket to keep it dim. It should last the night."

"Thank you." I gripped his hand, needing the touch in this strange place. I tucked the orb into my jacket, comforted by the buzz of magic coming off it. Mason lay on his back and the muffled gleam was just bright enough that I could make out his sharp profile.

"If you need to get out in the night, climb over me. You can't hurt me," he said.

"What do you think Simone is afraid of?"

"Let's hope we don't find out."

I shifted in my hammock, looking for comfort in the rigid ropes and hyper-aware of Mason pressed against my side.

"Are we close to sunrise?" I asked, just as I knew the answer. I felt his magic go still, like a church bell that lost its clapper. Ollie whined from the ledge above us. Angus had gone gargoyle too.

I lifted the light to examine Mason. He looked at perfect ease. He could have been sleeping except his eyes were open and they had dulled. There was no life there. I reached out to touch his face. The skin was warm and rough where stubble had turned to stone. Each hair on his head was distinct, and I gave into the urge to run my hands over it. In life, I imagined it would be soft. Now it was spiky and frozen in a curl across his forehead.

Neither of us had acknowledged my reckless embrace when he arrived at Annequin Lodge. Now my heart ached as if I'd lost him—lost him before I'd been given the chance to truly know him. Logic told me he wasn't dead, just in his curse-induced stasis, but he looked so inanimate, like the carving atop the sarcophagus of a great king. I laid my hand on his chest and dug deep with my keening.

*Yes, there.* It was faint, but I could just detect the murmur of his magic. I left my hand across his chest and tried to sleep.

A quiet grunting snore announced that Simone wasn't affected with the same insomnia. Even Ollie nodded off. Eventually the white noise of the waterfall lulled me and I slept.

The wind rustling through the trees woke me. I sat up. My hammock swayed erratically and I remembered where I was. No wind and no trees. But the strange noise was louder than the waterfall.

Simone's hammock creaked.

"Don't move," she whispered.

The sound grew, a shifting, clicking noise that raised every hair on my neck. I pulled Mason's gleam from my jacket. Its light was nearly out, but it was strong enough to illuminate the rocks six feet below. I peered through the ropes.

The ground was moving.

"What is that?" I hissed.

"Shushers," Simone said.

I could barely make out the individual bodies of the swift moving creatures. Each was as big as a shiny black walnut with crablike pincers and a tail curving up in a barbed point. They came from deep in the mountain and skittered across the cave floor toward the river. There had to be hundreds of them. Thousands!

They flowed over the ground, covering rocks large and small in their relentless tide. What if we'd been sleeping there? A couple of the creatures skittered up the ledge and over Angus's feet. They leapt onto Mason with pincers clacking, and I swatted them aside in a panic.

Ollie squeaked and jumped into my hammock, making it swing wildly, bumping us against Mason's still form. I grabbed the dragon and his claws scraped me as he scrambled for purchase. The hammock tilted with the extra weight and I crashed to the ground.

The fall shook the gleam and reactivated it. Suddenly I faced the shushers in their full, horrifying detail. The claws protected huge jaws and a row of beady eyes.

And they liked the light. The tide of chiton turned like one and made for the gleam.

Which I was still holding.

The shock of hundreds of critters crawling up my legs and body to get to the light blocked out all my other senses. I was only vaguely aware of Ollie tangled in the hammock above and Simone screaming.

Pinpricks of pain shot through me—stings on my legs, arms and face. My hands took the brunt of the bites as I frantically swatted the creatures.

"Throw the light!" Simone's words finally sunk in. I threw the gleam over my head. It bounced on rock, splashed into the river and sunk.

The shushers followed the light, and I scrambled away, putting my back against rock.

*Oh, what I wouldn't give for my pest kit and a good can of bug fogger right now.*

"*Imbécile,*" Simone said. Then she rolled over and went back to sleep.

Ollie fluttered down and landed beside me with a quiet chirp. The shushers were intent on the light in the river and left us alone.

"It's okay." I patted him with my hand that was pockmarked with bites. They hurt, but no worse than bee stings.

Ollie settled beside me with his head in my lap. I spent the next hour in the dark listening to the clack of chiton on rock, the shifty sound of thousands of sliding bodies and the faint splashes as they leapt into the river to be swept away through the underground highway.

# CHAPTER 18

I woke feeling cramped and sore from sleeping upright against the rock wall. The shusher bites had faded to nothing more than a few red bumps. They didn't even itch. I could have imagined it all, except for the litter of black bodies I'd crushed when falling from my hammock.

Ollie chirped at me from his perch on the ledge beside Angus. I wanted him to eat and get some water, but he wouldn't move until his friend woke up.

Simone was already awake and I joined her at the small fire she had going to heat water for porridge and tea.

"You must use this camp often," I said.

"It is the fastest route through the mountain." She had an odd way of not looking at me when she spoke, as if she could commit her words to the conversation, but not her thoughts. She was even twitchier today, jerking through the small movements needed to make breakfast.

"Those creatures last night…the shushers. Are they always here?"

She shrugged. "It's breeding season and they seek a mating nest. They're only dangerous at this time, otherwise…" She made a squishing motion with her foot. "Like cockroaches."

"Pretty scary for roaches."

Simone thrust a mug of hot tea at me, and I took it down to the river's edge. The gleam still glowed faintly underwater. I stretched to scoop it out, drenching my shirt to the elbow. It was too valuable to leave behind. I shook my hand to dry it and reactivate the light. Simone glanced up from the fire to glare, but she didn't rebuke me. The threat of the shusher invasion had passed.

Several of the creatures lay dead on the rocks. I examined one by the light of the gleam. Its carapace wasn't really black, but iridescent, like oil floating in water.

I took a specimen box from my pack and scooped it up.

"Only you would bring a cockroach home as a souvenir," Mason said from behind me.

"Not a roach. A shusher." I stood and showed him the creature in the plexiglass container. "I've never seen one before, have you?"

"No."

"A migrating horde of them visited us last night."

"Yes, I know."

"You mean, you're aware when you go…" I still wasn't comfortable with the gargoyle terminology.

"When I'm inanimate?"

I nodded.

"My senses are dulled. Sort of like being underwater. But I can still feel, hear, and see light."

"Oh." By the All-father, I wanted the ground to open up and swallow me right there. He knew I'd groped his face!

Mason grinned, enjoying my embarrassment. He took my hand and laid it on his cheek. His skin was warm and pliant. His five-day beard tickled my hand as he leaned into it, then he turned and kissed my palm.

"You can touch me any time, day or night."

I yanked my hand away. I wouldn't fall for that again. Mason was a terrible flirt, but he wasn't looking for more. His disappearing act after our first kiss last year proved that. And my heart wouldn't accept less.

I studied the dead shusher again to avoid the too-close-for-comfort conversation.

"It's kind of beautiful, don't you think?"

Mason barely glanced at the creature.

"You're a very strange woman, Kyra Greene."

"You don't know the half of it."

He watched me with his odd, intense gaze.

*Tell me you want to know more!*

My thoughts screamed so loud in my head, Mason must have heard them. But he just smiled sadly and turned away.

"Why do you do that?" I asked, stopping him.

"Do what?"

"Flirt with me. You made it clear you don't want a relationship."

"There are relationships and there are relations." His eyebrows waggled. "Carnal relations."

If I wasn't so annoyed by his hot and cold blustering, I would have laughed.

"In my experience, carnal relations usually lead to relationships."

"Then you're doing it wrong."

"I see."

He lost his grin.

"It bothers you, doesn't it? That I never contacted you after our encounter with the troll."

I folded my arms and tried to look noncommittal.

"I'm sorry." He reached for me, but stopped before taking my hand. "I know mortals get attached easily. It's just not a good idea for you to attach yourself to me."

"You think I'm mortal?"

Mason shrugged. "You said yourself, your heritage is a mixed bag. But you don't have that world weary look an immortal gets."

"Oh, I have been plenty weary of this world. How old do you think I am?"

"There's no good answer to that question."

"I'm seventy-eight." I had the pleasure of watching his jaw drop. "But I spent forty-six of those years in Asgard eating the Golden Apples of eternal life. They kept my complexion clear." I smiled fiercely.

Mason considered me for several long seconds.

"But without the Golden Apples, you'll age just like anyone else, right?"

It was a good question, one I had pondered a lot in my younger days. In the years I trained as a Valkyrie, I ate the famed Golden Apples every day. These brought youth, health and vigor to all who consumed them. They were the reason we went to Asgard in the first place, after conventional medicine failed to cure my mother's cancer.

When I returned to Terra, the entire world had changed, but I still looked eighteen. Twelve years later, my appearance had matured a bit. Did this mean I was mortal? Were the effects of the Golden Apples wearing off? Would I now age and die like any human?

The question of my lifespan was complex. Aesir were more or less immortal as long as they didn't take an axe to the brain. Dryads were long-lived, but not technically immortal. And humans, of course, had woefully short lives. I could go either way, but had long ago decided not to dwell on it. No one was truly immortal. Death could come for any of us at any time. If my Aesir genes meant that sickness and age wouldn't touch me, I could still have my throat cut in a dark alley one night. Life was precious no matter what, and I tried to live by that rule.

But I felt the weight of Mason's question. It was important to him, and I couldn't tell which answer he wanted.

I shrugged. "I like to take a wait-and-see approach to immortality."

His expression froze somewhere between curiosity and horror.

"Does that bother you? I might get old and wrinkly while you stay forever young and…" I stopped myself from saying "hot" but he saw it in my eyes and grinned.

"Even your wrinkles would be beautiful." His hand snuck around the back of my neck where his thumb found the vulnerable hollow. "But I have outlived three wives and ten children. I won't do it again."

He turned and went back to camp, leaving me with the feel of his touch blazing along my skin.

I felt sorry for him. How lonely to be so closed off. But was I any better? How many men had I let into my life since Aaric died? Oh, I'd had flings, sexual encounters that filled a base need, but no real connections. I'd filled my life with furred and feathered relationships instead.

"Hey, old man," I called out. He stopped but didn't turn around.

"Maybe we can revisit this conversation in a few hundred years, if I'm still around."

"Maybe we can."

# CHAPTER 19

There was no light at the end of the tunnel. We followed a narrow passage that sloped steeply upward, then turned down at a gentle angle and came out into a dark wood.

Simone didn't hesitate, but pulled out a machete and cut through the undergrowth. The rest of us followed, pushing branches out of the way. Behind us, the bushes and trees were already regenerating. Within a few hours there would be no sign of our passage.

These impenetrable forests were common in the world left after the Flood Wars. Wards spent as much magic fighting back the encroaching foliage as they did protecting themselves from rival wards. Alchemists spouted all kinds of theories for the bizarre landscapes in the Inbetween. Some proposed that the bombs dropped during the war damaged ley-lines and so the magic ran amok. Others suggested that the sheer number of dead twisted the burgeoning magic.

I had another theory. I could feel it humming up through the soles of my feet. Every leaf on every branch tingled with it. The magic of the world. Terra was alive and sentient. And she was pissed at the humans crawling all over her like vermin.

Sheet lightning flashed but only seemed to highlight the darkness under the trees. We stopped at a small stream to fill our canteens. No one spoke.

A branch cracked behind us and we all turned. The darkness was absolute. I held my breath, waiting for some giant mutant badger to jump at us. Five agonizing seconds passed and nothing.

Ollie whined and hid behind Angus.

"Just a wee night critter," Angus said. "Probably more afraid of us, than we are of it."

I doubted that.

We moved on, but I couldn't shake the feeling that something watched us.

An hour later, the forest ended abruptly at the edge of a cliff, like some god had taken a giant cleaver and cut away the land. Below us, cattle grazed on a massive plain where glowing grasses reflected on the low-hanging clouds.

"Look." Simone pointed to a section of blackened grass that the cows avoided. Lightning filled the sky and thunder rumbled in the distance.

"What is it?" Mason asked.

"Dragon fire," Simone said. "They came, burned the land and took the cows. We lost nearly a quarter of the herd."

I squinted into the darkness. The scorch marks looked odd.

"They're too regular, almost like footprints," I said. "Are you sure a dragon made these?"

"What else?" Simone scowled.

"Well, we'd better get all our ducks on the same page and check out those marks up close," Angus said. He was chewing on the root of some plant he'd found, and his words were even more mangled than usual.

Ollie peered over the edge of the cliff and I dragged him backward before he got any ideas about flying.

"Is there some way down?" Mason asked. He wasn't looking over the plains though. He stared into the shadows between the trees we had just left. So I wasn't the only one feeling the creeping stare of unseen eyes on us.

"There are stairs cut into the bluff," Simone said. "This way."

Even with the rough stairs, descending onto the plain was a tough hike with the effects of the vampire venom wearing on me. Mason brought up the rear of our group, slowing down to match my pace.

"Go on ahead." I waved him through. Angus and Simone were almost at the bottom. "I just need a short rest and I'll catch up."

"Not going to happen." Mason folded his arms and leaned against the rock face.

"I don't need a babysitter."

"No, but if you fall down those stairs, I'm going to either have to bury you or carry you the rest of the way. Both options sound like too much work." His grin was just a bit evil.

"Chivalry isn't dead," I muttered. Mason handed me his canteen and I drank. He watched me.

"I'm fine. Really. See? Ready to move on already."

Mason shook his head, not buying my bravado. Then he moved ahead, descending slowly, and I realized that he was being my buffer. If I fell, I'd fall on him first.

Simone waited at the bottom of the stairs, conferring with two soldiers, both female and heavily armed. They seemed to know Simone and spoke in whispers with heads close together. When she saw us, Simone shook her head as if to deny the guard's last words, then motioned for us to follow her.

"Why the guards?" I asked.

"Cows are precious out here. This is the only grazing land around, but it's too far from the ward, so we guard it."

"We?"

The tic on her face jerked.

"The Sanctuary Ward, about twenty kilometers east of here. I haven't lived there in many years, but the guards know I run this route a lot, so I don't get any trouble."

"Are there more guards?" I waved in the general direction of the fields.

"Probably." Simone shrugged. "Is that a problem?"

"No." But I felt very vulnerable. It occurred to me I knew next to nothing about our guide. Simone could be leading us into all kinds of nasty. But then, Nesi had vouched for her, and that had to be good enough.

The cows were drowsy, but a few were curious enough to come meet us. They stared at the strangers in their midst with that strange intensity that cows have. One lowed in protest. Simone petted its head and gently shoved it aside to make a path. I liked that. It made her almost human.

We moved across the plains toward the streak of black marks cut into the ground. The air smelled of ozone, sharp and tangy. One burn was massive, easily wide enough for all of us to stand within it. Mason's gleam hovered over our heads, and I bent to inspect the blackened ground, reaching out with my keening too.

"What do you think?" I asked.

"You're the creature expert," he said.

"I never saw a dragon before last week."

Ollie sniffed the perimeter of the burn mark, clearly agitated. Was he sensing his pack? Was it some other predator? Finally, he turned in a circle several times and squatted.

"I'll get that," grumbled Angus.

Simone made a face as Angus sifted through the dragon dung with a stick.

Mason and I moved on, following the trail of burned grass. It cut off about midway through the plains. What ever made it had either vanished or flown away.

Angus and Ollie joined us.

"Anything?" Mason asked.

Angus shook his head. "If he swallowed that stone, it's camped in his gut right good. Should have passed it by now."

"So where do we go now?" I asked Simone. "Nesi said you know where these creatures are nesting."

"This side of the mountains." Simone pointed along the mountain range we had just descended. "But north. We should be there by daybreak."

We weren't.

An hour before sunrise, Mason called a halt when we found a decent camp beside a river that flowed out of the mountains. I wondered if it was the same river that the shushers rode in their mating journey.

"We stay here for the day," Mason said.

"But we're less than an hour away!" Simone protested.

"We stop," I said. I wouldn't go on without Mason and I understood his reasoning. We might make it to the dragon den just in time for him to turn to stone. Better to rest here and meet the creatures after a good day's sleep.

"Some of us have lives to get back to," Simone snapped.

"If you want to turn back now, go ahead. We'll find our way without you," I said.

Simone stared at me, teeth clenched and cheek twitching. She threw her pack down and stomped off into the trees.

"I'm sorry to hold you back," Mason said.

"You aren't. We're all tired and I want to rest before we face whatever is nesting in that mountain."

He nodded, but I couldn't tell if he believed me.

As we settled in, Angus gave Ollie flying lessons again. The dragon climbed on top of a large boulder, then jumped off, flapping his wings.

"No, no!" said Angus. "You've got to do it with panache. Think of gliding instead of flying."

Ollie watched Angus as he demonstrated, then climbed up the boulder and flapped his wings just as frantically as before.

Angus smiled. "That's alright. You'll get it."

"I can't decide if he understands language or not," Mason said.

"I think he's learning. Maybe soon we can ask him about the bloodstone," I said.

"He swallowed something of yours?" Simone asked as she returned with an armful of kindling. "Is that why you keep looking through his shit?"

"A gemstone," I said, not wanting to give her too much detail.

"So cut him open. Only sure way to get it back." Her hard eyes made it clear she would help with this task.

"We're not in a hurry," I said. I'd met Simone's kind before. She might share her hearth with a dog, but if it got sick, she'd take it out back and shoot it. To her, animals were a means to an end, not beings with their own rights. There was no point in trying to reason with her.

"Whatever," she said and turned away to set up the fire.

"The sun is coming," Mason said quietly. It was hard to tell under the dense canopy, but I trusted him.

"I'll go sit in the trees over there, so I don't make you uncomfortable. Please, don't…" He ran a hand over his face and head, messing his hair. "Don't confront the dragons without me. I don't trust Simone to have your back."

"I won't." I watched him head into the trees and then listened to the keen of his magic until the sun rose.

I WOKE WELL before sunset, even though the days were still short. Simone puttered around the camp, collecting more wood for the fire. She wouldn't look at me and I didn't know if she still chafed at the delay or if that was her natural sunny disposition.

Ollie paced like a caged tiger. I hoped his fidgeting meant that he had to do his business again and we'd finally recover the bloodstone, but he just kept circling the camp with a determined air of impatience.

With nothing to do until sunset, I took out the shusher specimen and sketched it for my blog.

"Can you tell me about these?" I asked Simone, holding up the plastic case.

"They're vermin. Like roaches."

"They're not venomous?" I still had red marks from their bites, but nothing more.

"Like bees. One sting will hurt. Dozens might make you sick."

She handed me a cup of tea she'd been brewing over the fire. I wrapped my hands around the hot tin mug and sipped it.

Simone stood. "Still an hour of sunlight. Going to hunt mushrooms."

"Okay." I didn't think mushrooms would put up much of a fight. She slipped away, her tight form quickly disappearing into the shadows between the trees.

"It's just you and me, buddy." I scratched Ollie's ears. He whined. "How about a walk?"

A few steps into the trees, we stumbled across Angus sitting like a stone guard. Ollie zipped around him as if his exuberance could wake his friend.

"He'll be awake soon." I urged Ollie on. His nervous energy infected me and I needed to keep moving.

The trees in this part of the Inbetween were impressive. As we moved deeper into the wood, I passed trunks wider than my outstretched arms. A couple hundred years ago, these would have been impossibly wide. Back then, humans didn't let trees age long enough to create these massive boles before harvesting them for throwaway goods like paper or clearing them for yet another suburban development.

But this was the new world ruled by the whims of magic. Terra had taken herself back from the humans. Now any settlement that encroached too far outside its ward for supplies or nourishment got slapped by the hand of nature. The fast-growing forests and choking foliage that covered lost cities were a big "Fuck you" from Terra herself.

Even so, such immense trees were rare. I hadn't seen their like since I left my grandmother's home in the dryad forest down south. There, the dryads doted on the trees, mourning like after the death of a loved-one when a tree fell from age or mishap. I'd seen no sign of dryads here, but this forest was almost too perfect.

The lowest branches were dozens of feet above my head. Vines crept across the ground and wound around trunks. Dead leaves crunched under my feet, and the sound was unnaturally loud in the stillness.

My keening picked up a trigger of magic that none of my other senses detected. Something watched us from the shadows. So far, I'd put this feeling down to paranoia caused by the lingering effects of vamp venom, but now my magic rang like an alarm.

Ollie seemed oblivious to whatever stalked us. He hopped and fluttered, pushing his wings to hold his weight. I stopped him with a firm hand on his shoulder. His big copper eyes watched me intently.

Ahead of us the trees ended near a steep drop-off. The late afternoon light penetrated the thick canopy. Pretending to inspect the rough bark of a tree, I slipped back into the shadows and peered behind me.

The magic weaving through the wood was eerie and disturbingly familiar, but I couldn't pinpoint its source. It seemed to come from all around, manifesting from the trees and shadows—from the very ground itself. Then a pinprick of too-familiar magic stood out from the rest.

I stepped into the light.

"Jacoby, come out! I know you're there!"

I stared into the darkening wood while Ollie hid behind me. I didn't know how he'd followed us all the way from Montreal, even through the mountains, but I had no doubt the magic I tasted was Jacoby's.

Leaves rustled and a curly-haired head poked through a bramble of dead vines. Jacoby's bushy eyebrows arched as he tried to look innocent. He raised a hand and waved his multi-jointed fingers.

"Hiya."

"How long have you been following us?"

He shrugged. "I feels bad."

I frowned. He'd said that before, and it hadn't meant he felt sick. Jacoby was prescient.

"You feel something bad coming in the city, you mean? Is that why you followed me?"

"I feels bad for you."

He turned to stare into the trees, then whispered, "Kyra-lady, runs!" before disappearing into the shadows again.

But it was too late.

I straightened and drew my sword as six beings appeared from the shadows.

We were surrounded.

*Valkyriebestiary.com/shusher*

## SHUSHERS FROM THE INBETWEEN

*(May 3, 2080 - Posted May 16, 2080)*

I'm on an adventure outside our ward where I encountered some really interesting creatures.

The first one is a shusher. I have never heard of this creature before. They may be a hybrid, created in the magic flares during the war.

The shusher seems to be an arachnid. The sample I have (see sketch) is 4cm across the shell and 9.5cm from end to end. It has claws in front (for defense or capturing prey?) and over-sized mandibles. The long curving tail comes to a point and is used as a stinger, though I can attest that the sting is not fatal. My arms were covered in stings after my first encounter with these critters. They hurt and itched for a few hours, but no worse than a bad mosquito bite.

The shushers come together in a massive swarm to mate and travel great distances to find the perfect nest. The sound the swarm makes as it moves across the ground is sort of like the whisper of a strong wind in the trees. Is this the origin of the name shusher? Unknown.

They are drawn to light, but can navigate in the dark. And they swim. What do they eat? Unknown.

I have never seen a shusher inside my ward, and I hope they stay away. I can see how a swarm of these could do a lot of damage.

My only source for information about the shusher isn't very forthcoming, so all the info in this post is from my observation only. I'd love your input. If you've run into these creatures before, please leave additional information in the comments.

## Comments (5)

Does that mean you went outside your ward? In the Inbetween? That's five by five!

*DaddysGirl (May 16, 2080)*

> DaddysGirl gets 10 points for the Buffy reference! That's seriously old world, but you just made my day!
>
> *Valkyrie367 (May 16, 2080)*
>
> > Who's Buffy?
> >
> > *Daddysgirl (May 17, 2080)*

I'm not cleaning bug guts out of your jeans again. Throw them out.

*CapeBretonBanshee (May 16, 2080)*

A little chamomile oil will soothe those stings and keep them from getting infected. I like to mix it with a bit of aloe vera. Stay safe out there!

*cchedgewitch (May 17, 2080)*

## CHAPTER 20

I hadn't sensed them coming. Only dryads can move through the forest undetected by my keening because they're one with the forest. Their magic matches the energy of the trees and the soil.

But these weren't dryads. They couldn't be. For one, they were too tall and broad in the shoulders. Their faces held the same elfin grace as a dryad, but with flattened noses and deeply set eyes. And while most dryads boasted spectacular manes of hair, these creatures were bald with bony ridges crowning their sculls—ridges tipped in green as if covered in moss.

The biggest difference was their dress. They wore armor over short leather tunics and carried blunt clubs of hardwood. Dryads are nonviolent. They don't hunt game or seek war. They eat only nuts and berries and dress in natural fibers.

I let my keening reach for the magic of these odd creatures. It tasted like conifers and cold stone. And then I knew who they were.

"What do you want?" I asked in the dryad tongue.

The one in the lead stepped forward and cocked his head, examining me. He flicked a glance to Ollie, who cowered behind my knees.

"You have a dragon," he grumbled in the same language. His accent confirmed my suspicion. These were oreads, distant cousins to my dryad kin. They live in mountains, existing in the harsh terrain at the limit of the tree line. Unlike the gentle dryads, oreads are warlike. They often fight clan to clan and once in a while come together to fight a greater outside foe. I'd met only one oread at my grandmother's house. He was a belligerent guest, and Nana Greenleaf sent him on his way as soon as the guesting laws had been fulfilled.

"Give me the dragon." The oread's voice rumbled like an avalanche. He was standing a little too close to me, and I didn't like it.

"No." I nudged him back with an open palm on his chest. The oread's eyes widened. He gaped at my hand, poised to push him again.

Then he backhanded me across the chin. It was the swat of a giant with a noisome fly and it flung me backwards where I tangled in a heap with Ollie.

"Tie them up and bring them," said the oread as he turned back to his pack. Two others approached with thick ropes ready. I was sitting on my sword and couldn't pull it easily. My head rang from the blow, and I couldn't fight six armed oreads anyway.

I had a better weapon. My widget was still strapped to my belt. I held it up to the approaching oreads and they paused.

"You don't want to hurt me," I said in English. I was too stressed to keep up in dryad. "I have Lisobet Greenleaf on speed dial. She'll hear about this behavior."

I hoped the oreads were too primitive to understand that I couldn't call anyone in the Inbetween. But my name-dropping worked. The leader pushed aside the two with the ropes and stood over me. Ollie squeaked and squirmed away.

"What did you say?"

"Lisobet Greenleaf. If you hurt me, she will find you."

Dryads might be gentle creatures, but they were fierce protectors of their forests and their families. And none was fiercer than Lisobet Greenleaf. She was a legend among dryad kind, a bad-ass forest ranger, sheriff and priestess all rolled into one. If the dryads had a queen, she would be it. And while oreads didn't recognize her authority, the long arm of her reputation reached even into their camps.

"And how do you know Lisobet Greenleaf," said the oread, in near-perfect English.

I lifted my chin and met his eyes. "She's my grandmother."

A murmur rose from the other oreads, and the leader shot them a silencing glance. He paced around me, considering. I still sat on the ground, my sword uselessly wedged under me. I shifted, but no way could I unsheathe fast enough to do any damage.

"That would mean you are related to Timberfoot Greenleaf?"

Oh, crap. Dropping Nana's name was one thing. But Dad had a reputation on an entirely different level.

"He's my father," I said reluctantly. The oread stepped back to confer with the others. They spoke in dryad and I could make out only a few words like "redemption" and "present for the prince."

Still on my butt, I inched backward toward the trees. Jacoby had returned and he soothed Ollie by holding his hand and patting it. I could have kissed that dervish. He could have teleported away and left us.

"Jacoby," I whispered, "do you still have that bag of wind?"

Jacoby's eyes were wide and unblinking. His grizzled fur framed them like the petals on a ragged flower. He nodded.

"Get it ready."

The oread returned.

"You think we are stupid." He spat, and a gob hit the ground in front of me. "That we are primitive and ignorant. Call your grandmother." His lips parted in a terrible smile.

Damn. He called my bluff. I raised one arm in surrender, holding my useless widget, and used my other hand to push up from the ground.

"Fine. You got me. I'll come."

But instead of standing and submitting meekly, I yelled, "Now Jacoby!"

Jacoby pulled the cord, and the bag of wind trembled with the beginnings of a vortex.

"Throw it!" I yelled and grabbed onto a vine, hoping its roots were solid.

Jacoby tossed the bag. He had a good arm for a little guy. The bag arced over the oreads' heads and exploded.

We must have been standing on a ley-line or a pocket of rogue magic left over from the Flood Wars. Never had a bag of wind done so much damage. It blew debris far and wide, uprooting smaller trees and leaving a bare dirt clearing around us. Three of the oreads fell backward over the cliff. The others tumbled into trees and were knocked senseless.

Jacoby squealed with glee and danced around the space laid bare by the violence of the micro storm.

I clambered to my feet, head throbbing.

"That one no dud," Jacoby said with a grin.

"Where's Ollie?" A little chirp made me look up. The dragon perched on a thick branch twenty feet above us. I had no time to worry about him. The oreads were getting to their feet.

I unsheathed my sword.

"At least the fight is fair now," I said, "three against one."

"No," Angus said, emerging from the shadows. "It's three against three."

I hadn't even noticed the sun set.

Mason and Angus stood with blades ready. Ollie fluttered down to land at their feet and hissed out a thin line of smoke. The oreads decided to fight another day and slunk away into the trees. Ollie ran after them like a spitting cat, but Angus pulled him back.

"Yes, you're very brave," Angus said. He pointed his blade into the forest where the oreads had disappeared, then circled his wrist a few times before re-sheathing. "That was a good warm up. Now let's go hunt some dragons."

# CHAPTER 21

Simone was packed and ready to leave when we returned to camp. Mason made a good show of taking his time to eat and repack his supplies while Simone waited with barely concealed impatience, her glare throwing daggers at him.

"You're going to make her head explode," I whispered.

He grinned and slurped his tea. I rolled my eyes.

We didn't need to rush. The dragon nest was less than an hour's hike. So, I let Mason play his games with the tracker.

Angus—who never seemed to eat—was giving Ollie a flying lesson. Ollie could now hover for a few seconds, but his wings still weren't strong enough for more.

Back on the trail, we headed away from the bluff where we'd encountered the oreads, and up the mountain.

"You shouldn't have wandered off on your own," Mason said as we walked.

"I didn't know I needed your permission to take a walk." The path was becoming steeper and the trees more sparse. I wasn't fully recovered from my opji encounter and my legs already felt shaky.

"It's not a matter of permission. It's about safety." Mason held my elbow to help me over a tumble of rock and I pulled away.

"I don't need your help. I could have fought the oreads on my own."

"But why would you want to if you didn't need to?" His brow creased, confusion filling his dark eyes. He really didn't know why I would refuse his help, didn't get that we'd been here before, fighting the bad guys side-by-side, talking, laughing, flirting. But when the adventure was done, he'd sneak back into his gargoyle lair and completely forget about me, the insignificant mortal who amused him for a blink of his eternal life.

Gods, I was exhausted just thinking about it.

"Because you won't always be around to depend on," I said. "Better that I put on my big-girl pants and deal with things on my own."

We walked in silence for a while, then he said, "I like your big-girl pants."

I wanted to kiss him and hit him. Not necessarily in that order.

Simone crouched on the path ahead.

"Hey!" I said as I almost stumbled over her. She made a cutting motion with her hand. Behind us, Ollie trilled at Angus's teasing.

"Keep that thing quiet!" Simone hissed. I stepped back to alert Angus that we'd stopped.

"Ollie, be quiet now," I said. He jumped up and hovered about eye level, a big grin on his face. Gently, I pulled him down and held him there so he didn't try to fly again. He chirped a question at me.

"Shhh." I touched his mouth, hoping he'd understand.

"What for?" Angus asked. "If there be dragons ahead, he should greet them."

"What if it's not his thunder?" Simone's stories about the dragon taking off with an entire cow still rubbed me wrong. "You wait here with them." I pointed to Ollie and Jacoby. "We'll check it out."

I walked back to Simone and crouched beside her as she peered through a break in the trees.

"Are you guys done with your party? Or should I serve the hors d'oeuvres?" she whispered.

"Keep your voice down," I whispered back. "Before you alert every monster on the mountain that we're here." I couldn't help it. Simone was as irksome as a pebble in my shoe. She glared at me, twitching as she held in a retort.

Mason crowded into the small space beside us. In the clearing ahead, the rocky escarpment eased into a shallow gully that butted up against another rock face. A dark smudge among all the other shadows showed where a cave opened into the mountain. Moonlight shone down on bones littering the space between the trees and the cave. A rib cage—the right size to be a cow—

shone white in the moonlight. The other bones were too small and too far away to identify.

From within the cave den came a rumbling growl, low at first, like thunder heard in the distance, then blossoming into a raging howl.

A snake appeared. It didn't slither up the wall, but bobbed in mid-air near the top of the cave entrance. Suspended, its tongue flicked out, tasting the night air. Below it, a lion emerged from the shadow.

I blinked. The incongruousness of the pair was too much for my tired brain.

"*Sacrement.*" I knew things were bad when Mason reverted to cursing in old French.

The lion stalked forward. Its powerful front legs ended in gnarled, furless toes tipped with claws. It came into the light, and just kept coming. Goat legs that were feathered below the knees supported leathery wings folded along its scaled body. Two spiraled horns capped its head. And the snake? That was its tail. As we watched in awe, the snake unhinged its jaw and spat fire at the moon.

Excellent.

I tugged Simone backward and we slid down the incline, hiding the beast from view.

"You idiot!" I hissed. "That's not a dragon! It's a chimera."

Simone shuddered. "We must kill it anyway."

"We didn't come here to kill anything. We came to find Ollie's thunder."

The chimera bellowed. A mating call? Oh, hells. One chimera was bad enough. I didn't want to be stuck there when a second arrived.

"We need to leave. Now!" I tried to pull Simone away, but she yanked her arm from my grasp.

"Coward." She was already on her feet and moving.

"No!" My voice was drowned out by Simone's shriek as she attacked the beast.

# CHAPTER 22

Critter wrangler rule number three: Never take on a two-headed beast that can spit fire with one end and bite your head off with the other. It's just common sense. But Simone had never read the rule book. Before I could even scramble out of hiding, she screamed. Not a battle cry—a shriek of pain and terror.

I rushed at the chimera. It had Simone caged under one of its giant raptor feet, one claw piercing her shoulder. I grabbed a dead branch as I ran and stuck it in the chimera's mouth before it tore out Simone's throat. The tail whipped around to bite me, but Mason blocked it with his arm. The snake bit down on solid stone.

How had he done that?

"I'll take the back end," he grunted. His fist came down on the snake's head, breaking its fangs on his stone arm. The snake reared back and hissed fire. Mason dodged under the massive body. The chimera stamped its back legs, and the feathers on its hocks burst into flame.

Angus appeared beside me and hacked at the claws that held Simone with a short axe. Blood covered her chest and face. She was unconscious or dead.

"Where's Ollie?" I shouted.

"The dervish is keeping him back." Angus's wings fluttered as he whacked at the chimera's leg.

The beast shook its head, snapping the branch and showering me with wood shards. It turned a massive feline face toward me and roared. Rank breath and flecks of spit hit me, then teeth snapped only inches from my face.

Mason struck a blow to its haunches, diverting attention away from me for a split second. That was all I needed. I slashed at its head with my sword, but it ducked and my blade only sheared off a horn.

The paw holding Simone kicked her body away, backhanding Angus at the same time. He tumbled out of sight.

Huge yellow eyes turned to me again. The beast was angry. It was in pain, and it would kill me for it. I lunged as it roared in fury. My sword was already primed with magic and I rammed it into the chimera's mouth, slicing the delicate palate, pushing magic through my blade into the wound. The beast shrieked. Its tail whipped around and tried to bite me, but Mason hammered the snake head again. The chimera bucked once with those fiery back legs, but then the flames went out. The snake fell limp. The golden eyes glazed over and the beast fell, only inches away from crushing Simone.

She would have deserved it.

I braced one foot against the beast and pulled out my sword.

"Stupid, stupid, stupid!" I said, shaking out my arms, which were jittery from spent energy. "Why did she force this fight? Why did we have to kill it?" I looked at the chimera. Such a magnificent specimen, dead now because of one woman's what? Vendetta? Ignorance? Was she more involved than she let on with that Sanctuary Ward and its missing cows? Had this all been a setup? I might never know what forced Simone to this suicidal act.

I knelt by her side and pressed my fingers to her throat. Her pulse throbbed and her breathing was even, but she'd lost a lot of blood.

The bellow of another chimera echoed through the trees. The mate.

"We can't stay here," Mason said. "Help me move her."

Part of me wanted to leave Simone, leave her to her wounds and her foolishness. Leave her as an offering to the other beast in apology for killing its mate.

But, of course, I didn't. Instead, I crouched and grabbed under one shoulder while Mason took the other. Once we got her up, Mason slung her over his shoulder and we moved away from the cave, back into the relative safety of the trees.

Jacoby hadn't ported away. He was holding tight to Ollie to keep the little dragon from following Angus into the fight.

"Thank you for staying with Ollie," I said. I might have to reward him with a place in my menagerie after all.

"Kyra-lady stinks." He wrinkled his nose.

"Yes, I do." I was drenched in chimera musk, blood and my own sweat. Mason didn't look much better. Simone's wound still leaked, and her blood matted his hair and shirt. Neither the gore nor the weight seemed to bother him.

"We need to find a camp soon or she'll bleed out," he said.

We found a small creek and camped in the clearing beside it. It was a terrible spot to defend if it came to a fight. But we needed water and we needed to tend to Simone.

Mason laid her on the grass. She woke for a moment, groaned and fell unconscious again. That was for the best. Cleaning her wound would be painful.

Angus left to find kindling, taking the others with him. Mason and I peeled off Simone's jacket and shirt. The wound had started to clot, and the cloth of her shirt stuck to her.

"Can you sew up a wound?" he asked.

I nodded. I'd fixed up enough damaged critters over the years to be well versed in basic first aid. I prodded Simone's wound. The chimera's claw had pierced muscle just below the collarbone. She was lucky. A few inches lower and it would have punctured a lung. Removing her shirt had opened the wound again and it oozed dark blood. The claws of the average house cat were full of bacteria. Who knew what festered on a chimera's claws. They could even be poisoned.

"We shouldn't stitch it," I said. "I'm worried about infection. We'll dress it for the night and see how she is tomorrow." I took bandages and antiseptic from my first aid kit while Mason fetched water to clean the wound. The creek was cold and fast running. I could only hope that the water was clean.

We worked quietly. I cleaned the wound and dabbed it with ointment. It didn't look too bad, but puncture wounds could be deceiving. And Simone still hadn't regained consciousness.

"Why do you think she did it?" he asked.

"I don't know. Nesi said she's an excellent tracker. No way she could have mistaken chimera tracks for dragons."

"Agreed." Mason handed me the roll of bandages without being asked. He lifted Simone so I could wrap her shoulder. She was pale and clammy. I covered her with the mylar sheet from my kit. It was the best we could do.

My left knee protested when I rose. I'd wrenched it during the fight and crouching to tend to Simone hadn't helped.

Mason was glancing around the campsite.

"It's not the best place to stop," he said. Thick trees all around meant that we wouldn't see an attack coming. The burble of the creek blocked other sounds too.

"Can you cast a ward?" I asked.

"Not unless I have some of those alchemy toys you like. You?"

I nodded. Ward magic was deeply rooted to earth magic, something dryads excelled at.

"How about I fix something to eat while you set a ward?" Mason said.

"Mom always said to find a guy who could cook," I teased.

"If pulling out dry rations and boiling tea counts, then I'm a catch."

Angus, Ollie and Jacoby returned, and I warned them not to leave camp again as I collected rocks and twigs.

Ward work was never my forte, but I could manage a basic protection. Sympathetic magic works on the principals of desire and mimicry. Fix your objective firmly in your mind and then act it out. In the case of this ward, I placed fist-sized rocks in a circle around the camp, treating them as anchors. I filled the spaced between the rocks with broken twigs to link them together. It wasn't as simple as that though. I anchored myself, feeling my weight sink into my heels and beyond, down, down, down, into Terra's well of magic. There, restless power trembled with barely suppressed rage. The Flood Wars had ended over fifty years ago, but to the land that was barely a heartbeat. Terra remembered. She was vigilant now, and protective. And she didn't like humans disturbing her. I had to coax, to show that I was worthy of receiving her power. That meant opening myself wide. A tingle began in the soles of my feet and vibrated up my legs into my chest. I felt like I was glowing, spreading…diffusing. Terra's magic filled me. I was blessed. She deemed my request for protection an acceptable use of the magic that surrounded us.

I stretched my fingers and touched the line of sticks. Magic streamed along the boundary of sticks and rocks, making a full circle back to me, and the ward clicked into place. The magic eased from me. The ward disguised itself as the magic of the trees and rocks. I kicked leaves over the line, and in the dark, it was almost invisible.

"I'm impressed," Mason said, coming up behind me. "That kind of magic is the basis for the city wards. We just amplify it with some fancy alchemical gadgets."

"The Apex." I nodded, thinking of the gemstone that capped the tower on Perrot Island just outside of Montreal. It was the focus of the ward energy, a sort of battery and amplifier all in one. "The basics are the same. You have to ask for the right from Terra first," I said.

"You can talk to the Earth?" He cocked an eyebrow at me. "Isn't that a bit…I don't know, hippie-dippy?"

"Gods, you really aren't from this century. And that's the kind of thinking that caused the wars."

"I get that. No city takes more than the land can maintain anymore. It was a hard lesson, but we learned it."

"Did we?" Sometimes I wondered. Land management had changed in the last fifty years. Fossil fuels were a thing of the past. Cities had to be sustainable from an environmental point of view. If they weren't, magic intervened. Terra took back the land. So had we learned, or were we just captives of this new god's whims? When Terra tired of intervening in human affairs, would she roll over and go back to sleep? And would we remember the hard-won lessons?

As I lay down on my bedroll, the magic of the land supported me and fell on me like a soft blanket. It was so very…there. But I could remember a time, back before I left for Asgard, before I even knew about Valkyries or dryads, when I'd lived in a world without magic. Or at least a world where I was blind to magic.

How simple life had been then. The sheer responsibility of *knowing*, of understanding the needs of the world, could be overwhelming.

But with the stress of the day, even these thoughts couldn't keep me awake, and I soon slept under my soft cover of magic.

To be rudely woken by something hitting my face. I sat upright in a cloud of powder and sneezed. A cloth was stuffed in my mouth and a sack pulled over my head.

I fought and screamed through the muffle, but only for a few seconds before the powder knocked me out.

*Valkyriebestiary.com/chimera*

## Don't Mess with Chimeras

*(May 4, 2080 - Posted May 18, 2080)*

The fun continues. I came face-to-face with an actual chimera recently. Now before you all start sending me irate messages that the term chimera is generic and misleading, I agree with you, but bear with me.

Chimera (from the dictionary): *Any mythical animal with parts taken from various animals.*

I think we can all agree to do away with the "mythical" misnomer. (Really, it's about time someone updates the dictionary for this century!) I've caught glimpses of other chimera before, including an infestation of winged rats. I even rescued a basilisk once. (See the post on Clarence and his ongoing health battles.)

My dictionary includes another definition: *A fire-breathing female monster with a lion's head, a goat's body, and a serpent's tail.*

Apparently, these are kept as pets in the Olympus ward down south. Those crazy Greeks! But this description is more in line with the creature I encountered, though I can't guarantee it was female.

A few other details were different. It had goat legs, but a long scaled body, and horns like a gazelle. The lion's head didn't breathe fire. That came from the snake head on the end of its tail and it was more like spitting napalm than exhaling fire like dragons do.

Unfortunately, my first (and hopefully last) encounter with the chimera was not a happy one. Blood was spilled. That's all I'll say on the matter, so I don't get the trophy hunters who troll this site all excited.

I'd love to hear of your encounters with any kind of chimera. Leave your stories in the comments.

## Comments (4)

Did you at least bring back the horns? They'd look great mounted on my wall. So would you ;)

*Biggameguy21 (May 18, 2080)*

Ride safely, Valkyrie!

*DaddysGirl (May 18, 2080)*

You are doing god's work, ridding the world of such filth. Bless you!

*CampingWithJesus (May 19, 2080)*

I've come across a chimera. Not like the one you describe. It was a bunny-antelope mix, I think. Strangest looking thing I ever saw. But it made a nice stew :)

*Homesteader898 (May 20, 2020)*

# CHAPTER 23

Flowers pressed against my face. Their scent—thick and sweet like curdled perfume—made me gag. Still groggy, I pushed up on one elbow, sneezed and wiped my mouth. My hand came away covered in gold glitter.

Fairy dust. Someone had knocked me out. Had the others been hit too? I sat up completely.

The others were gone.

My mouth tasted like moldy sock and my head pounded.

Where in the hells was I? I'd fallen asleep under the stars, protected by my ward, and now I was in a…hospital? A lab? With a pile of rotting flowers as my bed?

I looked around the room. Scientific equipment neatly lined a counter along one wall. An island with a sink dominated the room, and a desk covered in notebooks and papers sat in the corner near the door. The far wall had cages stacked against it. Most were empty, but two held rats.

A fae wearing an alchemist's white coat turned at my movement and said, "Oh good, you're awake. I told those louts they used too much dust. Now you can tell me how this gods-damned sword works." He leaned over me and plucked a flower from the pile around me.

"Who are you?"

"Barton Kemp. *Doctor* Kemp, of course."

I didn't know any fae who used occupational titles like Doctor. Most didn't have the patience to complete the schooling, and they felt human designations were beneath them anyway.

But Barton—Doctor Kemp—had the stature of a goblin with a round, wrinkled face. His magic also had that odd sing-song feel to it that could only be fae.

I raised myself onto my knees, awkward because my hands were bound with rope in front of me. Standing, I got a better look at the room and marked the exits. One door, one window. Both closed.

Barton had my sword locked in a vise, blade sticking straight up from the counter. He ran the stalk of a white flower along the blade, splitting it in two.

"Don't cut yourself on that!" I lunged at him but a second fae—one I hadn't seen in my dazed state—grabbed my shoulders and hauled me backwards.

"Stay where you are or we'll bind your legs too," Barton said. The assistant was just a sprite, no taller than my elbow, but strong.

I yanked my arm away and glared. He smiled back at me with a toothless grin and fluttered his wings.

"I mean it, you draw blood on that blade and you'll regret it," I said.

"I know a soul-sucker blade when I keen it." Barton tapped the side of his nose. "I've been around the magics longer than any human lifetime. It's why the king chose me for this task. I think outside the box."

"What King? What task?"

He narrowed his eyes at me. "Wouldn't you like to know. But you can't. Not that it would do you any good. There is no way out of Underhill for you. Even if you managed to escape the castle, which you can't, you could run for days in any direction and Underhill would never let you go."

Underhill? There were no doors left to the old fae country. Queen Leighna had destroyed them all when they built Montreal Ward. It was the only way to protect the city from outside invasion.

"But time is wasting." Barton turned back to his work. He clenched his hands together like a gleeful child with an unexpected gift. "Now, tell me how to work this magnificent sword. It breaks magic doesn't it?"

Among other things, that was one of its talents. I shrugged.

"Of course it does. Extraordinary. How does it work?"

I shrugged again.

"No matter. I will discern the answer by a process of elimination—scientific methodology. It's what I do."

He clamped a second metal vise to the sword. A thin cable attached that to some kind of conductor. When he flicked a switch, magic pulsed. Another machine on the counter beeped and a needle jerked on its dial. It was a thaumagauge, an alchemist gadget that measured magic. I had never found them useful because my keening was a thousand times more sensitive.

But I understood what Barton was doing. He'd primed my sword with the conductor. Now he wanted to measure its magic in action.

Of course, that would never work. He tested another flower, slicing through the petals, then checking the thaumagauge to see if the sword reacted to severing the flower's magic. It didn't.

Barton swept the rest of the flowers off the counter in a fit of pique.

The door opened and a man stepped in.

At first, I didn't recognize him. He was a young man, unnaturally aged. His skin had dried and cracked, pulling his mouth into a permanent grimace. Blond hair stuck out in tufts from his bony scalp.

But when his blue eyes latched onto mine, I knew him.

The poacher!

His mouth tightened when he saw me. Our eyes met and I saw my loathing reflected at me. He raised one bandaged arm.

*I bet that hurts, asshole. But not as much as what you did to those dragons.*

"Joran, I have no time to look at your wound right now. The king wants this blade working yesterday."

"The king wants to see you in the hall. Her too." He grabbed my arm—I was really tired of being grabbed—and hauled me out of the lab.

Barton followed us down a long hall, muttering the entire way about joules of magic, wattages and other alchemical nonsense. Joran hurried, dragging me along. Still woozy from the fairy dust, I struggled to keep up.

The hallway was lit only by natural light coming from the far end. One side was lined with doors, presumably to other rooms like Barton's lab or bedrooms and sitting rooms. The other side was blank stone until we came to a wide doorway leading to an outer courtyard. I had only a moment to blink in the bright sunlight before Joran tugged me through another set of doors into a grand hall.

The glass domed ceiling provided an epic view of the blue sky dotted with picture-perfect clouds. Light filled the large space but it was strangely flat. And then I realized why. There was no sun in the sky. The light came from everywhere but with no visible source, like a stage lit from every angle to avoid shadows.

At first I didn't see the small cluster of people at the far end of the hall but as my eyes adjusted and Joran dragged me unrelentingly closer, I saw they were the usual assortment of fae courtiers, mostly elves, with a smattering of other class one fae.

On a low platform, one man crouched over a…pottery wheel?

From the back, he looked like a youth with ginger hair, long enough to curl over his collar. He wore traditional fae hose and deerskin boots, but no waistcoat over his white shirt. His hands were wet with clay and he shaped a curvy vase with his long fingers. A goblin pumped a pedal beside him to keep the wheel spinning.

"I brought you the girl and the sword," said a familiar voice. "And we agreed to double this price."

Joran pulled me through the audience to stand next to Simone.

Of course it was Simone. She'd been pinging my bitch radar since we met, but I gave her the benefit of the doubt because Nesi hooked us up. Oh, gods! Was Nesi part of this too? I didn't want to believe it. He'd had my back too many times. But the evidence stood twitching in front of me. In fact, Simone seemed even more twitchy and angry than usual.

"We made a deal. The fae always honor a deal." Her clenched fists pounded on the sides of her thighs as if she couldn't stand still. She'd changed out of her bloody clothes but she still looked awful. Her skin was thin and tinged green. A vein throbbed on her forehead. She stank of sweat, but her magic was worse. It reeked of desperation and fear, and it quivered like a widget screen that was slightly out of phase.

I'd seen these signs before. Simone was a junkie in serious need of a fix.

Her lip curled in a sneer when she saw me.

The oread chieftain stood beside her, still clad in his leather armor, but missing his weapons.

So that's how they got through my ward. Only someone inside it could have moved the rocks and stones to break the magic tie to the earth. Simone had been working with the oreads all along. For what purpose? To kidnap me and bring me to Underhill?

The man at the pottery wheel turned. His eyes were a shockingly bright blue.

"You will get half now and half when we get the bloodstone. That was the deal."

I blinked. That was Alvar Redrain. *Prince* Alvar. Queen Leighna's little brother. What was he doing in Underhill?

Most people had never been to another world and could not imagine that they existed alongside our own, just out of mundane reach. The godlings—those descendants of the various divine pantheons—knew of the other worlds, of course. Just as I had once found my way to Asgard, they could open doors to their pantheons. That was why the godling petition to start a new political party in Montreal was always denied. They couldn't be trusted not to create portals to Olympus, Omeyocan, or Meru. Or Asgard.

In the aftermath of the Flood Wars, Queen Leighna had saved her people the only way she knew how. She brought the fae to Montreal and sealed the door to Underhill with royal blood, so no other fae could open it. None but her little brother.

By fae laws, it was treason to set up a court without the queen's knowledge. And I was sure Queen Leighna had no idea what "King" Alvar was up to.

I looked around at the group, testing their magic. Three elves leaned against each other as if they were too bored to stand upright. A group of sprites fidgeted on the left, their wings always in motion. Two dwarves carried a fat chest, a gift for the prince (I couldn't bring myself to think of him as king). And beside them…my keening recoiled at the taste of magic coming off her.

An opji. Unlike the others, she stood tall and straight as if endlessly waiting on the prince was no hardship. Her white hair hung in a perfect silky curtain, halfway to her waist. She dressed all in black—hose, tunic and boots, so that the bit of deep red blouse peeking out of her collar was almost shocking. She was watching me as I watched her. Her black lips creased, exposing fangs in the vamp version of a smile.

What was Alvar doing with a vampire in his court?

"I brought you what you wanted!" Simone said. "I demand my payment!"

Alvar smiled, showing teeth that were too sharp to be mistaken for human.

"The deal was for the sword, the bloodstone and the gargoyles," he said.

"You failed. Consider yourself lucky that I am paying you at all."

"That wasn't my fault!" Her fists continued the relentless pounding on her thighs. "Those damned oreads wouldn't touch the gargoyles. Do you expect me to carry two tons of stone?"

"Enough!" Alvar stood up. His wet vase spun out of control and clay flew in all directions, splattering the goblin's face. "Clean that up!" snapped the prince. Overhead, the sky turned black as storm clouds rolled in.

"I expect you to do the job you signed up for. The gargoyles aren't here. So your payment reflects that failure."

Alvar snapped his fingers. "Pay her." Another goblin stepped forward and tossed a small pouch at Simone. She caught it and held it to her nose, inhaling with satisfaction. Her magic calmed and her fists relaxed.

"Half," Alvar said. "Now go before I take the other half from your flesh."

Simone turned, then remembered herself and bowed quickly to the prince, before limping away. The uneven clack of her boot heels was the only sound as she made her long exit across the marble tiles of the hall.

At least Mason and Angus were safe, or as safe as they could be in the Inbetween. Alvar probably didn't know that the gargoyles were aware of their surroundings when they were stone. Hopefully, they recognized the oreads and were already on the way back to Annequin Lodge for backup.

Was Herne a true descendant of the Wild Hunt? If so, he might be able to open a door to Underhill, but would they even know where the oreads had taken me? No. I couldn't rely on outside help.

The oread chieftain stepped forward, knelt and bowed his head. Alvar gazed at him, considering. Finally, he said, "Rise and speak." The oread unfolded his long twiggy limbs and stood.

"I am Esot, chief of the Oakfury. We bring you a great prize in humble supplication." He swept his arm back and pointed at me. "We bring you the daughter of your enemy, Timberfoot Greenleaf, he who allied with your sister in the great wars. Take her as your queen. With her at your side, all fae will bow down to the new king." Esot paused to look at me. His smile was just a quiver. "Or kill her. Her death would bring you great magic."

The crowd had gone silent. All eyes turned to me. Suddenly, Alvar no longer looked like a surly adolescent. He stood taller and his striking eyes commanded attention.

"Timberfoot Greenleaf was a great man," he said slowly. "A closer cousin to the fae than you are." He nodded at the oread. "An ally in a time when few could be trusted. Do you know how he died?"

Esot stood frozen under Alvar's gaze.

"Answer me!" The prince's voice was razor sharp.

"No, my lord!" snapped Esot.

"He was quite literally the cornerstone of the ward that my sister built." Alvar's eyes found mine. "I saw him die, you know. I was just a child, but I remember it. I saw it in his eyes. He knew death was coming for him. He knew it, and he embraced it so we—you, me, the blasted alchemists and the filthy humans—could all have a safe haven."

My legs felt weak, as if I'd run a four-minute mile. All my life, I'd heard rumors of my father's demise. My grandmother wouldn't speak of it, but a legend had grown up around him. The fae in Montreal were particularly superstitious about Timberfoot Greenleaf and their reactions to his name produced everything from rage to awe. It was the reason I changed my name to Greene.

"Timberfoot may have been my sister's ally," Alvar said, "but that doesn't make him my enemy. Still, I thank you for the gift." He nodded at Esot. "You may leave us now. Your generosity will not be forgotten."

Esot bowed again, then the band of oreads left the court.

Alvar beckoned for Barton Kemp.

The alchemist stepped forward. "My lord, we were right. The sword is a soul-sucker."

"Excellent!" Alvar said. "That is the last piece of our plan. Kill the prisoner and make ready to return to Montreal."

# CHAPTER 24

A guard standing next to the dais gripped my shoulder and pulled me away.

"My lord!" Barton said. "I mean no disrespect, but perhaps we should keep the Valkyrie alive. For a while at least."

Alvar pursed his lips and once again, he looked like a spoiled child.

"It is possible...I mean, I have to do more tests, but it's conceivable—"

"Spit it out already!" Alvar snapped.

"I think a Valkyrie sword's magic can only be tapped by an Aesir," Barton said, smiling like a sycophant. "And no one has seen another Aesir for years. I may need her once we find the stone. The sword will break it, I'm certain, but possibly by her hand only."

Alvar considered me. Then he turned to the alchemist and wiped the wet clay from his fingers on Barton's lab coat. Barton stiffened but his fake smile didn't waver.

"Very well. But figure it out quickly or I will have to kill you. I am tired of this place and wish to return home." Alvar smoothed down the dirty lapel of Barton's jacket and turned to leave, taking his bored entourage with him. The opji woman smiled at me and flicked her tongue like a snake before following the crowd.

Barton looked shaken as he led me back outside. Clouds boiled in black fury overhead, along with persistent, grumbling thunder.

Instead of taking the long interior hall back to the lab, Barton led me along a portico that ran the length of the castle's courtyard. A few people worked around the yard, mucking out stalls in a barn, pulling water up from a well, or sweeping the pristine cobblestones.

I heard a chirping cry, barely audible above the storm.

I knew that chirp.

Yanking my arm from Barton's grasp, I ran across the yard, to stop in front of a large fenced-in pen.

At the back of the pen, a run-in shed provided shelter from sun and rain. Something moved inside. I leaned against the fence and peered into the shadows.

"Ollie?" At the sound of my voice, the dragon sprinted forward, skidded at the fence and head butted my chin.

They'd taken Ollie too! Alvar wanted the bloodstone. That had always been his plan—the reason he sent Joran to dig up the graves behind Mason's home. He'd known the bloodstone was there. And now Simone had told him that Ollie ate the stone. Alvar wouldn't wait for the dragon to pass it. He'd gut Ollie for his treasure. And soon.

Ollie shook rain from his feathered crown. Behind him, another enormous beast crept into the light. Ruby, the red queen from the cemetery. She was too thin. Her wings hung limply at her sides, but her eyes were fierce.

*Fly!* A voice sung in my head. *Fly! Fly!* Ruby's voice. A clear image of dragons soaring in the clouds flit through my thoughts. She wanted me to free her.

And then I saw the dull metal collars around their necks. They were trapped here, same as me. I'd hoped Ollie was safe with Mason and Angus, but Simone had recognized his worth. And Ruby? The beautiful red queen had not evaded Joran's poaching friends for long. It made my heart hurt.

Ollie bounced and chirped, his useless wings stretched wide.

"I need my sword," I said, trying to conjure the image of my blade slicing off their collars, projecting the thought and hoping they understood. "Do you remember?"

Ruby cocked her head.

"I'll win back my sword and come for you. I promise."

Barton caught up to me, wheezing from the short run.

"Do that again and I'll have you shackled," he said.

"Where are the others?"

He looked back blankly.

"The dragons." He flinched when I seized his once-white coat. "Tell me what you did with the other dragons."

But he didn't have to say it. I could see it in the shift of his eyes. They'd slaughtered them all looking for the damn stone.

"If you were any kind of real alchemist, you would have known those dragons didn't have the stone."

"Yes, well." He licked his lips. "The tests were inconclusive. We had to be sure."

I slammed him up against the railing of the pen. Ollie jumped and hovered, squeaking in agitation. No one else in the yard came to help Barton. Good to know. He didn't have many friends here.

"You're hurting me." Barton choked as I pressed my fist into his chest.

"If you harm another dragon, I'll do more than hurt you."

His eyes watered. "It's the king! The king wishes it! I can only do…" He ran out of breath, mostly because I was squeezing it from his lungs. I let go and pushed him aside to pet Ollie.

"It's okay, buddy. I'm going to get you out of here. I promise." He settled down and I scratched his brow ridge. Behind him, Ruby stared at me with intelligent eyes.

Joran had caught up to us. Despite his cadaver-like appearance, he was still stronger than the alchemist. He grabbed me by the ropes binding my hands and hauled me to a door at the far end of the courtyard. Ollie's cries chased after me. Leaving him was one of the hardest things I've ever done.

Joran unlocked the door with a key from the ring at his belt, shoved me inside and slammed it, leaving me in total darkness.

From outside, Ollie's cry echoed my own thoughts.

# CHAPTER 25

My eyes slowly adjusted, though my temper didn't settle. They'd taken Ollie. They were going to kill Ollie. I couldn't let that happen.

My prison wasn't completely dark. Light leaked through heavy curtains covering one small window. The room was set up like a clerk's office, though it hadn't been used in a long time, probably not since before the Flood Wars—before the fae escaped this world to resettle on Terra. A small desk and chair took up most of the space. The only other furniture was an empty bookcase along one wall. I searched the desk, looking for anything to use as a weapon. I even pulled the bookcase away from the wall, hoping that something might have fallen behind it and been forgotten. Nothing.

The door to my prison opened and a small round woman entered, balancing a platter of food and a pitcher in one hand. Her magic tasted like dwarf. She dumped the food on the desk and left without a word.

My stomach ached for food, but the thirst was worse—an effect of the fairy dust. Awkwardly, because my hands were still tied, I picked up the pitcher and sniffed it. Water. I couldn't keen any spells on it. I took a small sip. There were many poisons that would be tasteless, but I was more worried about the stories of humans eating food in Underhill and never leaving. If I'd had a choice, I would have forgone the food, but I needed energy if I was going to escape. I drank carefully, not so much that my empty stomach would recoil, and ate a handful of nuts and some dried figs.

Then I waited. And I planned. Barton would get nowhere with my sword. I felt the blade's anxiety. It was a low level hum in the background of all my senses. It didn't like to be away from me and it didn't like Barton Kemp's experiments. But, with Alvar pushing him, he wouldn't give up. I had to find a way out.

I gazed around the dim room again. There had to be something I could use as a weapon. Then I noticed that the thinner wood backing of the bookcase was cracked. With a little effort, I pulled the wood apart and was working on splitting off a shim when a being manifested right in front of me.

I fell back on my butt before I realized who it was.

"Jacoby!" The little dervish flung himself at me and hugged my knees.

"I follows Kyra-lady when ugly tree-beasts takes you."

"You did well," I said. "Now help me get these ropes off."

The ropes were thick and well tied. As Jacoby tugged, the knots burned my chaffed wrists. He set his teeth to one rope and tried to chew it off.

"That's not going to work," I said. "You'll just break your teeth." I sat back in the chair and considered. The food and drink had restored me, and a small reserve of magic hummed through me. But my magic was limited. I could manifest a decent glamor when I needed to, and I had a touch of dryad magic, but none of that would help get the ropes off.

"Can you carry objects with you when you port?" I asked. Jacoby nodded. "Go find a knife and bring it back. But be careful no one sees you."

He smiled, his wizened expression turning sly. "I moves like wraith."

"Good, now go!" I shoved him just as the lock rattled. Jacoby disappeared. The door to my cell opened and I faced Joran. He shuffled in like a zombie and shut the door.

We stared at each other.

"You're the poacher," I said.

His mouth pulled a half grin. "My name is Joran Shulist. You should know the name of the man you killed."

"And the dragon?" I asked. "The one you and your friend slaughtered? What was her name?"

He shrugged. "It was a beast. It had no name."

I wanted to hate him for that callousness, but he started to cough and couldn't stop. He leaned on the desk, and flecks of blood spattered its surface. He pressed one shaking hand to his chest. When he finally got control of himself, he raised red-rimmed eyes to me in a silent plea.

"I'm sorry," I said when the silence became unbearable. "I didn't mean to cut you." Despite his actions, the dragon killings, his affiliation with Alvar and Barton, despite all of that, I was sorry. No one deserved to die this way.

His eyes narrowed, hatred plain in that gaze and, for a moment, I thought he'd attack me. Maybe that had been his plan. Maybe that's why he shut himself in my cell, alone. But he had no fight left. His hands trembled, and when he spoke, his voice rasped as if his vocal chords had atrophied.

"Come," he said. "He wants you."

"Who?" I asked, but Joran just turned for the door. I glanced at the bookcase with the half broken shim, but I wouldn't have time to break it off before Joran stopped me. So, I followed the dying poacher into the yard.

I had enough strength in me for one really good glamor, but I had to use it wisely.

Joran led me through the outer courtyard, under a sky that churned with black clouds. Lightning spiked in jagged streaks. We ducked under the covered walkway as rain pelted the copper roof. The sound was so loud, no one heard Joran scream.

He turned to make sure I followed and saw a bear coming at him and one massive paw raised to slash his face. His moment of shock was all I needed to barrel him into the wall. His head hit stone and he crumpled like a puppet with cut strings.

I let the glamor drop and sagged against the wall. That was big magic and I had few reserves. After my moment of dizziness passed, I searched Joran's belt until I found a small utility knife. Cutting the ropes around my wrists was awkward. The knife slipped and I sliced into the side of my thumb. Blood made the grip slick.

*Come on, come on.*

I sawed with deliberate care, even as my heart pounded. The storm had cleared the yard, but someone could come down this walkway at any time.

The ropes fell away. I dragged Joran into a room off the courtyard and tossed in my bloody bindings. Too bad the fall hadn't killed him. I had no time for that kindness. I turned away, cursing a prayer to the One-eyed Father, that he take Joran's spirit soon.

My left hand bled freely, and I squeezed it under my other arm, trying to staunch the flow as I ran back into the courtyard.

I couldn't leave without my sword—literally. Its separation anxiety buzzed like a fog of gnats around my thoughts. If I tried to flee Underhill without it…just the thought shot pain and nausea through my stomach.

"I'm coming," I muttered. Luckily, the sword's possessiveness meant that I could find it too. Just follow the flow of anxious magic.

I dashed along the portico, slipping inside at the first doorway, then along the hallway that led—I hoped—in the general direction of the grand hall. Barton's lab was behind one of the dozens of doors along that corridor.

The hallways dipped and turned, more like organic cave tunnels than a well-planned castle. Or perhaps they were designed to confuse intruders. If it weren't for the constant keening of my sword, I would have been lost. I ducked my head and tried to look like I belonged there when a servant hurried by lugging two buckets of water. But he was more concerned with not spilling and ignored me.

I headed down a staircase then back up another. The sword's keening pulled me onward, until I stood before a door like any of the others. I flung it open, and ran inside, hoping for the element of surprise. Barton's assistant hit my elbow with a broom handle, freezing the nerve on that arm, and I dropped the small knife, my only weapon.

"Nice of you to join us," Barton said from across the room. My sword was still locked in a vise, suspended above a counter in front of him. A pile of cut flowers lay nearby.

Before I could speak, two strong hands grasped my wrists. I turned to see the sprite snarling up at me. Barton's assistant wore a white coat with frilled lapels and holes cut for wings—a fae's idea of a lab coat. I tried to twist away, but couldn't. The little Igor was unnaturally strong.

"Bring her here," Barton said. The sprite shoved me forward until my knees slammed against the counter.

"Tell me why it doesn't work." Barton hadn't changed out of his clay-smeared coat. His eyes were a little manic as if he hadn't slept in days. Maybe he hadn't.

He held a flower to my sword. The blade easily cut through it, and pink petals fell to the counter. We were back to this game again.

Barton pointed to the thaumagauge attached to the sword.

"Nothing." He slammed the flower stem on the counter. "No matter what

I try, this damned sword remains inactive. No magic in it whatsoever." Clearly my keening was more sensitive than his tech because the sword screamed with elation now that I'd arrived.

Barton's assistant let go of my wrists, but he frisked me, looking for more weapons. He took his sweet time about it too, fondling all the right places. Then he picked up Joran's bloody knife, and grinning, he stood by the door to guard against my escape.

I turned my back on him to show that he didn't scare me.

"What were you expecting?" I asked Barton.

A sneer spread across his face. "I know all about you, Valkyrie. Your friend Joran gave you away. Did you see what your little sword did to him?"

I nodded.

"It's quite extraordinary. Like his soul is leaking right out of his wounds. Someone should really put that boy out of his misery. It's a terrible way to die."

"I'll get right on that," I said. Barton was examining the sword again.

"You see, his wound made me suspect your sword was more than an ugly hunk of metal."

In my blade's defense, I was insulted, but I let him rant on.

"We had the bloodstone, or at least we knew where to find it. But the last piece of the puzzle was a way to break it. And I'm certain your soul-sucking blade is the key."

He dropped into silence as he flipped through a notebook. I wanted to keep him talking, hoping he'd shed some light on Alvar's end game.

"You're a science mage." I inched toward the desk.

"I am." He flared his nostrils and stood straighter. "Do you have a problem with that?"He was touchy about being mocked for his pseudo-science. I could work with that.

"Only that it's a ridiculous idea." I was goading him now. "Science and magic don't mix. You can cherry pick aspects of each and deceive yourself into believing they are compatible. But in the end, they are two fundamentally different powers."

As I spoke, I scanned the schematics laid out on the desk. One image looked like a battery of some kind, but on a massive scale.

"You're bleeding." He pointed to my hand. Blood streaked down my pant leg from my thumb. I had forgotten all about the wound.

"Maybe it's not the sword," he mumbled, distracted by his own thoughts. "Yes, yes. It's the blood." He picked up one of the discarded flowers and grabbed my hand to smear my blood over the petals. "Valkyrie blood. Yes, yes." But the petals fell apart like the others and my pesky sword continued to fool the thaumagauge.

His eyes blazed with fury. I shrugged.

"It *is* about the blood. You're holding back." He turned to one of the cages that lined the wall and came back with a white rat.

"Hold her," he commanded, and the sprite clamped my bloody hand on the grip of my sword.

"There are no rats in Underhill. I had to import these all the way from Montreal." Barton held the squirming creature over the blade. "So, I'd appreciate it if you don't waste one. Use your mojo or whatever and let me see the sword's magic take a life."

He pressed the rat's neck against the blade. It squealed and I swallowed the bile that rose in my throat. Memories of Aaric forcing me into this same dilemma nearly choked me. Then, I'd used my magic to give Aaric what he wanted. I'd ushered his soul to Valhalla. I could do nothing else. But here, if I connected with my sword, Barton would understand my magic and he'd use it against me for a far greater evil. He'd force me to kill Ollie. And what would that do to the bloodstone in his gut?

I wouldn't do it.

The little rodent squirmed and I closed my eyes. It would be so easy to push my magic into the blade, to take the tiny soul and usher it onto rat heaven. But I couldn't.

I wouldn't let this monster understand how Valkyrie magic worked. I had no idea what he was planning with the bloodstone, but my sword and I would not be part of it.

The rat would have to find its own way to the afterlife. I consoled myself that animals were pretty good at that.

Barton was studying the thaumagauge with a frown.

The rat squealed and died as Barton thrust my sword into its heart. I held my magic tight inside of me.

Barton swore and shoved his face right into mine.

"I have more rats. I can do this all night." He stood back and a sly grin replaced his snarl. "But maybe I can find something bigger to kill. Something like a dragon. Yes, I see that hits home, doesn't it. I'll start with the small one. I was going to gut him anyway to get that pesky stone."

I wanted to punch him in the face. Only the fae assistant's grip on my wrist held me back.

"You don't like that idea?" Barton took another rat from the cage. "Good. Let's try this again then."

No. I wouldn't be the impetus for this man's madness.

The rat wriggled in his grip.

The fae held me immobile, but suddenly I welcomed the connection to my sword. Magic pulsed through us, but not from me to the sword.

The blade fed me.

Strength rushed into my arm, and I jerked free of Barton and his nasty little sprite. I wrenched the sword from the vise. The blade sang as I drove it into Barton's stomach.

"This is how Valkyrie magic works, asshole." I jerked the blade upward until I hit bone. Barton gasped, then sagged against the counter and my sword slid free. The rat fell from his grip and scurried away.

I turned to the fae guard. His eyes goggled and he ran. Jacoby stood in the doorway.

"Stop him!"

But the fae hurdled over the startled dervish and disappeared down the hall. I was out of time, but before I left, I opened all the cages. It was time Underhill had some rats.

# CHAPTER 26

"Do you know how to get out of Underhill?" I asked.

Jacoby nodded.

"Can you port out of here with me?"

He stuck a long finger in his ear and considered.

"No. Too far."

I knew his teleportation magic had limits, but I didn't know his range.

"Fine. We'll walk out." If Alvar and Joran could come and go, there had to be a portal to Montreal somewhere nearby.

I grabbed a pile of papers from the desk, folded them into a notebook, and shoved it at Jacoby.

"Whatever happens to me, get this to Mason. Understand?"

Jacoby's face was all eyes, but he nodded.

"Good. Let's go."

We ran down the twisting corridors. In this part of the castle, there was no natural light. The hallways were lit by gleams that illuminated only as we passed, so we were always running toward darkness.

We turned yet another corner that looked like all the others, and an alarm rang. Not an audio siren, a magic one. The entire fae court would keen it.

"Stop!" I bent over, pushing a thumb into the stitch in my side. I was running on empty, and we were lost.

"Have you seen the dragons?"

Jacoby nodded.

"Can you get back to them?"

His face lit up, and he stepped back, ready to port away.

"Wait!" My words competed with my need to draw breath. "You have to take me. Don't port!"

Jacoby looked uncertain, but he took my hand and pulled me toward a closed door.

"In there? Why?" I looked down the hall. We were alone for a moment, but voices echoed from somewhere ahead. Jacoby was already slipping into the room and I followed him, closing the door softly behind me and locking it.

We stood in a parlor. A card table with green felt dominated the room. A puzzle was laid out on it, partially finished, and the rest of the pieces sorted by color. Dust covered it all.

Voices rose from the hall. I grabbed Jacoby and ducked behind a couch. Footsteps thundered by, but no one stopped to look in our room.

"Do you have glamor?" I asked. Jacoby shook his head. Damn the gods. I didn't have the energy to cloak us both in a disguise, but we couldn't go back in the hallway without one.

"Kyra-lady, looks!" Jacoby climbed onto the back of the couch to push aside curtains. A window placed high on the wall filled the gloom with Underhill's strange flat light. I boosted Jacoby onto the window ledge and we both looked out at the courtyard. We were in a basement room, about two-thirds of it below ground. The rain had stopped, but fog had rolled in. It moved like smoke, hiding and revealing a red door across the yard.

I knew that door. It was the barn right next to the dragons' pen.

"Quick! Before the fog disappears." I cranked open the window, hoping against all hope that no one was watching. Jacoby easily slipped out the window that opened only a foot. I struggled to get up on the ledge, then squeezed my head and shoulders through the gap.

"Hurries! Hurries!" Jacoby tugged on my sleeve.

"That's not helping!" I hissed. It was no use. I was stuck. I backed up to stand on the edge of the couch again. "Go tell Ollie I'm coming. I'll find another way out."

The dervish, still clutching his treasure of papers, disappeared. I jumped down and listened at the door. More voices in the hall. This time they stopped outside and tried the doorknob.

I was out of time. I dashed back to the window and smashed through glass and frame with my sword, not caring about the noise. Shouts came from behind me as the fae guards broke the lock. I hauled myself through the broken window. My pants tore on ragged glass and a sharp pain told me I'd cut more than fabric.

Someone grabbed my foot and I kicked out. My fingers scrabbled on the slick cobblestones. But I was free.

I slashed at the hands reaching for me, too flustered for any other defense.

Then I ran.

*Fly! Fly!* Ruby's urgent request filled my head. I skidded into her pen and scrambled over the fence, falling in a graceless lump on the other side.

*Fly! Fly!*

"I'm here!" I gasped for breath. Ollie bounced beside me and Jacoby looked scared enough to implode. "Settle!" I clamped a shaking hand on Ollie's shoulder and slipped the tip of my blade under his collar. It fell away.

Ruby bowed her head and I freed her too.

"Go!" I urged, but she didn't fly. She bowed to me. Her wings spread, and her shoulders nearly touched the ground.

It was an invitation.

Fae were bursting out of the keep, pointing at us and shouting. I jumped on Ruby's back and pulled Jacoby up in front of me. He still held onto Barton's papers, so I clamped one hand around him and the other grasped the bony ridge on Ruby's neck as she lurched upward.

My stomach fell into my feet. Ruby pumped her wings, struggling to get airborne. An arrow hit the tough scales by my knee and bounced away. More arrows whizzed past us.

Ruby ignored them and climbed.

Ollie screamed.

*Oh, my gods!* I looked back and the little dragon hopped in the pen.

Angus had never managed to teach him to fly. And now it was too late.

Ruby circled back and called to him. Ollie jumped and floated for a second before crashing down.

A fae guard hurdled the fence and dove for the dragon. Ollie squealed and jerked away, his wings pumping. He rose a few feet.

*Come on, Ollie. Come on!*

Ruby let out a primitive roar and spat fire. The fae scattered. Ollie rose another few feet, too high now for the hands reaching to pull him down. He caught the wind, and he was suddenly flying.

Ruby cawed like a giant hawk, and Ollie chirped back as he zipped past us. We headed into a sky filled with storm clouds, but at least we were leaving the usurper king and his murderous court.

# CHAPTER 27

The clouds grumbled and we flew high enough that moisture seeped into my clothes. Below us, Underhill sped by, an unending landscape of hills, copses and winding creeks. Vast tracts of land were scarred by burns. The bombs that had decimated my world during the Flood Wars had damaged Underhill too. We flew past these monuments to the folly of both races in silence.

Lightning flashed in sheets, but Ruby seemed unconcerned. She flew steadily as if she had a destination in mind.

*Where are we going?* I tried to project the question from my mind to hers, the way she had intruded on my thoughts with her need to fly. But either I failed at mind-speak or she ignored me.

I hunched in the crook of her shoulders and waited out the ride. Jacoby shivered in front of me. His grizzled fur drooped with dampness. I tucked the notebook under my shirt to keep both our hands free. Ollie had spent the first part of the flight zipping back and forth, enthralled with his newfound talent. But as the minutes dragged into hours, his wings drooped a little more with each flap. Ruby snarled at him in a dragon scold, and he dropped back to fly off her tail where the wind resistance was broken by her flight.

Below, the land seemed to crawl with shadows. I squinted into the distance. One entire hillside teemed with dark bodies. As we flew overhead, I could make out upturned faces and hands pointing our way. A few of the figures rode horses, herding the others like cattle. I recognized one of those on horseback. The opji from Alvar's court rode in the lead, her long ash-blond hair streaming behind her.

The opji were marching their wojak army across Underhill.

I clamped my knees on Ruby's sides, urging her to fly faster. Did she understand the meaning of that horde? I needed to get home and tell the queen before the opji reached the door between our worlds.

We flew on, leaving the army behind.

The cold became a real problem. My stiff fingers could barely hang onto Ruby's slick scales. I hunkered down and prayed to the One-eyed Father.

I must have dozed and jerked awake when Jacoby squawked. I'd almost fallen from Ruby's back. My fingers gripping the bony ridge below her neck were blue with cold. I couldn't go on like this much longer. And just when I thought I would topple like a block of ice and shatter on the ground below, Ruby banked and began her descent in a slow spiral.

Ahead, a waterfall covered a wide cliff face, falling into a pool and filling the air with more mist. Ruby circled until we descended below the mountain's crest. I thought she would land on the bank, but she made one more turn and headed straight at the mountain.

"Whoa!" I yelled, but she dove through the waterfall. The cascade of water hit us like a torrent. I lost my grip on Jacoby and he slipped off. I screamed, sucked in water and choked, too scared of drowning to worry about the mountain we were about to hit. The blast of water knocked me backward. I fell.

And landed, choking and gasping on hard stone. Getting to my knees, I retched and shook water from my eyes and nose.

The stones beneath my hands and knees weren't the uneven ground of a cave. They were smooth and cut in uniform squares. Tiles.

I crouched on a marble floor.

Daylight and a cool wind blew in from one open wall…of what? I looked around, shivering. Polished glass, a wall of brass mailboxes, an old-school elevator, its door cracked open to show the blackness of the shaft beyond.

I was in the lobby of an office or apartment building. One entire corner of the building was missing, but the rest seemed intact and barely mistreated by the elements. That could only mean we were inside the ward, where the weather was carefully managed. I looked back at the wall of marble tile we had come through. If I reached out with my keening, I could faintly hear the rush of the waterfall it masked.

It wasn't really a wall. It was a door to Underhill, hidden in the ruins of an old building. Who else knew this door existed? Certainly not Queen Leighna or any of the other ministers. They would have destroyed it.

But Alvar probably knew of it. He most likely opened it.

I shivered just thinking about the possibilities. What good was a magic wall around the entire city if it was porous? What would happen if the city's enemies found this door?

And then my dulled mind remembered the army of wojaks marching this way.

I had to warn someone…everyone.

Ollie lay in a deflated lump on the tiles. Ruby rested beside him. She watched me with half-hooded eyes.

"Thank you for bringing me home." I bowed in a universal sign of respect.

Ruby slow-blinked and heaved a big sigh.

I stepped over broken glass toward the front entrance that was open to the street. Except there was no street, just a wreck of old concrete, buckled and broken from a long-ago quake. I peered left and right along the old road, trying to get my bearings. More rundown and vacant condominiums rose from the ruins. Something crawled among the tumbled stones. I froze. But it was just a lone goblin scrounging for bugs to eat. He startled at the sight of us and ducked into a hole in the ruins.

Across the broken street, the land fell away into Lake St. Louis, which was cold, gray and choppy in the morning sun.

Power shivered up my spine uncomfortably, and I gazed at its source.

The ward.

Straight ahead, about a kilometer out, the city's ward was anchored deep into the bottom of the lake. It might have been invisible, but it set my teeth on edge, like standing too close to those giant power-grid pylons when I was a kid. My teeth hummed with the magic. Even a mundane, blind and deaf to magic in the everyday world, would feel creeped out so near the tingling energy of the ward. That's why these edge neighborhoods were all vacant. After the war, when the water receded to reveal these crumbling neighborhoods, nobody bothered to rebuild them.

"Kyra-lady goes home?" Jacoby bounced over the cracked cement as I gingerly made my way toward the lake.

"Soon." I just had to figure out exactly how far away home was.

Despite my humming teeth, I pushed closer to the edge of the water, stepping over the old condo's broken sign—a slab of cement with *Aristo* cut into it like a tombstone. I stood at the edge of the land and shielded my eyes against the morning sun. Was that an island? Yes. Now I could orient myself. Dorval Island had once been home to a handful of hearty souls. The Flood Wars had decimated it, but the island emerged again. It was too close to the ward for inhabitants, but the alchemists had stationed a tower on it to sync with the Apex on Perrot Island.

With Dorval Island at my left, home lay to the right, about twenty minutes by car. Of course, I didn't have a car. I didn't even have my widget to call for a car.

I turned at the sound of breaking glass. Ruby pushed out of the condo's entry, demolishing whatever was left of the front door. Ollie followed, never too far from her side. He saw me and chirped.

I climbed back over the treacherous ground and crouched by his side to give him a hug. He leaned his chin over my shoulder and melted into me.

This was goodbye. My brain knew it was for the best, but my heart ached.

I straightened up and found Ruby watching me intently, trying to convey some message I was too tired to parse. Either she was warning me away from her baby or thanking me for freeing them.

"Take good care of him."

The red dragon flexed her wings and launched into the sky. An image of a thunder of dragons flying over a sunlit valley tucked between mountains flashed through my mind. Ruby was heading home too. I didn't know how she'd get through the ward, but I figured if she could find a way out of Underhill, she'd make it.

Ollie head-butted me one last time, then followed his red queen. Mason would be furious that his precious bloodstone was out of reach and I didn't care. From what I'd seen in Barton's notebooks, Mason had some explaining to do.

I watched the dragons until they disappeared into the sky. A bony hand slipped into mine. Jacoby watched me with big gray eyes lost in bedraggled fuzz.

Right about then, he was thinking that I would send him away too. I knelt in the rubble to look him in the eye.

"You were really brave when we faced those oreads. And again when you found me in Underhill."

He looked down. "I was scared. Not brave."

"I was scared too. That's what bravery is—being scared but doing the right thing anyway. You were brave." I poked him in the chest.

He was cute in an odd way, like a furry apple doll. I wanted to pet him, but I thought that might be offensive.

"Gita's probably worried sick about me. Think you could port home and tell her I'll be there soon?"

"Home?"

The look of pure hope in his eyes undid me.

"Yes. My home. Your home too."

Jacoby was family now. I had to stop fighting that idea. His fuzzy face split into a grin.

"I tells the banshee, Kyra-lady is safe." He disappeared with a keening pop.

I sighed. It would be a long walk home.

# CHAPTER 28

Three hours later, I limped into the parking lot of Valkyrie Pest Control, happy to see the building still standing. Gita met me at the door.

"You're home." She sniffed as if it was no matter to her.

"I lost my widget," I said. "I couldn't return your messages."

"So the dervish told me." She turned back for the kitchen. Gita might seem as cold as the briny ocean, but she showed her love in other ways. A stack of pancakes and a pile of bacon waited for me in the kitchen. And coffee. Gods, how I had missed coffee.

When my belly was uncomfortably full of carbs and syrup, I did a quick walk-through to say hello to my critters.

I needed to get in to see Leighna, but one didn't simply call up one of the three prime ministers of Montreal Ward and ask for an audience. There were protocols and I didn't have time to follow them.

But I knew someone who could get a message to Leighna. Unfortunately, for the next six hours he would be stone.

I asked Gita to wake me at seven p.m., then dropped into bed and slept.

I WOKE TO Gita shaking me with one hand while she wiped her drippy eyes with another.

"You should sleep some more, but no doubt the world needs saving."

It really did.

"Thanks." I sat up to peer out my window. The light was fading. I stepped over Jacoby, who—wiped out from excessive bravery—slept on the rug beside my bed and headed for the bathroom.

The face in the mirror was a stranger. At least I could stop feeling guilty about the pancake overindulgence. I'd lost weight—too much weight—and my eyes seemed exaggerated in my gaunt face. Even my hair looked tired. It hung limply, lacking any curl or the sheen that brought out my red highlights.

I had few indulgences because I spent most of my money on food and medicine for my critters, but the one thing I'd splurged on was a fancy massage shower head. After scrubbing the dirt out of every pore, I leaned on the tile and let the water beat down on my back until the hot water tank ran cold.

Then I inventoried my wounds: a cut on my thumb, another on my thigh, a bruised cheek where the oread had hit me, a twinging knee, and one nasty blister on my little toe from the walk home in wet boots. I put a bandage on that last one.

After grabbing a sandwich, I surprised Gita by giving her a quick kiss on the cheek.

"Thanks for taking care of everyone."

She nodded and shooed me out the door.

"Go, go! Get your business done so you can get home for a decent night's sleep."

"Yes, Mom."

I met Mason on the gravel driveway outside his manor house as I parked my truck.

"I was just coming to see you. I tried calling, then realized I have your widget." He held out my pack.

"Thanks." I reached for the bag, but he pulled me in closer. I fit perfectly into the crook between his chin and shoulder as if he was a puzzle and I the missing piece. His arms wrapped around me, and he laid his cheek against my hair.

"I was so worried. Woke up with a damn fairy hangover and you were gone. Ollie and Simone too. We tracked you through the forest for about a while, then the tracks just disappeared."

"It was Simone." I pulled back to see his face. "She betrayed us to the oreads. She must have opened the ward for them. They hit me with fairy dust too. I woke up in Underhill."

Mason nodded. "As soon as we realized you were gone, Angus and I came home. Do you think Simone planned this all along?"

"Feels like it. She's more unstable than we suspected. I think she's an addict. But Nesi…" Nesi had set up the whole thing. "I need to talk to him to be sure. And I want to petition Queen Leighna for an audience."

"With the fairy dust and the oreads, I already suspected fae involvement. I pulled some strings to meet with her. I'm waiting to hear back."

He looked me up and down, his eyes resting for a moment on the bruise that was purpling my cheek.

"I'm just glad you're safe."

I wanted to give in to the pressure of his hands on my arms, to the look of want in his eyes, but we had serious things to discuss first.

"Ollie's gone. I found one of his thunder. The others are probably dead, but I let them go free."

I waited for the backlash of anger when he realized his bloodstone was out of reach, ready to strike back with my own recriminations about how much he'd been hiding from me, but he only rubbed a hand across the back of his neck, and I realized how tired he looked.

"There's more." I held up Barton's notebook. "We've got a serious problem."

Mason's house wasn't what I expected. There were no Gothic fireplaces, intricately carved staircases or baroque settees. I don't know why I'd pictured him living like an eighteenth century Marquis. In reality, his tastes were modern and simple.

The front foyer opened to a large living space with one entire wall made of glass that looked out at a tidy garden. A fieldstone fireplace dominated the middle of the room, with a huge copper chimney rising above it. Couches, chairs and tables were set up in individual seating areas, all done in a palette of cool whites, brushed silver and pine, making the room seem much bigger. It was the decor of a man who lived in the dark but longed for the light.

"Drink?" Mason headed straight for a bar in one corner.

"Wine, if you have."

"White or red?"

"Surprise me."

He came back with a glass of deep burgundy. I took a sip and realized how long we'd been roughing it. Mason pointed to a couch by the fire, but I shook my head and moved to a card table set up with chairs. I opened the notebook and spread the blueprints.

"Where's Angus? He'll want to see this too."

"He's gone with Dutch to Marcella's to get my car." Mason picked up a page and frowned. "What is this?"

"This is civil war." I didn't mean to sound all doom-and-gloom dramatic, but I couldn't think of any other reason Prince Alvar would build a bomb.

I told Mason about waking up in his sham court and Barton's experiments with my sword.

"Not many people realize that my sword can cut through anything. Barton did his homework. And he seemed pretty excited to get his hands on a soul-sucker."

"I still don't understand this." He leaned both hands on the table and studied the blueprints. They showed a device like a giant tube with a dense core.

"Originally, they weren't after me or Ollie," I said. "They were after the bloodstone. We just got in the way. But after I cut that Joran character, Barton realized the potential of my sword. So in the end, maybe he was after both of us. But think about it. You said the bloodstone was indestructible."

"It is. I've tried to burn it, crush it. I even tried to dissolve it in acid. Nothing."

I nodded. "And you also said that it's a vessel. It holds life magic, right? And isn't that just a bad euphemism for souls? The damn thing holds souls."

Mason nodded again.

"So how many souls could it hold?"

"Theoretically? Thousands. Millions, maybe." His face was carefully blank. He knew where I was going with this.

"If one were to trap a million souls, and then crack the bloodstone what would happen? Where would all that life magic go?"

He studied the schematics again. "A bomb. They're building a bomb. The release of energy would be catastrophic."

"Enough to bring down a ward," I agreed.

"But why?"

I shrugged. "Why do megalomaniacs do anything? Alvar wants what he doesn't have. Power. And he thinks killing a bunch of people will give him that."

Mason dropped into a chair and flipped through Barton's notebook.

"It makes no sense. I thought Pierre was behind all this. He's been hunting the stone for so long," he said.

"Well, if Alvar succeeds, Pierre might get his wish. My sword will break the stone, but it will also release any souls trapped inside."

Mason wasn't happy about that. He paced the room.

"It still makes no sense. For their plan to work, they'd need to prime the bloodstone first. They'd need a lot of death to do that."

I told him about the wojak army coming this way.

"*Sacrement.*" He slammed a fist on the blueprints. "How long?"

"About eight hours as the dragon flies. Maybe three days on foot."

He considered that news and said, "It gets worse. I finally heard from my source about that transport truck they used to carry the dragons." His face looked bleak, like he'd just lost his best friend. "It was leased to GenPort Construction."

"So?"

"GenPort is owned by Gerard Golovin."

Oh, damn.

Montreal Ward was governed by a triumvirate of prime ministers. Queen Leighna Icewolf ruled for the fae, Jean-Paul Tremblay for the humans, and Gerard Golovin was the third prime minister, representing alchemist interests.

"Do you think Golovin knows about this? Or did one of his flunkies steal the truck?"

"We have to assume he knows. I think my office might have been searched too. Probably looking for the bloodstone. That means I can't trust anyone on Perrot Island."

"Maybe we shouldn't even trust Leighna."

Mason shook his head. "She has to know about her brother. If nothing else, there are holes in the ward that need plugging. She can do that."

"Right. So when do we go see her?"

"As soon as we get the OK." He held up his widget. I ground my teeth in frustration. I couldn't simply walk into the ice queen's court uninvited, but a clutch of worry in my gut told me we had little time to wait.

We studied the notes and schematics, looking for any clues I'd missed. At some point, Mason left the room and returned with a plate of cheese, bread and fruit.

"You look hungry." He was being polite. I remembered the hollow-eyed face that had looked back at me from the mirror. He watched me eat with an odd look of satisfaction on his face.

"I have something for you." He pulled a small glass terrarium from the bookshelves that lined one entire wall of the room. "In truth, he came along for the ride from the Inbetween without permission. I found him in my bag when I was unpacking, and I don't recognize the species. I'm afraid to put him in the garden and have him eat all my roses."

I peered inside the case. A small snail sat on a pile of leaves. It had a brilliant hued shell, all in jewel tones—green, pink and blue.

"You know most girls get flowers."

"Well, you're not most girls." He watched me with a worried expression, his eyes flicking down to my lips and back to my eyes.

"I love it." And I did. Mason could have squashed the gastropod under his shoe. He could have flushed it or left it outside in a strange environment to die. Only someone who really got me would understand that I would love to take in a lost little snail. I squeezed his arm and he smiled a small, tight smile.

We continued to study Barton's schematics until well past midnight before I made a move to leave.

"I want to confront Nesi in the morning about his involvement with my kidnapping. Simone might have played him too, but I need to know for sure."

"You shouldn't go alone." Mason rolled up Barton's plans, getting ready to leave with me.

"You still think I can't take care of myself?" I said, getting my back up for no good reason other than I was damn tired.

Mason shook his head. "We've been over this. I get that you're a bad-ass with a magic sword. That still doesn't mean that you have to go it alone. I started this with you and I plan to finish it. Let me help."

That last part was such a simple plea. I wanted to let him in, truly I did. But after being alone for so long—and being so good at being alone—I just didn't know how.

"Look." He handed me his widget. "Dutch and Angus will spend the day at Marcella's and return tonight. I won't be able to answer if the queen's secretary calls. But we've got a good four hours till dawn. Let's wake this Nesi guy up and get some answers. Then I'll crash at your place…" He held up his hands when I opened my mouth to protest. "Strictly business. I'll sleep on the couch. You can babysit my widget all day tomorrow in case the queen's aide calls."

It was a solid plan and I couldn't find any way out of it. I nodded.

"And by the way, his name is Bijou."

"What?"

"The snail. I named him Bijou."

Of course he did.

# CHAPTER 29

Even in the wee hours of the morning, Abbott's Agora wasn't quiet. The taverns never stopped serving wine, beer and mead, but the live music had ended, leaving only the die-hard drinkers. Most of the shops were closed, but bakers were already stoking their giant ovens and a few farmers had come early to get the best spots in the open-air market.

We walked along the winding path. I glanced at the sky and Mason read my thoughts.

"Don't worry. We've got time. After all these years, I can feel dawn coming down to the last second."

"You're not like other gargoyles though, are you?"

"What does that mean?"

"That thing you did when we fought the chimera. You changed only your arm to stone. I've never seen a gargoyle do that before."

"And you've known a lot of gargoyles, have you?" His grin suggested I might have a fetish.

"No!" I blurted. "I mean, it was just odd. And useful."

"I've always been able to do that. I come from a long line of geomancers. My grandfather was an extraordinary stone-carver and my father after him. No one knew they were using magic back then. But I spent my childhood in their studios. Working stone became as easy as breathing. And then I learned to change my hands and feet to stone. It was a great gift for street fighting. Polina thought it was a joke to corrupt that magic when she cursed me." He shrugged. "So the gargoyle."

"She sounds like a charmer."

"She was once." His face took on a far-off expression. Then he looked sharply at me. "She was my first wife."

I stopped walking and stared at him. He had the grace to look embarrassed.

"You imprisoned your wife for all eternity in a bloodstone? Why?"

I had visions of a marital spat gone too far. Domestic abuse was tolerated in the eighteenth century, but I didn't want to believe that Mason could be so cruel.

His face was hard. "She tried to kill my daughter. *Our* daughter."

"Oh." I hadn't expected that.

"Polina was beautiful and obsessed with her looks. The thought of growing old horrified her. So she found a fountain of youth spell. She needed the blood of our child to make it work. I wouldn't let that happen." His voice cracked. I had no words. He started walking again.

"I used to think the worst thing that could happen would be for her to break free of the bloodstone. Now, I realize it could be so much worse. I've been a fool…should have found a way to destroy that thing a long time ago."

I took his hand in mine, meaning to comfort him, but felt an immediate intimacy.

"We'll fix it. Now that we know about Alvar's plan, he can't do any more damage." And Ollie had fled with his thunder. I had to believe he was safe.

"I met Alvar a few times," Mason said. "Did he strike you as intelligent?"

I thought about the petulant, spoiled prince. "Not particularly."

"No. Someone else is pulling his strings. Someone who promised him a fae court in Montreal, but has bigger aspirations of their own."

"You think that's your friend Pierre?"

"Maybe. He wasn't ever the top of his class in brains, but something changed after Polina got her claws in him. He became consumed by some frenzied need to free her and exact his revenge on me."

"Has he tried something like this before?"

Mason shrugged. "The last time I saw Pierre was a hundred years ago and halfway across the world. I thought I was well hidden in Montreal. I guess I was wrong."

We stood in front of Nesi's door. "Well, let's get some answers, for both of us then."

I knocked, thinking I'd be there for a while, but Nesi opened immediately.

"What?" He seemed frazzled. A jeweler's loupe was strapped to his forehead, but he wore reading glasses too and had probably forgotten the loupe. "What do you want?"

"Can we come in?" I said.

"Whatever." Nesi flung the door wide and disappeared inside. The main room was a disaster, as if someone had broken in and destroyed the place. We found Nesi crouched in front of an ancient chest, his head buried deep inside. He tossed books and papers over his shoulder as he dug deeper into the chest.

"What are you doing?" I asked.

"It has to be here!" His voice was muffled. "Gods dammit! I know it's here."

"Uh, Nesi? Can we talk to you for a minute?"

Nesi's head popped up. He stared as if he'd never seen us before, then slammed the chest shut. Standing, he glanced over the ruin of shelves, started plucking books and shaking them out. The air bristled with anxious magic.

"Gotta be somewhere," he mumbled.

I was acutely aware of time passing. I needed to get him to focus.

"Nesi, stop." I grabbed his hand. Big mistake. Nesi was jumpy at the best of times. He shoved me hard enough that I fell against a standing birdcage. The brightly colored bird inside squawked and fluttered.

Mason grabbed Nesi by the shirt and shoved him against the wall.

"Don't do that," he said, his expression grim.

Nesi's eyes bulged. He gagged as if Mason were choking the life out of him, when in reality he was barely holding him upright. The walls of the shack began to shake. The cages rattled and the water in the aquariums rippled.

"Let him go!" I said. Mason felt the tremors too and dropped his hand. Nesi scuttled away like a bug. I knew I should have come alone. Nesi's paranoia was on high gear tonight.

"Go wait outside," I whispered to Mason. "Let me handle this." Mason frowned at Nesi, who now sat hunched in a corner, pulling at the frayed hem of his pant leg and mumbling about "the man."

"Trust me," I said. "I'll get him to talk, but not with you looming over him like a..." I ran out of words.

"Like a gargoyle?" Mason grinned.

"Exactly."

After he left, I crouched beside Nesi but didn't touch him.

"Hey."

He looked up. "Hey."

"You okay?"

I could sense the moment when the madness left him. The walls stopped vibrating and he focused on my face.

"Princess?"

"I'm here." I helped him stand and we shuffled through the debris to his table.

"I need to ask you some important questions. And you need to be honest, okay?"

He nodded, looking a hundred years old. His white eye wept tears into his beard.

"How did you hear about the dragons nesting in the mountains?"

"Dragons?" His voice sounded small. "I can get you a good price for dragon claws. Scales too."

I tried again. "Remember, you sent me to meet Simone and said there were dragons nesting north of the city. Who told you that?"

"Simone is a princess just like you…a long lost princess."

I was losing him.

Then he perked up.

"Did you find the dragons?"

"Yes."

He nodded. "Simone is the best. A tracker, you know."

"I know, but who told you where to find the dragons?" We were going in circles.

"Simone did. She knew."

What? "Simone called you?"

Nesi smiled. "Yes, yes. She's a princess, you know. From a dead planet. They stole her throne."

I sighed. "Can you at least give me her address? Does she have a place in town?"

He was too far gone down Paranoia Lane, but he said, "Fairview."

"The mall?"

Nesi nodded.

I squeezed his arm. "Why don't you get to bed?"

He touched the side of his nose and leaned in to whisper, "They'll come after you too, Princess. They always do. The man is in charge. You can't ever defy the man! He knows, he knows, he knows..."

I left him rocking and chanting among the mess he'd made and found Mason waiting outside. The black sky was tinged with dawn. As we hurried through the market, I told Mason what Nesi said.

"Do you trust him?" he asked. What he really meant was did I think Nesi had set me up.

I chewed my lip and nodded. "He's been good to me in the past. I have to give him the benefit of the doubt."

"Are you going after Simone?"

"Yes." I waited for the lecture about not going alone, but we had no time before sunrise, and I wouldn't wait another day. Simone could leave the ward at any time.

But Mason only said, "Good."

# CHAPTER 30

Soft noises. A burbling aquarium filter. The shuffle of a wing. Madras plumping their nest with hay. The muted sob of a banshee hiding in her closet.

I lay in my bed, late morning light streaming through the window, and listened to all these sounds of comfort. Sounds of home. The magic of dozens of little lives surrounded me like a favorite blanket.

I could have stayed in bed all day, if not for the pesky problem of an impending civil war between the fae.

Mason had given me his widget last night. I checked it for messages from the queen. Nothing.

Mason.

He was asleep in my living room. Or not asleep. I still couldn't wrap my head around the language. He was stone. But in the caves, he'd been aware on some level, so when I rose, I pulled a robe over the t-shirt and panties I used for pajamas.

A patio door filled most of the back wall of my living room. A plant stand for Gita's herb garden blocked half the door, but on sunny days the room was still bright. It was one of the things I loved about my humble apartment.

The outer walls of the main room were lined with shelves that held cages and terrariums of all sizes, but the floor space was split into two sections. A table with bookshelves sat beside the patio doors. Hunter's aquarium filled a low cabinet that separated this space from a seating area with a couch and chairs.

Mason sat on the couch with my cat curled in his lap. *Lucky cat.*

He was ghostly pale, but his magic still thrummed slow and even. Maybe cats had keening too. Willow certainly looked comfortable. Jacoby snored quietly from a chair opposite the couch.

I moved around the room, checking water dishes. Hunter was curled up in the ice sprite's terrarium. As I dropped him back in the aquarium, I couldn't help feeling that Mason watched me like one of those creepy paintings in old movies where the eyes moved.

I tried to ignore him, but his presence was just too large. He seemed to fill the room even though he sat in one small corner of it.

"You could have closed your eyes at least. Like a normal person," I blurted. Mason, of course, said nothing, so I continued my chores in silence.

Finally, I couldn't take the growing tension. I found an old fedora I'd used to dress up as a gumshoe for a Halloween party and placed it on Mason's head at a jaunty angle. He looked annoyed, and I laughed, breaking the tension.

The hat suited Mason. He was odd, yes. But I specialized in oddities. If I could find the beauty in a venomous moon-frog, I could deal with a gargoyle.

I let my finger trace the line of his jaw, knowing he could feel my touch. It was a small luxury I would have never permitted myself when he was awake. And if he asked, I could say I was curious about what his stone skin felt like.

It wasn't cold, but hard and smooth, and also warm, like beach stones under the summer sun. Willow opened one eye to watch me, then tucked her head under a paw and went back to sleep.

Talking to him felt right so I chattered on as I cleaned cages and filled food bowls, thinking out loud about Barton's notes and what it could all mean. Alvar's plan nagged at me.

"It still makes no sense to me why they went to so much effort to get the bloodstone. I mean, I get that it has the potential to be a bomb. Right? But you said it would have to store hundreds or thousands of souls before breaking it would release enough power to cause any damage. Even with the opji on their side, that could take weeks."

It seemed like a plan full of holes. Or we didn't understand the motivations behind it. That was what worried me. I checked Mason's widget for the hundredth time. Still no word from the queen.

"I'm going to let Clarence out. I apologize in advance if he jumps on you.

He has bad manners." As soon as the basilisk was slithering around, Willow stalked off to find a quieter bed and Jacoby woke up. He played a kind of hide-and-seek with Clarence, except Clarence gave away his hiding spot each time with a screeched out "Gobble! Gobble!"

I left them to it while I showered and got dressed. I still needed to find an assistant, but that could wait one more day.

After shutting Clarence back in his pen, I said goodbye to Mason. On the way out the door, I plucked my sword from the umbrella stand, hoping I wouldn't need it.

Few buildings taller than ten stories survived the wars. When the city-states started protecting themselves with wards, they could only muster the power to cover ten stories or so. The upper floors of taller buildings were left vacant. But some of the early battles between cities had been vicious. Drones dropped bombs. They couldn't break through the wards, but they decimated these taller buildings. Over time the debris could wear down a ward, so skyscrapers had mostly been pulled down, their stones and steel repurposed for other projects.

Long, low buildings like malls were better suited to ward living, and Fairview Mall had been refitted for living quarters.

As a kid, I remembered coming to Fairview to shop for school clothes every fall. Back then—nearly three-quarters of a century ago—the mall was a mecca for fashion, consumerism and consumption. It showcased the great divide between the haves and the have-nots with window displays of sparkly goods and contemptuous-looking mannequins who seemed to say "You can never look as good as me, but you can try."

I once begged my mother for a t-shirt with a *Lumineers* album cover on it, but she refused. The shirt was forty dollars—a hefty price even back then for a piece of fabric that was so thin it was almost see-through.

"That will never last the school year," Mom had insisted. Looking back with adult eyes, I understood and agreed with her reasoning. But as a tweenie, I was convinced that t-shirt was the only thing standing between me and school popularity.

Walking through the doors of Fairview still made me feel insignificant.

The window displays of shiny things I could never have were gone, but the apartments built in their place were palatial compared to my humble garage-office-apartment combo. The mall itself had been redecorated to feel like a downtown street, with lampposts and benches. Each storefront-turned-apartment had its own entrance, some with gardens out front, others with porches and swings. The entire complex was roofed with skylights, giving it an open air feel.

Simone, it seemed, made good money as a tracker if she could afford a place in the mall.

I found the mall registry and scanned the listing for S. Bellantier. She was on the first floor at the far end. I passed a pair of elderly women out for a stroll and kids playing street hockey in a park area before I found Simone's place. It was a small apartment, probably a food concession in the old mall. The front was paneled in faux-brick with a white door and one shaded window.

I knocked on the door and waited. After a minute I knocked again, then moved to the window. Through the crack at the edge of the blind, I could just make out a dark interior—a couch, chair and breakfast bar. Everything was oddly tinged in blue. Nothing moved.

"She's home."

I turned to see the two mall walkers. One woman was older and leaned on her companion for support, but her voice was strong.

"She's probably sleeping it off. Shameful for a young woman to be carousing so late." The women unlocked the door two apartments down. "She woke up the entire street with her yelling, at what? Two in the morning?" She looked to her companion for confirmation. The younger woman nodded.

They sized me up, taking in my jeans and work shirt. Their eyes glanced off my sword without noticing it.

"She a friend of yours?" The old woman squinted at me as if I was tainted by mere association to Simone.

I considered a moment. I could pretend to be there for a job, but friends got more information than business associates, so I nodded.

"Well you'd better check on her. She was fighting with some man. Boyfriend or dealer. Or both."

"Thanks." I turned the knob on Simone's door and it opened. I left the mall walkers thinking they'd done their good deed for the day.

As soon as I entered the apartment, I knew something was wrong. The room was saturated with magic, like when I found a home infested with termites. Only this wasn't the magic of thousands of tiny lives living in the walls. This magic had the stink of fae with a hint of rotten food and vomit. Blue light from a wall screen, which played a screensaver of dolphins swimming underwater, tinted everything in ghostly tones.

"Hello? Simone?" My voice fell like a wet rag in the gloom. I stepped over cartons of takeout and dirty clothes toward the two doors at the back of the apartment. The first one opened to a bathroom with a faucet wasting water into a small steel sink. I turned it off and opened the second door.

She lay on the bed, but she wasn't sleeping. The room was too still. The only magic pulsed from a small leather sack on the bedside table. The same sack I'd seen Alvar's goblin toss at her.

Simone had overdosed on fae magic.

To my shame, my first thought was, *Damn, that's one lead down.* Then, my conscience kicked in. This was a person. A life. Chewed up by this hard world and spat out again. I didn't know what lay at the heart of Simone's trauma, what made her so angry and unlikable. It didn't matter. She'd been alive and now she was gone. The utter certainty of death never failed to shock me.

I fished my widget from my pack and called my contact at Hub. If the police were going to be all over this scene, I wanted it to be someone I knew, someone who wouldn't mind if I sifted through the evidence.

# CHAPTER 31

Hub took their sweet time getting there. Near death was an emergency. Actual death could wait.

Simone's apartment was officially a crime-scene until they ruled her death an accidental overdose, so I was careful not to leave fingerprints as I searched for ties to Alvar.

The bag of fae drugs was a big, glaring link, but I was looking for something more informative. A letter outlining all of Alvar's plans and naming associates would have been excellent. Of course, I found nothing like that.

Neither did I find any explanation of Simone's suicide run at the chimera. A photo of her with two smiling women on her nightstand gave me a hint. One of the women in the photo was the guard we'd met at the grazing grounds in the Inbetween. The three women locked arms like sisters or best friends, and Simone's relaxed expression seemed at odds with the tracker I'd known. It made me think that some tragedy had befallen her since that photo was taken. Maybe it was the reason she left the Sanctuary Ward for Montreal. Or the reason she went hunting chimeras.

I stared at the photo, but it wouldn't give up its secrets, and after a few more minutes of searching, I went out to the mall court to wait for Hub.

A small crowd gathered, following the paramedics wheeling in a gurney. The two mall-walking women stood at the front of the gawker line. Detective Benoit Giroux pushed his way through the crowd.

"You found the body?" he asked.

"Yes."

"Wait here while I secure the scene, then I want to ask you some questions."

Two hours later, Ben asked me the same question for a third time.

"Why did you go out to the Inbetween?"

I sighed. Ben was nothing if not thorough. The first time we worked together was when a murder victim sprouted spoors that turned into nasty stinging bugs about the size of hummingbirds. Hub called me in for all those fun cases.

I repeated my answer, stamping down on my impatience. "I was trying to find a thunder of dragons to bring back an orphan." I'd related the story as truthfully as I could, leaving Mason out of it, and ending with the chimera fight, letting him think Simone and I parted ways after that.

"A thunder," he said. "Of dragons."

I smiled sweetly.

"You know, Kyra, if anyone else tried to feed me that story, I'd lock 'em up. But you're just crazy enough to do it. So do you have any idea where Simone got the fae drugs?"

I shook my head. I couldn't tell him about Alvar. Not before I spoke to the queen. I trusted Ben. He was one of the good ones, but that didn't mean the people he reported to were.

"Can I go now?" With the skylights overhead, I was acutely aware of the fading light. My gargoyle would be awake soon.

"Sure," Ben said. "Just, you know, be available if I need to question you again."

"Don't leave town. Got it."

Two paramedics pushed a stretcher out the door, followed by the coroner. I took a moment to watch them wheel Simone away in her body bag. The group of gawkers was also silent. The two mall walkers glared at me as if they'd known right from the start I was bad news.

As I left the mall, a widget buzzed in my pocket.

"Hello?" I answered, before realizing it was Mason's.

"Is this Henry Mason's phone?" asked a smooth female voice.

"I'm sorry, he's not available. Can I take a message?" I glanced at the number but didn't recognize it.

"My name is Merrow Farsigh, secretary to the queen." There was only one queen in Montreal, Queen Leighna Icewolf of the Winter Court.

"Her Majesty will hold a late court tonight, I believe that would be suitable for Mr. Mason?"

"Yes. What time?"

"Ten o'clock. Please don't be late."

"We'll be there."

I parked my truck at Morgan's, a small but convenient market less than a block from my house and took out my canvas shopping bag from the back of the truck. We needed to eat before heading across town to the fae court, but I had nothing at home.

I laid spaghetti noodles, Morgan's homemade sauce and fixings for a salad beside the register.

My sword hummed.

Morgan, a grizzled old fae with pointed ears that poked through his wild mane of white hair, looked up sharply.

By habit, I kept a glamor on the sword, just a small, sly spell that made mundane eyes slide off the blade without taking note, but some fae could see through glamors. Morgan had never complained about me bringing the weapon into his store, but the humming was hard to ignore.

"Wassat?" he asked in his guttural hiss, glaring right at the sword.

I smiled. "It's singing the song of my people. Nothing to worry about."

But I was worried. My blade only made that noise for one reason. It had unfinished business and its quarry was nearby.

Joran.

I paid for my food, grabbed my bag and hurried outside.

It was a perfect May evening. The sun glowed red just above the horizon, tinging the empty street in soft warm light. I glanced up the road toward Abbott's Agora and Gallop Bridge beyond, then eastward, toward my place. Nothing.

Except for a small figure barreling down the street. Jacoby?

The dervish ran with unnatural speed, like a cartoon bird I used to watch as a kid.

"Kyra-lady!" He fell on me, sobbing and panting. "Come! Come! Bad man!"

I dropped my groceries and ran the half-block to my house, my heart hammering, sword screaming.

The front window was smashed. A big man with dark hair had Gita restrained. I pulled my blade, ready to skewer him to save my banshee, but Jacoby stopped me.

"Bad man inside!" He pointed through the broken window, where I could hear more glass shattering and Clarence screaming. That's when I realized the big man wasn't restraining Gita. He was trying to comfort her. I had no time to question him.

My blade all but pulled me through the broken window.

Inside, my critters were agitated. My office had been ransacked. The pile of folders lay scattered across the floor. Desk drawers were pulled out and upended.

Mr. Murray pounded on the floor of his apartment.

The door to my apartment was ajar. I nudged it with my foot.

"Joran, you can stop now," I called out. "The bloodstone isn't here."

A loud crash came from inside, then a muffled curse. My sword led me, and I stepped over the debris lying in my entryway.

The room was a disaster. Cages were toppled. My kitchen chairs and table were smashed. Broken bits of dishes and books were strewn around. Hunter's aquarium was cracked and dripped into a puddle on the floor. The little kraken watched the commotion with his face pressed against the glass.

The plant stand in front of the open patio door had been pulled down, and the potted plants trampled, spilling black earth everywhere. Clarence darted around the room on a manic loop.

Mason had toppled off the couch and lay face-down on the floor while Joran ripped into the couch cushions with a small knife. He might be looking for the stone, but he'd been vengeful about it.

I took a deep breath. Despite the rage building inside me, I needed to be the diplomat here.

"You look like shit," I said.

Joran looked up from his busy work and laughed. It was a wet, unhealthy sound. His eyes had sunken into his skeletal face. His arm was still bandaged, but the wrappings were dirty and tattered. Beneath them, his muscles had shrunk to the bone. And he stank like rot.

"Look, I'm sorry about…well, everything. But I can help you." I took a step into the room. He backed up, putting the ruined couch between us, and waving his knife in the air.

"No closer!"

"All right." I held up my hands as if in surrender, but my right hand still held the sword, so it didn't have the same effect. Joran squinted at me.

"Where is it?"

"I told you the bloodstone isn't here. The dragons are gone. Give up now and I will help you with your wound." It was a lie. Nothing could fix him now.

He considered my offer. Or maybe he considered his odds against a healthy woman armed with a sword.

"Tell me, is this bloodstone worth it? I have Barton's notes. I know what you're planning. But without my sword, you'll never break the stone."

He zeroed in on my blade, greed plain in his eyes.

"You won't take it from me. You couldn't best me before. And now you're as weak as a child."

He coughed into his sleeve, flecking it with blood. He saw the stains and laughed again. Clearly, he'd gone mad.

"Barton told me all about you…Valkyrie. You're nothing more than another god's cleanup crew."

This was good. Keep him talking until I could get around the couch. Or until the sun set and Mason woke up.

"My grandmother is a goddess. She can kill you with a thought."

"Is she here?" I pretended to look around the destroyed room, as if she might be lurking in the shadows.

"She's trapped in that damn stone." He jammed the tip of his blade into the couch. "But when I free her, she'll come after you and your abomination of a boyfriend." He tried to spit on Mason, but couldn't muster enough saliva. In his frustration, he kicked something toward me.

A tiny, fat body.

*Oh, my gods. Theo.*

Another mangled lump of fur was half-hidden under the couch stuffing. Alvin.

Clarence ran by and Joran sliced at him with his blade, shearing off part of the basilisk's comb. Clarence screamed and ran out the back door.

"Enough!"

I lunged at Joran. He kicked the couch and took off after Clarence. I stumbled over the couch and slipped on the wads of cushion batting. By the time I made it outside, Joran had disappeared. Nothing moved in my small backyard. The tumbled patio furniture told me that Joran had run toward the garage. I waited a long minute to see if he was hiding in one of the neighbor's yards. My entire being focused on the pursuit so I wouldn't have to think about the tiny bodies inside.

Joran was already dead, his body just didn't know enough to lie down and give into the rot. He wouldn't last much longer. The necrosis had spread up his arm. Once it hit his chest, he'd be done. In reality, I didn't need to chase him down. A second strike of my sword would release his soul to the afterlife, but I no longer felt any desire to be merciful to him. He could wallow in his own rotting skin until his heart burst for all I cared.

But neither would I let him back in my home to terrorize my family again. So I waited out the silence, making sure he was truly gone.

After five minutes, I moved around to the front of the garage, my sword still primed and ready.

The dark-haired man still stood in the parking lot. He had the stance of a fighter, weight distributed evenly, knees slightly bent, and his eyes roamed the terrain, looking for an attack. Gita sat in a ball at his feet, holding Jacoby. He was guarding them.

"Who are you?" I called from about twenty feet away. I didn't know this guy, and right now, I didn't trust anyone.

"Gabriel Devi. Gabe. I called about the job opening but no one got back to me."

He didn't look like my normal applicants. He looked like he should be modeling jeans in a fashion zine. Tall and slim, with just enough muscle to bulk out his shirt, his skin was golden brown and his dark curls fell onto his forehead like someone had mussed them.

Just then, Clarence came hurtling by me, bleeding and hissing. Gabe's hand shot out and caught him by the throat.

"This is yours?" He held out the squirming, spitting basilisk.

"You're hired," I said. "You start now."

## CHAPTER 32

Mason, Gabe and I sorted through the debris of my life. Mr. Murray had come downstairs to complain about the noise in person, but he took one look at the damage, then the expression on my face and retreated without a word.

Gita sat in the corner by the kitchen with the dead madras in her lap. Oddly, she didn't cry. She made no sound, and her only sign of life was the long-boned hands stroking the little bodies over and over again.

I couldn't help her. Alvin and Theo would never drive us crazy again. Just the thought of it made me want to break something, except there was nothing left in the apartment to break.

Eventually, Gabe crouched in front of Gita and spoke softly. After a moment, she nodded, and he plucked the madras from her.

"Do you have a shovel?" he asked. I led him through the office to the garage that I had set up as a workout space. Thankfully, Joran hadn't made it this far. At the far end of the garage, I unlocked another door. Here, garden supplies lined one wall. The other wall held weapons—spears, blades, guns. Some traps. Ammunition and the heavy-duty magical weapons were locked away in a cage.

Gabe raised one eyebrow at the array. "Right about now, I'm wondering what kind of extermination business this is."

I showed him my teeth. "Sometimes the vermin are really big."

I handed him a shovel, then examined the guns on the wall. Normally, I didn't bother with guns. They had little effect on magic, and so weren't useful against the things I usually hunted. But I'd tasted Joran's magic. He was pure mundane. His grandmother might have been a witch, but that gene had skipped him. Bullets would work just fine on Joran.

*His grandmother.* Oh, no. Mason had been stone when Joran spouted off about the bloodstone, but he'd heard it all.

The witch in the bloodstone was Joran's grandmother. How could that be? Maybe Polina was his great-great-many-greats-grandmother. But that meant he was descended from Mason too—Mason who still mourned the deaths of all his children. And I had sentenced Joran to death.

"Dig a couple of holes, but wait for me," I said to Gabe. "I have something to do first."

Back inside, Mason was sweeping up the dirt from the toppled plant stand. The aquarium's leak mixed with the potting soil to make a mud puddle. Hunter gripped the rim of the glass with two tentacles and peeked over the edge to watch. His other six arms swayed back and forth with each sweep of Mason's broom. He was helping. Tucker, the abaia eel slunk through the fake grasses in the slowly diminishing water at the bottom of the tank. I needed to find alternate accommodations for both of them soon.

"I think I can fix the aquarium," Mason said. "We've been working on a new adhesive that should do it."

I took the dustpan from his hands and forced him to look me in the eye.

"I'm so sorry."

He watched me with a look of resignation.

"I never wanted this power. I tried to leave my sword in Asgard, but I couldn't. I can barely stand to leave it in another room. I didn't mean to cut him. Mason, I'm so sorry. He's your grandson, or great-great-great-something grandson. And I killed him—"

"He's not mine." Mason cut me off. He gripped my arms as if willing his words into me. "Polina and I were estranged for many years after our daughter was born. There were rumors that she was living with another man, even rumors that she'd had his child. Of course, I knew about her and Pierre, but I didn't give the rumors much credit. She resented being a mother the first time. I couldn't imagine she'd let herself get pregnant again."

My mind whirled with the possibilities.

"So Joran isn't your descendant, but hers. That still seems like too much of a coincidence."

Mason nodded. His dark eyes were unfocused as if he looked inward, searching for answers. "I agree. They brought those dragons to the cemetery for only one reason. To find that bloodstone. I don't know how they found me or when Alvar got involved, but I don't think he's running the show. It's Pierre. I'm sure of it."

That reminded me. "The queen's secretary called. We have to meet with her in…" I looked at my widget, "in less than two hours."

Clean up would have to wait, but I had one task before leaving.

"Gabe is going to bury Alvin and Theo in the backyard. Would you… would you stand with me?"

This was more than a request on my part. It was a test of character. If Mason made a joke about funeral rites for rodents, I'd know he wasn't the one for me.

Instead, he nodded and reached for my hand. We gathered the others and went outside. My property didn't have a lot of bare ground, so Gabe had chosen a site on the side of the garage where a bit of scrubby grass was starting to turn green.

We all stood around the two small holes in the ground: Mason, still holding my hand, Gita, tucked under Gabe's arm, and Jacoby, who held onto Clarence's tail. Some were new acquaintances. Some had been with me for years, but they all felt like family. Not the family I was born into. But the family I chose. The family who chose me. Even Willow sunned herself on an old picnic table nearby, pretending she wasn't curious about the gathering.

"Wait!" I dashed into the garage, filled a bucket with water, then ran inside to fetch Hunter. Back outside, I plunked the sloshing bucket beside me. The little kraken grabbed onto my pant leg to prop himself on the edge of the bucket and watch the proceedings.

"Okay, go," I said.

Gabe cleared his throat. "Does anyone want to say something?"

Jacoby stepped forward. He wrung his hands in front of him.

"Alvin and Theo likes to tease me. This sometimes made me sad. But not so sad as now." He stepped back and I nodded my approval at him.

"Alvin and Theo wouldn't want this to be a solemn occasion," I said. "They would have preferred that we crack jokes and throw confetti. But I find that I have nothing funny to say."

After that, we stood in silence until Gita started to wail. She began with a low keening that grew into a glorious, multi-hued cry. Every hair on my body stood on end. The sound filled our yard and kept growing. Faces peeked out of windows. Doors opened along the street and people came out to listen. It was beautiful, haunting, and a perfect tribute for my lost children.

When her song ended, the world seemed strangely quiet. Gabe filled in the holes and I turned to Mason.

"It's time for us to visit the queen."

# CHAPTER 33

Queen Leighna's Ice Palace filled an entire block in the north end of the city, not far from the Crystal Bridge. The title "Ice Palace" was a misnomer. There were no columns of ice or sweeping ice staircases. No frozen sculptures of fae heroes. The anteroom where we waited was plain, like waiting rooms everywhere—a few chairs, a low table, a water dispenser and a reception desk, which was empty at this hour.

A tall, sleek fae let us into the waiting room. His hair was thick, brown and glossy like an otter's. That and the webbed fingers made me think he came from the Riverhelm tribe, a type of fae often found at the confluence of two rivers.

"Leighna will see you shortly." He bowed curtly and left.

"Leighna?" I said when we were alone. "Isn't that a bit informal?" The Ice Queen was the last remaining fae monarch in Montreal and one of three prime ministers of the triumvirate.

"What did you expect," Mason asked. "Her Majesty? Leighna doesn't roll that way. You'll see."

Great. Now I couldn't help wondering how Mason knew the way the queen rolled. My foot started tapping as I turned my thoughts to other things.

We'd left Gabe and Gita to clean up the worst of Joran's invasion and settle the beasts. Gabe had promised to board up the broken front window and call the glazier. I didn't want to leave the new guy alone, but not because I didn't trust him. Gita had an unerring sense of people and she'd taken to Gabe immediately. I was just worried that I'd dropped him right into the deep end, hoping he could swim. My track record with assistants wasn't stellar, and at some point I had to ask, was it me or them?

"I'm the one who should be sorry," Mason said, startling me out of my self-recriminations.

"You? Sorry for what?"

"For Joran." He sat forward in his chair, arms leaning on his knees while he fidgeted with his widget. "I could hear everything. I even felt myself tipping off the couch. But I could do nothing."

The widget flipped in his hands, over and over. He raised his eyes to me and I saw the depth of his pain.

"Simone was right. I held you back in the Inbetween. I couldn't stop them from taking you. I couldn't stop Joran."

His hands closed around the widget as if he might crush it.

"More than anything, that's why I hate Polina. She did this to me. She made me into this half-man to mock me. I should have killed her when I had the chance."

"I don't expect you to save me." How to find the right words to make him understand how amazing he was? He lived in the shadows for centuries and was still be the kind of person who wanted to help others. But the fae attendant returned and told us that the queen was ready to see us.

Once again, the queen's inner sanctum was underwhelming. Instead of the grand court I'd imagined, she met us in an old-fashioned parlor. She sat on a couch with six baroque-looking chairs forming a semi-circle around it. A low table set with tea sat between them. The walls of the room were lined with bookshelves, filled with books that looked well read and hummed with magic, like each title was whispering its contents. The far wall behind the queen's couch was covered in a subtle print of bluish-white on white, like crystalline ice on glass. I blinked. The pattern crawled. The crystals blended and morphed in a shifting pattern that was mesmerizing and nauseating if I looked at it too long.

I focused instead on the queen. Her simple dress of pale blue highlighted her startling eyes. Alvar's eyes. She wore no jewelry except for a silver necklace with a tree-of-life pendant. Her only claim to ostentation was her white-blond hair that was intricately braided and piled on her head in an elaborate style.

"Your majesty." I didn't even attempt a curtsy, but bowed slightly.

"None of that." She waved me toward a chair. "Please, just call me Leighna. Mason, it is so good to see you again." She reached for his hand and kissed both his cheeks. Mason nodded and kissed her back. I wasn't jealous. Really, I wasn't.

Leighna introduced the others already seated.

"Merrow is my executive director." She pointed to the fae woman seated to her right. Merrow sat forward on her chair so her charcoal wings could flutter behind her. She was small for a fae, slim and dark haired. She wore all black. I felt like I was looking at a live calligraphy glyph, all well-shaped smooth lines of black ink.

"And of course, you know Minister Okorafa."

I nodded to the burly senator. Everyone knew the outspoken minister. He was nominally a fae senator, one of seven, but as a godling of the Anansi pantheon, he was at the forefront of the reforms to create a new political party that would be the voice of all godlings in the ward. That he was part of Leighna's inner circle intrigued me.

Okorafa watched us with dark eyes, first sizing up Mason, then me. His gaze rested over-long on my sword, which should have been masked by my glamor. Clearly, I wasn't fooling him.

"And Minister O'Grady." Leighna smiled tightly at a ruddy-haired giant of a man who looked like he would be more comfortable with an axe in his hand than the delicate teacup that rested on his knee.

I keened each of them. Okorafa kept his power wrapped snugly around him, so he was hard to suss. Merrow's magic breathed in and out like her wings. O'Grady was hiding something. His magic felt puffed up, and I was convinced that he wore a glamor. He was probably no bigger than a gnome under all that lumberjack bluster.

After the introductions, the queen poured tea for us, and then dug right into things.

"Merrow tells me you have news of my brother. He is well, I hope?"

"Yes, your Majesty…I mean Leighna." It felt wrong to call her by her first name, but I stumbled on. "When I last saw Prince Alvar, he was fine, but…" How could I say that her brother was a traitor?

"But he's been up to no good. I understand, Kyra. May I call you Kyra?"

"Of course," I said.

Her smile was genuine and full of warmth that belied her ice-queen nickname.

"Good. Please don't feel the need to sugar coat things with me. I love my brother, but I am not blind to his faults. If he is causing you strife, I must know about it."

Causing me strife? That was not the half of it. But I gathered my thoughts, trying to ignore the fact that Merrow watched me with hawk eyes while Okorafa texted someone on his widget.

"I'm afraid to tell you that your brother has opened a door to Underhill."

I told her everything, starting with the poachers in the cemetery. When I got to the part about the bloodstone, I glanced at Mason, but he just nodded. We'd already agreed that Leighna needed to understand the full import of Alvar's plan, and she couldn't do that without full disclosure. As I spoke, I handed Barton's notebook to Leighna who glanced through it then passed it to Merrow. I finished with my trip to Simone's and finding her dead of an overdose from drugs she procured at Alvar's pseudo-court.

O'Grady started to laugh. *Laugh!*

"He's always been such a high-spirited lad!" He leaned back in his chair. "I bet he's just having a bit of fun."

"Fun?" Merrow's tone whipped like cold wind. "He breached the ward. That's treason. And if these schematics are real, he's planning something much worse."

"Bah! He's just fallen in with a bad crowd as boys do," said O'Grady. "But he's a bright lad. He'll figure out his own business."

Merrow pinched her lips tight. Her wings fluttered, and Leighna laid a hand on her knee to still her.

"I believe things have gone past boyhood pranks," she said. "My brother is over two-hundred years old. It's time I stopped treating him like a child." She sipped her tea and her thoughts turned inward. Everyone in the room watched her, waiting for a verdict. Behind her, the crystalline pattern crept faster along the wall as if it were linked to the queen's agitation.

Leighna put down her cup and turned her attention on me. "In his last days, your father made sure that Underhill remained closed. The security of the entire ward depended on it. There are many among the fae who miss the simplicity of our old life and would return. But only one of royal blood can open a door to Underhill. So even if my little brother has been influenced by someone else, he is the one that cut through the ward." She sagged back in her chair. "Honestly, I didn't think he had the power to do it."

After a moment, she mustered herself again and turned to Mason. "Please explain this bloodstone to me. How does it work?"

"In truth, it is nothing more than a vessel to hold magic. Not unlike the Apex gems that store magic and then disperse it to our ward system," he said.

Montreal had four Apex gems, massive uncut rubies that capped a tower on each of the bridges, and another, the master gem on Perrot Island. Between these were dozens of smaller towers and gems, like the one on Dorval Island. Together, they created a web of magic to fuel the ward. The bloodstone was only a fraction of the size of the Apex gems, but size didn't matter when pure magic was involved.

"Over three hundred years ago, I trapped the spirit of a necromancer in the stone. She was an evil woman, and, I am ashamed to say, my wife, Polina."

That got a raised eyebrow from the queen. Even Okorafa looked up from his widget.

Mason spread his palms in a show of defeat. "She threatened my daughter's life—our daughter's life. I had no other choice. I couldn't kill her. I could only imprison her."

"So you've been her gaoler for the last three centuries?" O'Grady said, as if it were a delicious secret.

"Yes. I tried to keep the bloodstone safe."

"But my brother found it. How did he know where to look?" Leighna asked.

"I believe he isn't working alone. I have enemies from that time. Friends who supported Polina over me. Her lover, Pierre, was like a brother to me, until she turned him against me. He has been looking for me ever since I put her in that bloodstone. It's possible Prince Alvar is working with him."

Mason wouldn't look at me, and my heart ached for him. He thought this mess was all his fault, and nothing I could say would change that.

"And what is this Pierre's full name and ward?" Merrow was taking notes on a digital notebook.

"Pierre Garnier," Mason said. "At least that was what he called himself back then. "I don't know which ward he lives in now. I tracked his movements for years, but lost him during the war. Before that he was still in France, in Marseilles."

Merrow nodded and made another note.

Okorafa finally put his widget away. "If I understand you correctly, the bloodstone cannot be broken except by Miss Greene's sword, there." He nodded at my blade in its sheath at my hip. I knew he could see it! "And the stone itself has been lost since the dragons disappeared, is that right?" Mason and I both nodded. "So what exactly are we worried about?"

"There's a hole in the ward!" Merrow was losing her patience. But I watched the queen and her ministers to see if any of them understood the bigger implications. O'Grady's foot tapped on the floor. Okorafa's heavy brow lowered over his eyes as if he was puzzling out an intricate formula. The frost pattern behind the queen slowed and I knew she understood.

"Breaking this bloodstone would release your necromancer, correct?" she asked.

Mason nodded.

"As uncomfortable as that might be for you, your wife's reappearance would hardly be cause for general alarm, agreed?"

"Agreed." Mason's face was blank.

"So we should assume that my brother had other plans for the bloodstone."

"We believe that he planned to harvest more souls, trap them in the stone, and then use the Valkyrie sword to break the stone and release the spirit magic all at once," Mason said.

"And this could do what?" Okorafa was interested now.

"With enough souls, it could have the effect of a bomb, like the magic incendiaries dropped during the Flood Wars."

Those bombs had devastated entire countries. The fighting reduced North America to a handful of city states with vast tracts of uninhabitable hot-spots in between. Europe and Asia fared no better. No one wanted to go back to the days of magic warfare.

Merrow broke the silence. "And how many souls would they need to feed this bloodstone in order to create a bomb?"

"Hundreds," Mason said. "Thousands."

"Well, there you go," O'Grady said. "We'd notice if a few thousand people went missing inside the ward, now wouldn't we?"

"The opji," Merrow said. "That's why they're rounding up homesteaders."

"We think so," I agreed.

"That's nonsense! I won't sit 'ere and have the good name of our prince slandered with talk of calludin' with vampires!" O'Grady's lilting accent grew thicker in his agitation. He stood and loomed over me, his glamor making him seem even bigger than normal.

"I saw an opji at his court," I said, clenching my fists and pounding my knees in frustration. "I saw an army of wojaks traveling through Underhill!"

"That's when you were riding the dragon, right?" sneered O'Grady. "And were the vampires riding unicorns too?"

I just stared at him. They didn't believe me!

"Sit down, minister." The queen laced her command with magic, and O'Grady's knees buckled. He sat, but not willingly.

"It seems that only luck and this woman's bravery have saved us from invasion by the opji." Leighna smiled at me, but it was tight. "Merrow, please round up the usual suspects for questioning. I want to know how deep Alvar has sunk himself. But we must prepare for an attack. He may have lost his special weapon and the element of surprise, but that won't stop him. It will only make him more determined. He'll attack soon with whatever army he has in reserve."

She set down her teacup and turned to Okorafa. "You will brief the parliament?" The minister nodded. Then Leighna turned to Mason. "Can we expect support from the alchemists?" I'd left out the part about the dragon transport truck originating with the leader of the alchemists. But Leighna had her own concerns about Gerard Golovin.

"You will have my support and the Guardians," Mason said with a curt bow. "I can only hope my fellow alchemists will do the right thing."

Leighna nodded as if she had suspected as much, then she turned to me. Being under the Ice Queen's scrutiny was like enjoying a brilliant sun on a winter's day.

"I thank you for bringing this news to us," she said. Whoa! Thanks from a fae was a big deal. The fae didn't do favors. Everything had a price. I had done the queen a service, and her twisted sense of propriety demanded that she compensate me for that service.

"Will you help us again? I mean to close that door, even if it traps my brother in Underhill."

"Of course. I can take you there as soon as you need."

Leighna inclined her head. "And for your service, you may choose your reward."

All eyes in the room turned to me. I was acutely aware of the agitated crystals on the wall behind Leighna. I closed my eyes to still my thoughts.

Choosing a boon from the fae was tricky business. If I was too greedy, they'd twist the favor to teach me a lesson. If I didn't ask enough, they would feel slighted. But there was really only one thing I wanted from the queen of the fae.

"I ask in return for my service that, once this affair with Alvar has been settled, I may return to visit you and hear the story of my father's last days."

Leighna smiled. "That is a wise request. It will be granted."

# CHAPTER 34

Mason had to leave me outside the fae court. He needed to gather the Guardians, and I had to take Merrow to see the Underhill gate.

"You'll be all right?" he asked. The wind blew his unruly hair into his eyes, but he didn't blink. He stared me down until I nodded.

He was asking if I could lead the fae emissary to the gate on my own, but the question had deeper undertones. Tears were close to the surface, and I fought to hold them back.

He traced the line of my chin with one finger. "When this is all over, if you need to talk…I mean, we *will* talk." His confidence was reassuring. I wasn't certain we'd survive the next few hours.

As I watched him walk away, an icy wind blew off the floodplains to the north. I shivered and pulled my coat tighter.

I waited for over an hour in an all-night coffee shop next to the queen's court. The sleepy-eyed fae waiter filled my cup three times before Merrow knocked on the cafe's window and beckoned me to join her.

She wore only a light sweater, but didn't seem to feel the cold. My hands shook, but more from excess caffeine and lack of sleep.

"I ordered us a car," she said as two vehicles pulled up to the curb. We got into the first one. "Lakeshore Road, Dorval," she said to the AI system. The car pulled away and drove down the empty street. The vehicle behind us transported a dozen armed Hub officers.

"I guess we're not aiming for stealth," I said.

Merrow twisted a frown at me. "Who knows how long that gate has been open." She seemed to take Alvar's treachery as a personal insult. Her magic didn't hum, it shifted and slithered like snake bodies twining over and around each other. It gave me the heebie jeebies. And like always, when I was uncomfortable, I asked intrusive and awkward questions.

"So how do you like working for the queen? Been doing it long?"

She side-eyed me. "Since before you were born."

That was possible. Fae weren't immortal, but they could be very long-lived.

"Do you know Alvar well?"

"Again, since before you were born."

I wouldn't get much else out of Chatty-Cathy, so I watched the city pass by outside the window. Somewhere on the horizon, the sun was just arriving. In the next hour it would crest the buildings, but it already washed the city in a pink glow.

I loved this time of day. On a normal week, this was when I'd be waking, drinking coffee and greeting all my rescues. Clarence would brush his rubbery comb under my chin as I tossed a hunk of spoiled meat into his pen. Hunter would stretch his little tentacle out of the tank for a high-five. Alvin and Theo would…My thoughts screeched to a halt. Alvin and Theo wouldn't be chittering and causing trouble ever again.

And here came the waterworks. Merrow was oblivious to my pain or she thoughtfully gave me space to grieve. I chose to believe the latter.

Gods, I was so tired. I couldn't even remember the last time I'd slept. I rubbed my eyes and sniffed. Was that me that smelled like rank sweat, smoke and garbage? The queen must have been really impressed.

By the time we reached Lakeshore Road, I'd packed away my feelings. I had a job to do, but once this was over…I thought of Mason's promise. Yes, once this was over, we'd have time for talking.

Steel beams and chunks of concrete blocked the road access, and we left the transports three blocks away from the crumbling mess that was once a row of luxury condos. The officers from the second transport fanned out and stood ready to shoot anything that popped out of the rocks.

Stepping over the debris, the rising sun hit our backs and lit the buildings with sharp yellow light. To my left, the lake frothed with choppy steel-gray waves. A sea-serpent breached the surface. Its massive body rolled over the waves, impossibly long until the tip of a forked tail splashed down and disappeared. Calling St. Louis a lake is a throwback to before the wars. In truth, it is simply a wider section of the St. Lawrence seaway that runs like a superhighway from the Atlantic ocean. And like the Inbetween, it's full of creatures born from spikes of magic.

The hum of the ward anchored offshore grated on my nerves. I turned away to find two figures waiting for us by the fallen *Aristo* sign. One was Detective Ben Giroux.

"Twice in two days," he said when he saw me. "I always knew you were a trouble-maker."

"Takes one to know one," I said, channeling my inner eight-year-old.

"This is Susanna Coulter," he nodded to the blond woman waiting beside him. "She's a researcher for Hub. And her assistants Julia and Raymond something-or-others."

The something-or-others crouched by a pile of rocks, taking dirt samples. Julia pulled a plug of dirt with a device like an apple corer. Raymond held a sample bag open to receive it. His glasses had fallen down his nose, and he tilted his head way back to see me.

"Hey."

"Hey," I said back at him, then shook Susanna's hand. She smiled. Her blond curls and round cheeks gave her a cherubic look. She already had a gadget out—like a widget, but bigger—and she scanned the debris for some arcane reading.

"You an alchemist?"

She nodded. "Ben said you found this gate. It's amazing. I'd like to hear all about it."

"So would I." Ben squinted at me. "Funny how you didn't mention it yesterday."

Was that only yesterday? It felt like months had passed since I found Simone's body.

"Since this is fae business, I felt I should inform Queen Leighna first." I waved to Merrow. "This is the queen's advisor, Merrow Farsigh."

Ben nodded. Merrow glared.

"Where is the gate," she said.

"That way." Susanna pointed her gadget up the hill to the crumbling front doors of the condo.

Merrow looked to me for confirmation and I nodded.

As we climbed over and around debris, I spotted several more Hub agents lurking about. Ben wasn't taking any chances.

"This is amazing," Susanna said. "These readings. I've never seen anything like it! These are like the old NASA readings from Mars or another planet. But that's not possible!"

She scrambled over a chunk of cement and ran toward the building.

"Whoa, there!" Ben jogged to catch up. "Let the tough guys go first before you run in and get yourself all dead and stuff."

"Sorry." Susanna looked sheepish. I had a feeling this wasn't the first time the detective had admonished her for being impulsive.

Inside the building, the hum of the ward dimmed, replaced by another itchy magic, this one coming off the open gate between worlds.

"Where is it?" Susanna demanded. She tapped the screen of her gadget a bunch of times as if the readings had gone haywire. "It's got to be here."

"It's right there." I pointed to the waterfall tumbling down the marble wall. Merrow was already standing before it, her head tilted back as she gazed up at the amazing sight. The two images were overlaid, filling the same space so that the rock face and waterfall seemed to grow naturally from the marble wall. Water crashed at Merrow's feet before evaporating into mist, and yet the stones of the old condo's lobby were dry.

"Right where?" Susanna's face scrunched in confusion. She couldn't see the other world gate. It was cloaked in a glamor that I could see through. Merrow too.

Susanna advanced to stand beside Merrow, still taking readings on her gadget. Raymond had wandered closer too, lugging a backpack that was already full of dirt and stone samples.

"It's cloaked," Merrow said. "But Alvar could never hide his magic from me. I was his tutor once." She smiled, a tight, cold smile.

"So why can I see it?" I asked.

"You came through it. The door will always be open for you now."

That meant anyone Alvar brought through would also have access to our city.

"Can you close it?" I asked. Merrow turned to me. A sneer flickered across her face. It was there, then gone.

"Closing a gate to another world isn't that simple. It will require a significant output of power. The queen is working on it, but a solution may take some time."

"Really?" I tried to sound genuinely curious. "I had no idea it was so involved."

When I broke Bifrost, the bridge from Asgard to the human realm, I hadn't worked on a solution. I'd simply reacted in rage and fear, slicing through the bridge's bindings with one furious slash of my sword.

Could I close the Underhill gate the same way? Possibly. But my sword's magic was unpredictable. And this was pure fae magic. No way to be sure how it would react. I could create an even bigger rift if I tried. Or worse. I could collapse this dimension on itself.

So I would let the fae sort it out. It was their mess anyway.

A figure leapt through the gate and sunk its teeth into Raymond's neck. The tech screamed. The vampire tore out a chunk of flesh and tossed him aside. Blood gushed and Raymond's wide eyes were dead before he hit the floor.

The vampire turned to us and grinned, his mouth smeared in red. A mindless wojak already looking for the next kill.

Merrow dropped her glamor like shedding a too-warm coat.

In her true fae form, she stood over seven feet tall, charcoal-skinned with natural armor plates covering her face and chest, and long wings flaring behind her. Black hair swirled about her head as if floating in water. Her muscular arms ended in razor-sharp pincers. She reached with one of those and slashed the wojak, killing him with one blow.

But more vampires were already falling through the gate.

"Get back!" I pushed Susanna, even as I stumbled over Raymond's corpse. No time to give him last rites with my sword.

I looked back once to see Merrow fighting off a dozen vamps. Ben was retreating too, and Julia was nowhere to be seen. I hoped she'd gotten out.

"What are those…" Susanna's question ended with a squeak. A wojak dropped from the rafters and landed in front of us, grinning his malicious intent.

"Go!" I pushed her toward the door and slashed at the vamp. He hissed when I cut him, not liking the feel of true life coming back to his veins. No matter, I didn't let him suffer long.

I backed up to the door. Susanna huddled just inside it. Had any vamps escaped? I didn't know.

"Take this." I handed her my hunting knife. "Do you know how to use it?" Susanna shook her head. Sweat matted her blond curls to her face. "Just keep slashing. Eventually you'll hit something vital."

Wojaks weren't easy to kill, but cut off enough parts and they'd go down.

Another one leaped at me, clawed hands outstretched to rake my face. I slashed and she fell, handless, black blood pulsing from the stumps. I cut her throat and she lay still.

My sword sang a triumphant song. It hadn't had this much fun in a long time.

We backed up a step. More vamps appeared through the rift. One got behind me as I took down another. Susanna screamed, but I had no breath to spare for her as three more attacked. I swiped at their knees, severing tendons, and two fell. The third latched onto my shoulder. I rammed the butt of my sword under his chin, smashing teeth and jaws. His claws raked my shoulder and pain flared hot and red. I kicked out and the vamp fell to a crouch, ready to spring again.

My sword was slick with sweat and blood, but I hung onto it. The vamp leapt and impaled on the blade. I lost precious seconds trying to pull the sword from the corpse. Then, two hands on the grip, I slammed it down on the second vamp still writhing on the ground. The third tried to scuttle away and I stabbed her in the back.

I turned, expecting to find Susanna down with her neck torn out. Instead, she crouched over the body of a wojak, her arm bloody to the elbow as she slashed and slashed and slashed.

I grabbed her wrist.

"Stop!"

She stared up at me with manic eyes.

"He's dead. It's done. Fall back." She scrambled to her feet and out the door. I followed. The sun was a welcome friend, but my eyes took time to adjust. Ben and his officers were lined up down the hill with guns pointed at the wreck of the door.

Not enough officers. Not enough guns.

"Hold!" Ben's voice rang out when he saw us. I stumbled through the courtyard, pulling Susanna behind me.

"Someone get her medical attention," I said as Ben reached us. "She's in shock."

Ben snapped an order, and an officer took off his own jacket to cover Susanna as he led her away.

"You're bleeding," Ben said.

I ignored that. "Merrow's still inside."

Ben nodded. "I called for reinforcements. Can't send anyone else in. Not without armor. Fucking vampires. No one mentioned vampires."

It seemed unbelievable. Fifty years ago, the triumvirate set up the ward to protect against exactly this kind of threat. Back then, vampires had ruled the Inbetween, hunting and feeding at will. Humans and fae banded together against this threat. And not since the ward's inception had the city fallen prey to vampires.

A roar of pure rage came from inside the condo, and the remains of the front door exploded outward. Merrow burst into the morning light with two vamps stuck to her back like leeches.

Light seemed to disappear in the blackness of her armor plating. She grabbed one of the vamps stuck to her back and ripped him in two. Organs spilled from his trunk as she tossed the halves to the ground. She roared again, a sound that keened with power and shook herself. The last vamp fell and scuttled back inside the condo.

Merrow limped away. The Hub officers stepped aside to let her pass.

More wojaks slipped out of the building and clustered in a ring around the door. They favored the shadows, and there were many of those within the broken mounds of concrete.

Ben swore quietly. "They're all wojaks."

I was thinking the same thing.

"Advance scouts. They're here to secure the gate."

Ben nodded, then walked off to talk to his superiors again. Merrow had wrapped herself in her usual glamor and sat on a block of cement talking into her widget, her free hand snapping in furious agitation. That was the joy of glamors. She looked as well put together as ever, black hair falling in a neat bob, pantsuit immaculate, as if she'd just stepped out of a boardroom—not a fight for her life.

The wojaks, at least two dozen of them now, didn't advance. They ringed the doorway and waited.

I found Susanna sitting beside the transport truck, now wrapped in a mylar blanket. She squinted into the sun.

"They killed Raymond," she said.

"I know. I'm sorry." I had no platitudes that would make it better.

Ben came up and held out a water bottle. Susanna shook her head, but he insisted. She drank, then held the bottle to me.

"Has anyone seen Julia?" I asked.

"She took off before the paramedics got here," Susanna said. "I couldn't stop her."

"Everyone deals with fear differently." I just hoped she wasn't hurt.

As I watched the condo, one lone ghost ambled past the ruins. He was dressed in ripped jeans and a t-shirt, with a backpack slung over one shoulder. Just a kid walking home from school. Kid ghosts were the worst, but soon, this whole lakeshore would be filled with spooks, if the opji had their way.

"They're just going to stand there and watch us?" Susanna pointed to the wojaks that blocked the ruined entry to the building.

"They're waiting," I said.

"For what?"

"For night."

"Oh, right. Aren't they allergic to sunlight or something?"

"No. That's just an old story. But they don't see well in full light. They're holding the door and waiting for sundown. That's when we can expect a full attack."

"Then we'd better be ready," Ben said.

## CHAPTER 35

I tried to make Gita stay home, but she could be as stubborn as a cat.

We stood in the parking lot of Valkyrie Pest Control as I loaded my truck with weapons.

"I will avenge their deaths!" She stood tall and willowy and blew her nose on a soggy handkerchief. She'd dressed for the occasion in extra layers of gray rags, and pulled back her hair into a bedraggled ponytail.

In the last day, she had turned Alvin and Theo's cage into a shrine, covered in flowers, twigs and odd little stones. The floor in front of it was washed in her tears.

She was adamant. Nothing would keep her from this battle. I looked at Gabe for help, but he just shrugged, so I put my foot down.

"I'm not taking you with me. Forget it. No way are you getting in this truck."

Gita's wrinkled face melted in a sly grin.

"Fine. Gabe will drive me." She marched over to the sleek silver vehicle Gabe called a car and got in.

"I thought you took orders from me," I said to Gabe. "Isn't that how this whole boss-employee relationship is supposed to work?"

He handed me the last box of ammunition. "She reminds me of my Gran. I can't say no."

"Whatever." I waved him away and studied the cache of weapons in the back of my truck. I wouldn't use all those guns and knives, but packing them gave me a sense of confidence.

In reality, my sword gave me the best chance of killing vamps. And the shock in their eyes when it struck blood and caused their hearts to come alive again…well, that never got old.

It was possible my sword's bloodlust was starting to affect me.

I shut the truck's hatch and turned to find Jacoby. At least I'd convinced him to stay home.

"You'll take care of everyone while I'm away, right?"

The little dervish stood as tall as he could. No one had ever given him authority before, and he liked it.

"Yes! I wills make sure everyone eats supper and goes to bed on time!"

"Thank you." To his surprise, I hugged him. Life is too short not to hug your dervish before going into battle.

I wanted to give him instructions in case we weren't back by morning. But I realized if we weren't home by then, it would mean the vampires had overrun the ward. I had no instructions to help with that.

Hub had set up a staging ground on Lakeshore Road, just east of the old condo. The sun was setting, lighting the lake in brilliant shades of pink and purple. Officers stood in huddled groups, holding cups of coffee, trying to stay warm in the fishy wind blowing off the lake. The grating hum of the ward only added to the unease. Even the humans would feel it, like an itch between their shoulders. They would call it intuition. Foreboding.

Up the road, the condo was backlit in the twilight. The shadows in front weren't still. They shifted and swelled as more wojaks poured from the gate to fill their ranks. Squinting into the light, I counted. There had to be a hundred of them now. Darkness hid their faces, but I keened the angry magic boiling down from their masses.

The fae were here, led by Queen Leighna in full armor. She wouldn't sit on the sidelines for this battle. The humans rallied around Detective Ben as he gave last-minute instructions.

A group of alchemists were setting up a ring of spotlights, all pointing at the ruined condo. Susanna was among these techs. She waved and gave me a shaky smile. I returned it with a thumbs up.

The alchemists were led by Gerard Golovin the third Prime Minister in the ruling triumvirate, the man who owned the transport company that had hauled captive dragons for Joran.

I eyed him with suspicion.

Golovin wasn't dressed for battle. He wore a blue suit with even darker blue rosettes embossed on the fabric. When the light hit him, the rosettes shone. He finished the ensemble with shiny black shoes and a thin, jeweled tie. He looked ready for a meeting of his shareholders.

Then a couple of alchemists set up a ring of tripods around his transport vehicle and fitted them with devices. When engaged, they gave off another blast of magic.

Gerard Golovin had brought his own ward. Fancy chickenshit. He didn't intend to engage the opji at all, but only direct the battle like a general behind the lines.

We hadn't told Leighna about the transport because we had no other proof he was involved, but I was going to go out on a limb and say I didn't like him.

I caught Leighna watching this set up too. Her lip curled up in the faintest disapproving sneer.

"Have you met our fearless leader?" Mason said, handing me a cup of coffee. I hadn't seen him arrive, but he must have been nearby. The sun had only just dipped below the horizon.

"Thanks." I held up the cup, enjoying the heat and coffee fumes. "No, I haven't met him yet. Do I want to?" We watched Golovin yell at one of his techs for scratching the side of his transport with a tripod case.

"Probably not." Mason pulled me aside. We crossed the broken road where the briny smell was stronger.

"Look at them." He nodded back at the groups of people waiting in the fading light. Fae, humans and alchemists didn't mingle. The factions were painfully obvious. The humans wore synthetic body armor and carried an arsenal of weapons—mostly old-school guns with actual projectile bullets. History had proven that these worked better than modern blasters to take out vampires that healed laser burns too quickly. I wondered if they'd plundered the archives to find so many antique weapons.

The fae were a smaller group. Some carried knives or swords, but most didn't bother with armor or weapons. These would drop their careful glamors when the time came and fight with claws, teeth or other magic. The alchemists were the smallest group. Their weapons were all tech. They weren't here to fight but to try and contain the opji. Mason's Guardians were nominally part of this group, but the dozen or so gargoyles stood apart from everyone.

"Where do you fit in with that lot?" Mason asked. It was a startling question.

"What do you mean?"

Mason gripped my shoulders and turned us so his back was to the crowd. Over his shoulder I could see Montreal's little army with the crumbling condos in the background.

"Tell me which of those groups you fit into. Who will have your back during this fight?"

His fingers pinched my shoulders and his eyes glared down at me. But he wasn't angry. His magic beat with tension. He was scared. For me.

I glanced over his shoulder again. He was right. I had no clan. I was the only Aesir in Montreal. The only one outside of Asgard that I knew of. Dryads weren't exactly fae, and my link to that heritage was tenuous at best. And I might look human, but I didn't fit with them either.

"Promise me you'll stay close," Mason said. "The Guardians will protect you." I opened my mouth to protest, but he cut me off. "Don't start with the whole 'I don't need protecting' crap. Tonight, we all do. I'll have your back and you'll have mine. Agreed?"

"Agreed."

He smiled and released me.

"I have something for you." He handed me a velvet pouch bound with a cord. I untied it and dropped a heavy silver bracelet into my hand. Holding it, gave me a familiar antsy feeling.

"It's a null ring." Mason flashed a quick smile at me.

"You made this?"

He shrugged. "The poachers did most of the work. I just adjusted it."

He'd adapted one of the dragon collars.

"You made this for me?" I asked.

"Yes." His smile held a hint of boyish delight. "You might need it tonight."

I slipped the bracelet on my wrist. The constant background hum dimmed. I was so used to magic pummeling me from all sides that its absence felt odd.

"Thank you." I didn't know what else to say. I might die tonight, but no way would I become some opji's helpless bitch again. I turned away to wipe a stray tear from my eye.

"Gita and Gabe are here too," I said in a level voice.

"Good. With Angus and the other Guardians, we'll be our own army."

Angus found us then and half-hopped, half flew over the broken road, swinging an axe as long as he was tall.

"Kyra! Aren't you a sight for desperate eyes!"

Hugging Angus was like hugging a bramble bush. Twigs and leaves scraped my face, but I didn't care.

"I thought I'd lost you and the wee dragon both! But we made it through, didn't we? And now we face the big guns, standing here like a bunch of blood bags, just waiting for the other cake to drop."

"Um, right. It's good to see you too."

He leaned in and whispered, "Do you think the wee one is safe?"

"Ollie?"

Angus nodded. "I worry about the damned stone, but mostly I want that little bugger to be far away from this mess."

"He found at least one of his thunder. We have to hope that is enough."

"Aye, we can only hope. But damn me if this standing around isn't going to kill me. When do we get this party started?"

"As soon as the army arrives." Hub officers opted to wait until reinforcements came in from militia outposts. I didn't want to take on the wojaks with anything less than an army, but as the night wore on, I didn't think the vamps would give us that choice.

I saw Gabe standing with the Hub officers and went over to him.

"You shouldn't be here."

He shrugged. His dark hair was pulled back in a queue and he looked every inch the warrior.

"It's okay." He grinned. "*Celebrity Homesteader* is between seasons anyway. There's nothing good to stream. Might as well fight."

I eyed him. "Seriously, promise me that if things go really bad, you'll get Gita to safety, even if you have to throw her over your shoulder kicking and screaming."

"I will, boss."

"You should be getting hazard pay for this, but I really can't afford it."

A murmur went through the crowd and Ben spoke.

"Listen up! We're waiting for more guns and reinforcements, but the vamps are moving up there. We may have to move in before we're ready. Kill shots only. Head or heart. They're not easy to kill but put enough lead in them and they'll go down."

"Boo-ya!" someone said.

The vampires had the high ground, and they circled the door to the condo. Now they swelled, pushing down the hill.

*Here we go.*

Weapons were drawn. Eyes strained in the growing darkness. My null bracelet dulled my keening, but I didn't need it to know that the fae were priming their magic, ready to fight.

The alchemists' spotlights kicked on, falling on the condo's facade with a harsh blue glare.

Wojaks cringed in the brightness. The light only enhanced their hideousness. These beings who were once human—homesteaders, perhaps, or refugees traveling between wards—murdered by the opji just to be brought back as undead soldiers.

The opji didn't bother to clothe them, and their bodies had wasted to bone with tight coverings of gray flesh. Lips had withered, drawing back to expose yellow teeth. Those that still had hair left it matted in clumps. The wind shifted and their rotting stench washed over us.

The night fell silent. They were waiting.

Someone's boot scraped on the gravel. One of the fae let loose with a premature arrow. It struck a wojak in the chest and the creature crumpled. The others in line ignored their fallen comrade.

"Hold your fire!" Ben shouted.

The line of wojaks parted and another group appeared. These were taller, opji by the looks of them. Seven in all. A male and female opji led the way with Prince Alvar between them like a prisoner or a revered guest. Their body language gave nothing away. I recognized the female opji as the one who'd taunted me at Alvar's court.

A few other fae followed behind them, Joran in their midst. Gita hissed beside me.

"Greetings!" Alvar's voice rang out. He stepped forward. The fae in our group raised their bows, but Leighna waved them back.

"Hello, sister." Alvar smiled. "I'm glad you're here. It's time we had a chat."

Leighna didn't deign to answer. She released the bowmen. Arrows flew and wojaks fell.

"Don't want to chat? Then I'll do all the talking." Alvar's expression hardened. In the few days since I'd last seen him, he'd aged. It was something in the way he held himself. Tall and straight, but with bravado instead of confidence.

"For years, our countrymen and women have come to me when their voices would not be heard in your court. And I would say, 'What can I do? I am just a prince.' 'But you have the ear of the queen,' they would say. Of course we know that isn't true, don't we, dear sister? Because you never listened to me. You never believed that some fae would agree with me, that they could even *prefer* me to you."

By the One-eyed Father, was he going to dredge up every imagined hurt? Did Leighna take away his toys? Send him to bed without supper? Around me, others were as impatient. Feet shifted. Arms flexed, holding knives and guns.

"But I listened to those voices, the ones that the *queen* refused to hear." He pronounced *queen* like it was a curse word. "And those voices want change. They don't want to rule or be ruled by weak humans anymore. So I found the means to that change." He opened his arms as if to embrace his fanged army.

"I am bringing a new regime to Montreal. One that won't bow down to humans or anyone else. One that will—"

The female opji leaned over and snapped Alvar's neck with a deft twist of her hands.

Leighna dropped to one knee like she'd been sucker-punched.

Then the wojaks swarmed down the hill.

# CHAPTER 36

They killed Alvar's fae court first. None in that group had the magic to stand up to an opji, and I didn't know how Alvar thought he could rule the vampires.

The wojak soldiers killed the fae with efficient ease, then stepped over their bodies, ready for more blood. Only Joran was left, hiding behind the opji entourage.

Ben's officers took the first line. Their guns fired nonstop. The bigger rifles took chunks off flesh and bone, sometimes dropping a wojak, but mostly not. The handguns were only minor distractions for the army of the undead.

As the wojaks broke through this human line, the fighting began in earnest. My sword sang for a taste of undead blood. Even the null bracelet couldn't hide its joy from me. We'd been together too long.

Leighna and her entourage disappeared inside the condo. Her only mission was to close the gate and stop the flow of incoming vampires. Merrow's roar came from above as she protected her queen on this quest.

I cut and dodged. Angus sliced through bodies with his axe as if he were cutting hay. Mason turned his left arm to stone and clubbed the vamps. His other hand held some kind of glass knife. He stabbed a vamp in the eye and twisted. The blade flared red and the vampire's head ignited. Mason withdrew and the flaming wojak fell.

Fancy. I nodded in appreciation, then turned my back, trusting that Mason would keep the wojaks from blindsiding me. My world dissolved to base reflex. Cut. Block. Cut. Cut. Block. The bright lights cast the scene in stark clarity. I stabbed a wojak in the neck. His gray face seized, eyes widened. Every craggy line on his face etched in my memory. I found his heart and finished him, turning to the next one.

The undead were odd foes. They didn't scream or cry out. They only grunted or hissed in surprise when my sword took them, and that was barely audible above the constant barrage of gunfire and human cries of pain.

A wojak slipped past me, but I couldn't stop. Behind us, the alchemists made up our last defense. I had to hope their gadgets could keep the vampires from overrunning the city.

Another vamp fell on me, her fangs finding skin through my jacket. I fell under her weight, felt hot, rancid breath on my face. Her skeletal body shouldn't have been heavy, but it was. And unnaturally strong. I struggled to heave her off.

The gruesome face leered down on me. She might have been pretty once. A homestead girl with fine bones and big eyes. But now those eyes were hollow and black. Her lipless mouth pulled back in a grisly grin as she strained to rip out my jugular.

I struggled, risked letting go with one hand to punch her. My fist glanced off a bony cheekbone, and the vamp latched onto my wrist. Fangs sank deep. Pain burst along my arm. The world went red. I gasped for breath as the vamp drank.

No. I wasn't going down this way. I fought through a fog of pain. My right hand still gripped my sword that quivered with the need to kill. I sliced it along the back of her neck. She reared back, hissing.

I didn't give her time to feel the life burning in her veins. I slashed through the leathery tendons, and her head toppled to the ground.

I rose on shaking legs. The wojak's venom was blessedly weak. Either she'd juiced out on the dozens of other victims in her wake or they weren't bothering with subduing their victims tonight. They just wanted the kill.

I'd become separated from Mason and the others. I scanned the field, looking for them. The harsh lights showed every fallen body in detail. Blood. So much blood. A pink-haired fae lay twisted and broken, her jaw hanging from a thread. Three of Ben's officers were sprawled in a heap, blood pooling beneath them.

Something slammed into my back. I fell and rolled, not wanting to get pinned again. I came up slashing and severed the vamp's arm, then pierced his heart.

At the head of the hill, the opji generals stood watching the melee. More wojaks poured out of the condo. Leighna was still inside. Was she dead? Why wasn't the damn gate closed?

The fae weren't numerous, but they fought with otherworldly tactics. One had dropped his glamor. His true form was a twelve-foot tree-being that stomped among the fighters, bashing vamps with a club-like arm.

A group of pixies had exploded into clouds of bright glitter. It was an effective defense, but did little harm. Then I saw the pixie cloud swarm and confuse a wojak, giving another fae with a long spear time to impale it through the heart.

On a pile of cement blocks, an ice troll was being strangled by an opji, and struggling to turn his foe into a block of ice before he succumbed.

I watched all this happen in a moment. My bitten arm was numb to the elbow and it hung useless at my side.

And still they came.

I fought, thrust and blocked. I couldn't keep up this pace. There were too many. I jumped over a fallen boulder, chased by three more wojaks. Jumped again. My strength failed and my boot didn't clear the rock. I fell, landing hard on my knee. The wojaks circled me. Easy prey.

A hawk-like scream came from above, and the night filled with fire. The three wojaks burst into flame, and a great shadow flew by. As they flailed and dropped, trying desperately to put out the flames, I looked up to find my savior. A magnificent red dragon.

Ruby circled the killing field, blasting clutches of wojaks with her fiery breath. Ollie followed behind, trying to imitate his queen, but blowing mostly smoke.

They made another pass, searing undead flesh. Wojaks exploded and the few remaining men took heart. They pushed forward against the tide of vampires. Ruby flew by again, but the effort cost her. Her fire wasn't strong and she had to fly low to make contact with the enemy. One of the opji sprang into the air and grabbed her wing. Ruby fell. Ollie screamed and dove at the opji, claws raking across his face.

The last I saw, Ruby and Ollie were flying away into the night, Ruby favoring one wing. I hoped they stayed away.

The ground in front of the condo was a dangerous mix of burning bodies, fallen rock and injured allies. One spotlight fell over and exploded in a burst of sparks. The other spotlights—all linked in a chain—went out, leaving the field in blackness.

Curses and screams punctuated the dark as we all fought to gain our night eyes. Ben ran by me and I grabbed his arm.

"We need to get the injured out of the way," I said. "Before the fires burn them too."

Ben turned haunted eyes on me. "There's no one left to move them. Not until backup arrives."

We both knew that backup wouldn't matter.

Ben raised his gun and fired. A wojak fell at our feet, hands clawing at Ben's boots. He aimed at her head and the gun clicked. Out of bullets.

"Shit." He threw the weapon aside. I finished the vamp with one jab.

"Do you have a blade?" I asked. He nodded grimly and pulled the wicked knife from his belt. We fell back into the fray. The fires made the ground even more treacherous. I stumbled over rocks, skidded on broken glass. A wojak pressed me back, and I stumbled into a fire. My pants smoked, and I wasted precious time putting out the flames.

Ahead, Gita and Gabe fought back to back. She barely reached his shoulder. He fought like a guy who knew his way around a blade. Mason and Angus were by their sides. I half crawled, half ran toward them and slashed at a vamp just before it struck Mason.

He kicked away the body and pulled me into their ring.

"There's too many." He grunted and lunged at another attack. We had the high ground for the moment and our little band stood in a circle, blades out. The darkness had isolated us from the others. We were alone and surrounded. Five exhausted fighters against a dozen vamps. Two dozen? They kept coming.

From the corner of my eye, I saw a dark body lunge at Gita. I swung and slashed. The undead face turned to me and struck, knocking my sword from my weak grip. Fangs aimed for my throat.

"No!" Gita's cry was harsh.

I struggled to keep the vamp off me. My hands circled his neck and squeezed.

Gita started to wail.

*Not now! Don't lose it now!*

Gita would be an easy target if she gave into her banshee instincts, but I could do nothing to help. I could only squeeze the undead throat in my grip, waiting for bones to break. My hands shook. The vamp squirmed and bit, his teeth hitting the null bracelet.

I squeezed.

Around us, fires burned. Men and women died.

Gita wailed.

The sound rose like a sad song, then turned sharp and cutting. It was a sound bigger than the night, like the lament at the madras funeral, only bigger, filling every shadow, piercing every heart and stopping the blood cold.

The wojak in my grip seized. He bucked once then went rigid, mouth pulled back in silent agony. I let go and he fell like a plank on the rocks.

Gita's scream shredded magic.

Mason and Angus turned to stone. One minute they were fighting. The next, they were stone gargoyles. Vamps toppled like felled trees.

Light burst from my sword, then it went dark.

Gita's voice rose, hitting a furious pitch. I clutched the null bracelet and scrambled away. And still she screamed. Gabe lay at her feet, gazing up at her, a trickle of blood leaking from his nose.

Gita's head was flung back, arms thrown wide. She no longer looked like a crone dressed in rags. She was beautiful. Her hair fluttered in some unseen breeze. The wrinkles smoothed from her face and she glowed with an inner light.

Everyone around me—humans, fae and vamps—all were frozen or dead. Gita's pitch soared above what human ears could hear.

Then a rumbling, grating sound accompanied her song, and the condo crumpled. Rock, steel and glass fell in an explosion of dust, crushing everyone left inside.

# CHAPTER 37

The humans recovered first. For once, their paltry innate magic work for them. Slowly, some bodies began to stand. They brushed off dust and looked around with owl eyes.

Those whose lives depended on magic took longer to rise. Most of the fae were unconscious. Angus and Mason looked shocked to still be in stone form. The wojaks, who were nothing more than necromantic constructs, stayed down.

The few humans who could walk set about cutting off wojak heads before they could rise.

Gabe crouched beside Gita. He brushed the hair from her eyes. She was back to her crone form—gray-skinned, wrinkled and filthy. But like me, I suspected Gabe would always see the goddess shining in her from now on.

"Take her home," I said. Gabe nodded and picked her up. Gita looked like a child's rag doll in his arms.

I stumbled toward the ruins of the old condo, dispatching wojaks whenever I found them.

*I have to get to the queen.* It was a crazy, futile thought. The queen was dead under tons of rock. Was the gate still open? I couldn't tell. My null bracelet blocked magic better than any ward I could build. It was the only reason I was still standing. I took it off and my keening went into sudden overload.

Burned magic filled the air. The dead and dying leaked magic with the blood spilling on the ground, and dozens of ghosts appeared, milling about, lost and aimless.

Ahead of me, I keened that the gate to Underhill still gaped like an open maw. I was the only one left who could close it, and I had to do it now, while the enemy was down.

I tripped over an arm. It lay in the path, severed by a clean cut. The stringy sinews over bone told me it was a wojak arm. A few feet away, the vamp stared with dead eyes at his appendage. Beside him lay Detective Ben, his throat a ragged mess, blood soaking his uniform.

His ghost sat at his side, but in pure Ben fashion, it mourned for another fallen officer, not its own body.

My eyes were hot and sore with unshed tears. Gently, I scraped the tip of my blade across the back of Ben's hand, drawing a thin red line. His ghost looked up, smiled, then vanished. I keened the moment his magic popped out of this world.

A young woman sat up next to Ben's body. She wasn't dead after all. She coughed and winced, then her eyes fell on Ben and she started to cry.

"Who's in charge now?" I asked. We had no time to mourn.

"I…I am." The woman gripped Ben's hand.

"Then start acting like it." I channeled Aunt Dana's whip-like voice of command. The woman sat up, tears shocked into submission.

"We have five minutes, maybe less, before all these vamps spring back to life. Put some blades in your soldiers' hands and get this field cleared."

Snot streaked from her nose and a mass of blood-matted hair stuck to the side of her head, but she nodded and moved off.

I climbed over slabs of concrete and bent steel beams, with no idea how to reach the gate, only knowing that I had to try. The building had toppled westward, leaving the front entrance relatively clear. But there was no door, no way inside the mass of unstable rock and metal.

As I stood, scanning the debris for an entrance into the building, the gate's distinctive magic signature flared, then disappeared. My ears popped and my jaw ached as if I'd eaten something sour.

Someone had closed the gate.

Did the opji retreat and seal it behind them? Was the queen alive under all that rubble?

I had no answers.

Then I spotted Joran.

He sat holding his head with a ring of unconscious vampires around him. Joran had recovered quickly. The only magic in him was the wound from my blade.

He saw me and stepped away, eyes darting left and right. He scuttled like a bug into a crack between two slabs of fallen concrete and I followed, stopping only to dispatch the opji. The blond woman wasn't among them.

Behind me came the groans of pain as people woke. I scanned the ruins, but Joran had disappeared into the shadows. I took heart that his wound would kill him soon. That would have to be enough. The living needed me.

I retreated through the wreckage to find Angus and Mason dazed but alive. Angus was pissed. He didn't like being turned to stone by a banshee.

"Well, don't that beat the fork that broke the camel's back." He took out his frustration by lugging wojak corpses to the space Hub had set aside as a pyre. The alchemists were already arguing about the best way to torch the bodies.

"He'll be okay," Mason said when he found me watching Angus with concern.

"It's just unsettling. We expect the change at sunrise and can prepare for it. I didn't even know it could be forced upon us like that." He rubbed the back of his neck as if he spoke about nothing worse than a kinked muscle.

Dirt and ash covered his clothes and brought out the lines around his eyes. He looked older, but also more real. I reached out to brush a wood shard from his shoulder. He caught my hand and pressed it to his lips. He seemed to breathe in my scent. My dirty, bloody scent.

After a moment, he released me. "You should get home to Gita. We'll finish cleaning up here."

Another Guardian stumbled over to us. I recognized him from the night I found the dragons. He held one arm against his chest and his face was pinched in pain.

"Berto, you're hurt," Mason rose to inspect his friend.

"Got caught in the rockfall, Captain," Berto wheezed. "Just a busted arm and a few cracked ribs. Maybe a punctured lung. Nothing the sun won't cure."

Mason turned to Angus. "Take him back to our camp and get him fixed up. Leave the medics here to deal with the human wounded."

For once, Angus had no witty retort. He wedged his shoulder under Berto's arm and helped him away.

"Will he be okay?" I asked.

"Sure. One shift to stone and back again will take care of him." He smiled wearily. "It's a gargoyle's life."

We wandered through the rubble looking for bodies. It was gruesome, exhausting work with little reward. We found none alive. Some bodies we carried back to the tent that had been hastily erected as a triage. Others were buried under too much stone, and we simply flagged them.

"Is that a jacket?" I pointed to a flap of fabric under a pile of broken concrete and glass.

"Looks like it." Mason heaved a stone aside to get a better look. My sword hummed stridently. Rock exploded by his head.

I whirled in time to see Joran fire a second shot. The bullet went wide. I had my sword out before I could even think of it. Joran could barely stand and his hands shook. Two more shots blasted the rocks beside me.

"You stupid bitch!" he shouted. A gob of spit hung from his lip. His red-rimmed eyes were sunken into his emaciated face. "You ruined everything! For what? A couple of dragons? I'll hunt them down…I'll gut 'em…" He staggered, the hand holding the gun flailed. Blood covered his pants. Sometime during the battle, he'd taken a second wound on his leg.

"He said…he said not to come home without that damn stone. So I won't…I *will* be the one to free her…" He wiped his nose on his sleeve and staggered forward. "My goddess…I will free her."

"Joran, listen to me." I said. "Put down the gun and we'll talk about it."

He seemed to remember that he was holding the weapon and pointed it at me again.

"Joran…"

He fired. My blade jerked up on its own to block the bullet that came too close. It pinged off metal. Joran continued to fire wildly until he pulled the trigger on an empty chamber. He swore, threw the gun down and limped away.

"I should go after him," I said. Mason didn't answer. I turned and saw him crumpled against the pile of stone.

"Mason!"

He held up one bloody hand, and I dropped to my knees.

"You're bleeding." A ricochet had hit him in the side. I pushed his shirt away and pressed my hands to the bloody wound.

"I'm fine. Go stop him before…" His eyes closed and took a long, painful breath. "Before he goes after the dragons."

I looked west to where Joran had disappeared along the beach, then back at Mason who struggled for each breath.

"Go. He won't stop." He shoved me weakly.

Damn. I pressed his hand against the wound.

"Hold that. Hard. And don't die before I get back."

I left him to run after Joran. Adrenaline is an amazing drug. I was exhausted, heartsick and bruised in a dozen places, but being shot at had given me my second wind, or maybe it was my third wind. I'd lost track.

Joran had a good head start despite his limping gait. I skidded on the sand by the lake and found him a good quarter of a kilometer ahead. A cold wind blew off the lake, rustling the dead grasses along the shore.

My knee screamed when I twisted it on the uneven ground. My left arm was still numb from the vamp bite, but I wasn't letting Joran get away again.

His death would no longer be a mercy killing. It was revenge.

I jogged west, my feet sinking into the wet sand with each step. I spoke to the grasses. They weren't trees, but my dryad magic might make them listen. I keened their interest and urged them to help me. I didn't know what to expect. Maybe that vines would sprout from the ground and wrap around Joran like rope? That didn't happen, but ahead, he stumbled and fell.

By the time I reached him, his legs were tangled in a clump of sea grass washed up on shore. I'd take my small miracles where I could get them.

"I should just let you die out here," I said. We were alone, completely isolated from the medics and cops who still sorted through the rubble at the condo.

Joran had lost his jacket and torn off his shirt to staunch the blood on his leg. The bandage on his arm was gone. That wound was black and rank. Necrotic tissue gaped like crepe paper and oozed yellow fluid.

His breath hitched with panic as he desperately tried to hold in his life. But there was too much blood. He must have been wounded in the building collapse too, taken a shard of wood or glass in the leg. And running from me had exacerbated it.

I had precious few minutes to get answers.

I pointed my sword at his head. "Why are the opji protecting you?"

He flinched but didn't answer.

"Tell me! Who are you working for? Not Alvar, or you'd be dead already. Why did the opji let you live?"

"They are letting me die." He laughed out a wet sound. "Die to come back. I found a way…" A fit of coughing seized him. I waited with itchy fingers. "I found a way around the curse of your blade, *Valkyrie.*"

He sneered that last word, as if I should be ashamed of my heritage.

"They're going to turn you into a wojak!" Those mindless drones that had only one need: to kill and drink blood. Was that better than dying? Would it even work? In all my years, I'd never seen the Valkyrie curse bested.

But wojaks could heal any wound except a pierced heart or a severed head. Maybe they could heal a wound from a Valkyrie blade. Or maybe Joran would continue to rot away as an undead, until he was nothing but blood-thirsty bone.

"I could kill you now," I pointed my singing blade at his heart. "Or I could leave you to die slowly. No one will find you here. You'll die alone and in pain." He glared at me with hate-filled eyes. I stared back at him in disgust. Even the fishy smell of the lake couldn't mask the stink of death coming off him.

"Your arm is nothing more than rotting meat. That's how you'll die. You'll watch your body rot until it hits your heart. No one will come for you. The opji are all dead. They can't help you now. You'll die here and your spirit will haunt your bones even as scavengers pick them clean of meat."

Joran wept. I didn't care.

I gazed out at the lake that had stilled into a sheet of black glass. The gentle lap of waves breaking on the shore seemed somehow wrong. So much blood had been spilled this night. But the lake didn't care. It was eternal. Men would come and go, even men who lived for hundreds of years. To the waves, these were nothing more than a blip of time.

It didn't matter. The opji were dead. The gate was closed. I would finish this here.

His wheezing sobs pulled me back.

"I *should* let you die, without any last rites or thought, just as you did to the dragons, to Alvin and Theo."

He blubbered. Tears, dirt and blood streaked his face. Then he gasped one last time and went still. He'd taken my friends, my family, and now he'd even taken my revenge.

In the end, I stuck his corpse with my sword and released his spirit because I was a Valkyrie. That's what we did.

I wouldn't tell Gita.

I found Mason right where I'd left him. A makeshift bandage was soaked with blood, but when I lifted it, the wound only oozed.

He opened his eyes and smiled.

"I'm going to get a medic," I said, but he grabbed my hand.

"No. I'm fine. The sun will come…" He hissed out a breath. "Let the medics care for those who need them."

"Fine." I sat beside him in the gravel. "Joran's dead."

"Good." He closed his eyes and leaned back.

We watched others pick through the debris, looking for survivors. I had nothing left to give. A medic came over to look at our wounds. He dressed the bite on my arm, but Mason waved him away when he went to peel off his blood-soaked shirt. The medic grumbled about ungrateful patients and left us with a bottle of water to share.

The blond woman I'd found next to Ben's body was Lieutenant Beth Carter. Once her initial shock wore off, she turned out to be a competent leader. The backup that Ben had promised came just in time for cleanup. They led the wounded away and hauled vampire bodies to be burned.

The old Aristo condominium was nothing more than a pile of rubble, too unstable to venture inside for bodies. A ring of militia were stationed around its perimeter in case any more wojaks made it out of the ruins.

As the alchemists studied the heap of rock, trying to decide the best way to stabilize it so they could recover the bodies of Leighna and her entourage, a roar of pure animal rage erupted from the wreckage. Rock shifted. Stone fell away. A steel beam screeched as it grated against rock. Something moved in there. Something big.

Another roar and Merrow pushed through the ruins in a ball of protective magic. Her hair was a matted nest. Bloody wounds crossed her arms and back, cutting into the thick plating that covered her body. And she carried her dazed queen. Leighna had done it. She closed the gate, but it had cost her. Of the dozen fae who went into the building with her, no others came out.

Merrow set Leighna down and steadied her. Already, she was shrinking, replacing her magic ward with an innocuous glamor. Leighna stepped forward and saw the line of bodies—humans, fae and alchemists. One of them was her brother. She gazed down at his lifeless form with a frown, then stepped over his body and moved on.

The night wore on toward morning.

"Why are you still here?" Mason said. His head lolled back against the rock. I dribbled more water between his lips.

"I'm waiting with you until the sun rises."

"You don't need to. Go home. Check on Gita."

"She'll be fine. Gabe's with her." I held his hand, so warm and full of life.

"I don't need help."

"Of course not. That doesn't mean that you have to go it alone," I said, throwing his own words back at him.

"Stubborn." He smiled weakly.

"Right back at you."

We sat like that until the sky purpled, then pinked. When the sun peeked over the horizon, lighting the lake in a thousand hues of red and yellow, I felt his magic slow and his hand turn to stone in mine.

*Valkyriebestiary.com/dragon*

## Dragon Talk

*(June 8, 2080)*

Okay, folks. Let's talk dragons.

There's so much information and disinformation out there, it's hard to know what is true and what is myth. Not only that, but how do we know if there are different breeds of dragons? I have very limited experience with these amazing creatures, so I'd like to pool our knowledge and create a database of sightings and info. Who's up for that?

I'll start with my recent encounter. A few weeks ago, I came across a thunder of dragons being poached. My first thought was that they would be slaughtered for their scales and hides.

But in the end, I learned that the dragons were reared like pigs, kept captive so they could root out magic artifacts. It seems that's what they eat.

Anyone else come across magic-eating dragons? Are they a new hybrid?

## Comments (8)

You should stop filling the world with your falsehoods. Magic doesn't exist. The true Lord will judge you for your blasphemy.
*Carousella (June 8, 2080)*

How did they keep the dragons captive? I mean couldn't they just fly away?
*DragonRider (June 8, 2080)*

> The dragons had their wings magically clipped. I don't want to go into it more than that.
> *Valkyrie367 (June 9, 2080)*

Dragons are majestic creatures and should never be treated this way. Were you able to help them?
*cchedgewitch (June 9, 2080)*

> Yes. Thanks for your concern. I was able to free all but one dragon. I'm sorry to say, the poachers killed that one before I could intervene.
> *Valkyrie367 (June 9, 2080)*
>
>> Poachers should be tried as murderers. Thank you for helping these unfortunate creatures. May the Lady's light shine on you for your courage.
>> *cchedgewitch (June 9, 2080)*
>>
>>> :)
>>> *Valkyrie367 (June 9, 2080)*

I have some information about a dragon sighting. I'll be in touch.
*DaddysGirl (June 10, 2080)*

# EPILOGUE

Gabe was already the best assistant I'd ever had. Two days after the vampires attacked, he had my work schedule sorted and all the messages answered.

"Your entire week is booked." He tapped his widget to mine to transfer the work orders.

"I should stay home and get this place put back together." My apartment was still in shambles. The glazier couldn't come until next week to fix the front window, and we'd barricaded it with plywood.

"No way. Gita and I got this." The banshee walked by with a broom and dustpan. "Right?" He held out a fist for her and she bumped it.

"Fine. But I'm still taking Wednesday afternoon off to take Clarence to the vet." His gizzard stones hadn't resolved.

"And I noted that on the calendar." Gabe's smile was infectious. I found I couldn't stay sad or angry when he was around. Just drinking in his tall, dark handsomeness was like a shot of caffeinated cola.

The timer in the kitchen dinged, and I went over to take out a batch of peanut butter cookies from the oven. Jacoby bounced from foot to foot, too excited to wait for them to cool. I slapped his busy hands away.

"You'll burn yourself."

Normally, I wouldn't waste time baking when there was so much work to do, but these were a peace offering. As soon as they cooled, I pulled a plate out of the cupboard, dumped Hunter (who had been lurking in the cupboard to ambush me) into his aquarium and arranged the cookies on the plate. Then I climbed the back stairs to Mr. Murray's door.

I knocked and waited. He was standing on the other side of the door, deciding if he wanted to open it or not. His magic was as familiar to me as Gita's or Clarence's.

"I brought you cookies, Mr. Murray!" I knocked again. The door was snatched open. Mr. Murray was four-feet of grizzled annoyance. A gnome had almost certainly snuck into his family tree at some point. One of his eyes was squeezed in a permanent squint, and his white beard looked like two rats had fought for dominance on his chin.

"What do you want?" His sharp nose twitched when he smelled the cookies.

I held out the plate. "These are for you."

He grumbled, but a cookie disappeared so fast, I didn't see him take it. Crumbs appeared on his lips.

"Sorry about all the noise. Things will be quieter now."

He grumbled something that sounded like a curse and took the plate. The door shut in my face.

I sighed and made my way downstairs. Bags of debris and dirty cage litter were piled beside the front door. I grabbed two.

"Let me help with that." Gabe grabbed two more bags, and we headed for the dumpster, only to find a pair of scrawny legs sticking out of it.

Jacoby was busy retrieving many of the broken things, chucking bits of wood, a lamp and cardboard back onto the driveway.

"What are you doing?" I dropped the bags of garbage. Jacoby jumped out of the dumpster.

"I makes my own house, right here in the yard. I keeps watch over Alvin and Theo." Jacoby smiled shyly. "And you."

Gabe knelt and Jacoby shied backward. He still wasn't sure about this unfamiliar man in his life.

"I think that's a really good idea," Gabe said. "But why don't we get some new lumber and build you a proper house. I'll help."

Jacoby squinted at him, then nodded. They went inside to draw up plans.

I sighed and started reloading the garbage. As I tried to mash more bags into the dumpster, I heard a familiar chirp. I spun and Ollie nearly bowled me over. He still needed to practice his landing.

He danced and head butted me, knocking me back into the dumpster. It seemed impossible, but he'd already grown a foot taller.

"Hey, buddy!" I rubbed the bony ridge above his eyes and ruffled his crest of feathers. Those seemed thinner too. As he grew, he'd lose those baby feathers.

"I thought you'd be long gone by now. Is everything okay?"

He chirped again. He seemed fine, but restless. After sniffing the ground, he turned twice and squatted. Magic blossomed in the air. His face pinched, then he smiled and stood back like a proud papa.

A huge pile of dung steamed on the cement and there, like a cherry on top, gleamed the bloodstone.

## Acknowledgments

As I write this, we are in the middle of the COVID-19 pandemic. Quarantine has shown me that I'm a bit of a hermit because my life hasn't changed much. Of course, my greatest joy is that I can stay home and write the stories of my heart. Others aren't so lucky. I am deeply grateful for those people on the front line, first responders, doctors, nurses and all the workers who keep us fed and our supply chains going during this difficult time. My heart also goes out to those who have lost friends and loved ones.

This book was a long time coming and I have many people to thank for their support during its creation: my daughter, Genevieve Chatel, who has always been my sounding board and was as excited about Ollie as I was; Vicki Pinkerton for being my first reader and cheerleader; Elaine Jackson for being a tireless proofreader (all remaining typos are from my clumsy fingers, not hers), as well as a constant champion for all my books; Pamela Francescut for capturing my vision of Ollie and Kyra on the most beautiful cover; my mother, Claire McDougall for being a beta reader, but mostly for never complaining when I brought home a new critter; my husband Louis Chatel for keeping himself busy while I hid in my office during quarantine to write; and finally, for my dearest friend, Larry Weller, who passed away before I could put a copy of this book in his hands. Larry often shared his unique sense of humor and the secrets of Abbott's Agora.

And thank you, dear reader, for spending time in Kyra's world. I hope you enjoyed it as much as I did.

*Kim McDougall*

## What to Read Next?

Sometimes you just need to hug your fire dervish. Like when he protects you from brownies. Or goes down into the scary basement with you because he's proud to be your apprentice.

Or when he saves the world.

Kyra Greene, pest controller to the extraordinary is back with a new adventure!

A Guardian is dead. Fae are missing. And someone has let a golem loose in town. Ride along with Kyra Greene, the only pest controller qualified to deal with the strange and wonderful creatures that come out the shadows when magic flares.res that come out the shadows when magic flares.

***Dervishes Don't Dance*, Book 2 of the *Valkyrie Bestiary* Is now available.**

## Reviews Help Everyone

You probably know that authors love reviews, but do you know why? Reviews are important to every author, for the following reasons:

- They help other readers know what to expect from the book.
- They let me know how my books are received by readers.
- They help booksellers decide which books to show to new readers.

To leave your review for ***Dragons Don't Eat Meat***, visit your favorite retailer or wrongtreepress.com/review.

# About the Author

If Kim McDougall could have one magical superpower, it would be to talk to animals. Or maybe to shift into animal form. Definitely, fantastical critters and magic often feature in her stories. So until she can change into a griffin and fly away, she writes dark paranormal action and romance tales, from her home in Central Ontario. Visit Kim McDougall online at www.KimMcDougall.com or visit sendfox.com/wrongtreepress to sign up for her reading group and get the latest news about new releases, plus your free starter library.

www.ingramcontent.com/pod-product-compliance
Lightning Source LLC
Chambersburg PA
CBHW030358310726
48979CB00001B/362